Summer on the Turquoise Coast

Lilac Mills lives on a Welsh mountain with her very patient husband and incredibly sweet dog, where she grows veggies (if the slugs don't get them), bakes (badly) and loves making things out of glitter and glue (a mess, usually). She's been an avid reader ever since she got her hands on a copy of *Noddy Goes to Toytown* when she was five, and she once tried to read everything in her local library starting with A and working her way through the alphabet. She loves long, hot summer days and cold winter ones snuggled in front of the fire, but whatever the weather she's usually writing or thinking about writing, with heartwarming romance and happy-ever-afters always on her mind.

Also by Lilac Mills

A Very Lucky Christmas
Sunshine at Cherry Tree Farm
Summer on the Turquoise Coast
Love in the City by the Sea

Tanglewood Village series

The Tanglewood Tea Shop
The Tanglewood Flower Shop
The Tanglewood Wedding Shop

Island Romance

Sunrise on the Coast
Holiday in the Hills
Sunset on the Square

Applewell Village

Waste Not, Want Not in Applewell
Make Do and Mend in Applewell
A Stitch in Time in Applewell

LILAC MILLS

Summer on the Turquoise Coast

CANELO

First published in the United Kingdom in 2017 by Lilac Tree Books as
Elephant and the Pinky Moon

This edition published in the United Kingdom in 2022 by

Canelo
Unit 9, 5th Floor
Cargo Works, 1-2 Hatfields
London, SE1 9PG
United Kingdom

A CIP catalogue record for this book is available from the British Library.

Print ISBN 978 1 80436 019 4
Ebook ISBN 978 1 78863 273 7

This book is a work of fiction. Names, characters, businesses, organizations,
places and events are either the product of the author's imagination or are
used fictitiously. Any resemblance to actual persons, living or dead, events
or locales is entirely coincidental.

Look for more great books at www.canelo.co

Printed and bound in Great Britain by Clays Ltd, Elcograf S.p.A.

I

For my hubby, Rob, for his support, and without his daft name for Ephesus and Pamukkale, this book wouldn't exist.

Chapter 1

'But, Gran,' Nina shot her mother a helpless look. Alice sent her exactly the same one back. No help from that direction, she guessed.

'You do know he's gone, don't you, Gran?' she asked, hoping this wasn't the start of something more serious. She knew her grandmother could be forgetful, but surely, she couldn't forget something as significant as *that*?

'Who's gone?' Flossie asked, her attention on a half-eaten packet of biscuits on the table in front of her.

'Grandad.' Nina was starting to worry, and so was Mum, Nina saw. Alice sat there, thin-lipped, worry clouding her eyes, and her hands were clasped together so tightly her knuckles gleamed white.

'Gone where, dear?' Gran asked, dunking a chocolate Hob Nob in her tea and chewing noisily.

Nina and Alice exchanged meaningful looks. No wonder her mother had called in the cavalry, Nina thought. This wasn't looking good. Nina's heart dropped to her boots when she considered how her grandmother was going to react to the "news" – though it wasn't really news was it, considering Grandad had been dead for four months.

'Grandad's no longer with us. He's passed on, Gran,' Nina said, as gently as she could, then braced herself for the ensuing hysteria.

'I know,' Gran said calmly, demolishing another biscuit, her false teeth clacking as she munched.

'You know?' Nina replied, mouthing "she knows" at her mother over Flossie's head and waggling her eyebrows in a "what-on-earth-is-going-on" fashion.

'Of course, I know.' Flossie dropped what was left of her soggy biscuit on the table, where it instantly disintegrated, and put a wrinkled hand over her heart. 'I was there when he breathed his last.'

'I don't understand,' Nina said to her mother. 'You told me she's planning on going to Turkey, next week.'

Her gran didn't give Alice a chance to answer. 'That's right, dear, I am.' Flossie attacked another Hob Nob with determination. 'But I'm not *planning* – I'm *going*.'

'See,' Alice hissed, twirling a finger next to her temple. 'Ga ga.'

'I saw that! I'm not senile yet, you know,' Flossie said and added, 'It's *Lady* Gaga to you.'

Nina wasn't so sure about the senility part. 'Let me get this straight; you've booked a two-week package holiday to Turkey? For two? For you and Grandad?'

'Yep.' Flossie slurped her tea, staring challengingly over her cup at her daughter and granddaughter.

'And you're going on your own anyway?' Nina continued.

'Your grandad can hardly come with me, can he?' the old woman pointed out.

'Er... no.' Nina sent her mother another "help-me-out" look. Her mother pointedly gazed out of the kitchen window, a martyred expression on her face, silently refusing to be roped into the conversation.

'He planned on coming,' Flossie said, 'but he died, so that's that.'

'When did you book it?' Nina asked, thinking she saw a light at the end of this proverbial tunnel.

'A couple of weeks before he passed away.' Flossie ate yet another biscuit. She had managed to demolish over half the packet in less than five minutes.

Alice let out a strangled sob and dabbed at her eyes. Mum had taken Grandad's death hard.

Nina shook her head in confusion. 'He was really, really ill at that point,' she said.

'I knew it and he knew it, but it gave him something to aim for. He made me promise to go without him, if he…' she trailed off, her lips pursing like a drawstring bag.

'Gran, going on your own isn't such a good idea.' Nina was trying to be diplomatic, but she suspected she was about to fail big time; her gran wasn't going to take kindly to be told she was too old.

'Why ever not?'

Nina paused as a thought occurred to her. 'Ah, I get it. Is it one of those escorted, organised *Saga* trips?' That wouldn't be so bad. *Saga* were used to old people and the millions of things which could go wrong with them. Plenty of widows went on *Saga* holidays so Flossie wouldn't really be on her own.

'Bah! Not flipping likely. *Saga* is for old people,' her grandmother declared.

Nina rolled her eyes. Her gran was eighty-four, just how old did you have to be? 'What have you booked, and who with?' Nina imagined a cruise, or a sedate hotel catering to wrinklies.

'Here.' Flossie grubbed around in her over-sized shopping bag, pulling something out, peering at it, muttering to herself, then thrusting the object back in, before delving in for another item. An apple, a hammer, a copy

3

of Penthouse (really???), a sticky packet of humbugs, and a tape measure were all pulled out and examined myopically, before being returned to the Tardis depths of the bag.

'Got it!' Flossie announced triumphantly, slapping a tattered holiday brochure on the table. 'The estate agent in the High Street booked it for me.'

'You mean the travel agent,' Nina said, trying to read the name upside down. "*Athena Holidays – For the More Discerning Travel Lover*". That didn't sound too bad. In fact, it sounded quite up-market. She had visions of blue rinses, sherry before dinner, and more beige than you could shake a walking stick at.

'Do you want me to contact them for you?' Nina asked.

'What for?'

'To see about cancelling. The insurance should cover bereavement. You won't get all your money back, because I think you'll have to forfeit your deposit, but you should get most of it.'

'I'm not cancelling, I'm going.' Flossie crossed her arms over her bony chest, and stared defiantly at the two women.

Alice let out a huge sigh. Clearly this argument had been raging for a long time before Nina arrived. No wonder her mother had called her to 'come sort out your grandmother, because I'm washing my hands of her.'

'Besides,' Flossie added, 'there isn't any insurance.'

'No insurance?' Nina was flabbergasted. Her mother looked resigned, and Nina suspected Alice knew this already. 'Everyone has to take out insurance when they book a package holiday, don't they?'

'Not if you tell them you've already got it,' Flossie said.

'You just said you *haven't* got any!' Nina let out an exasperated sigh. The old woman was going loopy. 'Have you, or have you not, got insurance?'

'Nope, none.'

'That's... that's...' words failed her. 'Why?' Nina wailed.

'Because your grandfather couldn't get any, not with him on oxygen and being terminally ill.'

'But you went ahead and booked a holiday anyway?' Nina rolled her eyes again. If she kept going at this rate, her eyeballs would end up stuck in the tops of their sockets, but she couldn't seem to help it.

Flossie nodded enthusiastically. 'Now you see why I've got to go – because I can't get my money back.'

'Gran, you can't go on your own,' Nina argued for the umpteenth time. Maybe she should solve the problem by breaking into Grannie's house and hiding her passport – let the old biddy try to get out of the country without it!

'Don't be silly, Nina love, I've been abroad loads of times. I'm hardly a travel virgin.'

Nina struggled to hold her temper. It didn't help that she wanted to laugh, too; travel virgin indeed! 'You've never been away on your own,' she said. 'You always had Grandad with you.'

'You really didn't know your grandfather very well,' Flossie muttered. 'I might as well have been on my own, for all the use he was.'

Nina closed her eyes, hoping when she opened them again, she'd be in her own house, doing a bit of essay marking, or cleaning the oven, or even pulling her finger-nails out – any of the above would be preferable to this surreal conversation. Were all old people this stubborn?

'Whether he was any use or not,' Nina said through gritted teeth, 'Grandad was still with you. You. Weren't. On. Your. Own. What on earth were you thinking of, booking a holiday when you knew he'd never be able to go on it?'

'Don't you lecture me, young lady. What I do is none of your business.'

'It will be my business if I have to fly out to visit you in a foreign country because you've broken a hip,' Nina retorted.

'I could break a hip regardless of whether your grandad was with me or not,' Flossie retorted with a huff. 'And I'm not asking you to fly anywhere.'

'No, but I am,' Alice interjected.

'Finally decided to speak, have you, Mum? Thanks for the input and – hang on, what do you mean "I am"?' Nina blew out a lungful of air. 'That's a relief. Why the kerfuffle then, if you're going on holiday with her?'

'I'm not going. I can't fly,' her mother said. 'Not with my ears.'

'What's wrong with your ears?' Nina demanded.

'I've got dodgy ears. They told me I can't fly with them.'

'Since when have you had problems with your ears?' Nina asked, scratching her head. This was news to her, because her mother usually loved sharing any, and every, health issue with anyone who'd listen.

Alice waved a hand in the air. 'Oh, for a while now.'

'Have you had any tests, and when you say "dodgy" what exactly do you mean?'

'Tinnitus, vertigo, dizziness, and… er…'

'Meniere's,' Flossie piped up, her backside in the air as she rooted in the cupboard for another packet of biscuits.

She came up clutching some bourbons. 'I see you've not got any custard creams. I'm not too keen on these ones.'

'You ate them all the last time you were here, Mum,' Alice said.

'You should buy some more,' Flossie retorted, tearing open the packet and tucking in with such enthusiasm anyone would think she hadn't seen a biscuit for days.

Nina asked her mother, 'You've got all those things wrong with your ears?'

'Yes. No. They're not sure. I've got to go back for more tests, but they were adamant I'm not to fly.'

'She's under the doctor,' Flossie declared.

Nina let out a snort at the phrase – it sounded like a doctor was sitting on top of her mother, not that Alice was under the care of one. An image of old Dr Edwards astride her mother, popped into Nina's mind. She shook her head to clear it.

'Your *grandmother's* not asking you to fly – *I'm* asking,' Alice said to Nina. 'I'd like you to accompany her.'

Nina looked at her mother in confusion. 'Me? Why me?'

'Someone's got to go with her,' Alice said. 'I can't, so you'll have to.'

'What about Aunt Mabel?' Why hadn't she thought of Gran's sister earlier? Two old biddies together was the obvious solution.

'Mabel isn't well either,' Flossie said. 'I'll be surprised if she lasts the month. On death's door, she is. Nope, I'll go on my own.'

'Tell her she can't go,' Nina protested.

'I've tried that, and so have you. It didn't get us anywhere did it, and we can't stop her going,' Alice added, giving Nina a significant look. 'Not when she's still got all her marbles.'

'That's debatable,' Nina growled. 'We can always hide the old bat's passport.'

'Listen. She wants to do this,' (Flossie nodded so hard her teeth rattled loosely in her mouth) 'and we all agree she can't go on her own...' Alice said.

'No we don't. *I* don't agree,' Flossie interjected. The other two shushed her.

'...so I suggest you go with her, Nina,' Alice finished with a flourish, akin to a magician pulling a dopey old rabbit out of a battered top hat and shouting "ta dah!"

'No, not me,' Nina squeaked.

'Yes, you,' Alice said.

'But—'

'But what? Too busy working, are you?'

Nina shook her head at her mother's sarcasm. The school summer holidays had started on Friday and Nina taught history in a secondary school, so of course she wasn't working.

'Is your boyfriend whisking you away for a couple of weeks?' her mother continued with a relentless lack of mercy, and Nina narrowed her eyes in irritation. Her last proper boyfriend had been two years ago, a fact her annoying mother was well aware of.

'No boyfriend,' she said, through gritted teeth, 'I'm concentrating on my career.'

Between rolling her eyes and gritting her teeth, Nina guessed she was going to need some serious work on her face to put it back the way it had been half an hour earlier, before she'd walked into this madhouse her mother called home.

'It's about time one of my grandchildren got married and produced some babies,' Gran said randomly. 'It'll give your mother summat else to think about and take her mind off me.'

'Gran, Ben is only eighteen!' Nina cried, the image of her younger brother holding a baby making her shudder. She'd never known anyone as clumsy as Ben. And *she* certainly wasn't ready for children – she saw enough of the little darlings at work. Besides, there was no man on the horizon, and if she was going to have babies, she'd like to do it the old-fashioned way and get married first.

'Are you sure? I could have sworn he was older. Not him then, if he's only eighteen,' her gran said. 'He's gotta play the field a bit, he needs to try before he buys. But what about you? You're old enough. In my day, you'd be a bit too old to be having your first baby at your age. What's your excuse?' Flossie countered.

'Well?' Alice folded her arms and stared over the top of her spectacles.

'I refuse to answer that. I don't have to justify my love life to either of you,' Nina declared.

Gran said, 'I've got a vested interest – the way you're going I'll probably be dead before you find a bloke to marry, and I've got a lovely hat I want to wear.'

'I wasn't talking about marriage and babies,' her mother said, 'I was talking about whether you'll agree to go on holiday with your grandmother?'

Nina blinked as she tried to get her head around the simultaneous conversations, and decided to answer her mother, as the lesser of two evils. 'Do I have to go?' She was aware she sounded as teenagery as the kids she taught, but she couldn't seem to help it. Her mother often reduced her to fourteen.

'Yes.' Alice nodded firmly. 'Just think of all the lovely things she's done for you. It's the least you can do for her.'

Nina screwed up her nose. What was it exactly her grandmother had done? Once, she'd made Nina spend a whole summer when she was fifteen picking blackberries so Gran could sell them by the pound to passersby ("character-forming" Flossie had retorted when Nina complained about scratched arms and legs) – was that supposed to have been for Nina's benefit? Or the time when Gran had blackmailed Nina into singing solo at the Old Age Pensioners' Christmas dinner, when her Gran was well aware Nina was tone-deaf? Nina would never forget the way one old gent had stuck his fingers in his ears to shut out the din. Or the time Gran persuaded Nina to wax her grandad's back, because he'd entered a body beautiful competition (the senior category, so that was okay then – *not*); his yells had affected her hearing for days afterwards.

'Besides,' her mother added, 'you heard your gran, she's getting on a bit and—' Alice dropped her gaze and bit her lip.

Nina held up a hand. 'Stop it with the emotional blackmail.'

Do mothers develop guilt-trip skills when they become pregnant or do they take courses in it, Nina wondered.

'If I go, and I'm not saying I will, I'm not sharing a room.' Nina shuddered. She loved her grandmother, but there were limits to what she was prepared to do in the name of that love. She needed her privacy, and a place to escape to when her grandmother's company became a bit too much.

Flossie turned to Alice. 'See? It's impossible. She can't come.'

Alice snatched the brochure off the table, went straight to the relevant page, and read. 'All rooms have twin beds, a private bathroom, balcony or terrace, blah, blah, blah. An additional charge is made for single occupancy. *Single occupancy*! Next excuse?'

Nina cast around for one. 'Ha! I haven't got a passport.'

'Yes, you have.'

'I haven't seen it in years.'

'That's because it's in my dressing table drawer,' Alice said.

'What is it doing in there?'

'You left it at home after the last time you went abroad.'

'Six years ago? Surely it can't still be in date?'

Alice smiled like a Cheshire cat on happy pills, and Nina realised her mother had set her up. 'It is, I checked.'

'Okay, okay, I'll go,' Nina said, giving into the inevitable, sounding more like she was spending two weeks in prison rather than two weeks in a hotel for the discerning traveller.

'Is Nina coming?' Flossie asked Alice, cupping a hand around her ear.

'Yes, Gran, I'm coming,' Nina shouted, plastering a smile on her face and trying to make the best of it. After all, what could be so bad – sun, sand, sea, and total relaxation for two whole weeks? All she needed to do was load up her iPad and plug her ear buds in when the bingo and karaoke started.

Despite the way her mother had railroaded her into going (she'd get her back sooner or later), Nina had a sneaking suspicion that she was starting to look forward to it. Then she realised how sad that sounded, when two weeks babysitting her gran was going to be the highlight of her summer. Great.

Chapter 2

'Let's have a look?' Nina held her hand out and Flossie passed her the brochure, already open at the correct page. Nina smiled – her gran was so looking forward to their holiday. She wondered how many people had been subjected to the dubious pleasure of having the old woman shove the brochure under their noses. Everyone at the Salvation Army she guessed. Gran wasn't a member, but she liked to go along to their meetings on Wednesday afternoons because they did "a lovely cream tea", though the singing was "a bit of a nuisance", the Old Age Pensioners ('I only go to keep the old biddies company,' Gran argued), and anyone else in the village who was unfortunate enough to come within ten feet of her.

Nina studied the brochure whilst trying not to walk into any other pedestrians. Or lamp posts. She narrowly missed smacking straight into a post, as Flossie grabbed her arm, almost yanking her off her feet. For such a little woman, her grandmother could really pack a punch.

If the photos were anything to go by, the hotel looked gorgeous; right on the beach and a stone's throw away from the lively main street. The interior was tasteful, and it had a little courtyard and a fountain, and boasted a Turkish bath, though Nina had no idea what one of those was). It also had an impossibly-blue pool, and the rooms seemed spacious, though she suspected the single rooms wouldn't be quite as nice.

'I'll come in with you, shall I?' Nina offered, as the pair of them came to a halt outside the travel agent's shop.

'It's alright dear, I can manage. You go and find yourself a nice bikini and I'll meet you in Marks and Sparks when I'm done. I'm in desperate need of some new knickers.'

Right, she can sort those out on her own, Nina decided.

She kissed her grandmother on her softly wrinkled cheek, reminded her to see if the booking could be amended from a twin room to two singles ('I don't mind if it costs extra – I'll pay,' Nina said), and headed off to search for suitable swimwear, with a little butterfly of anticipation skipping about in her stomach. It had been a long time since she'd been beachwear shopping, and she had no idea what suited her, nor what other clothes to buy.

The sales assistant in Debenhams was lovely.

'Where are you going?' the girl asked.

'Turkey. I can't remember the name of it, but apparently, according to my gr— friend, it has a beautiful blue lagoon.'

'Ooh, I know it. Me and my boyfriend went there a couple of years ago. It was lovely. The water in the lagoon is like bathwater.'

'Will the weather be hot?' Nina asked with trepidation. She wasn't too good in the heat, or the cold. She didn't like rain much either, come to think of it. Rain made her hair stick to her head like it was painted on whenever she was forced to put her hood up, and she broke every umbrella within a few days of purchase. No, she wasn't too keen on rain.

The assistant nodded emphatically. 'Really, really hot.'

'Should I take a cardi?'

'Nah. I took a couple of bikinis and lots of skimpy dresses. Oh, and a baggy T-shirt to pop on over my bikini for when the sun got to be too much and I wanted to cover up. Tell me what size you are and I'll bring you a selection of things.'

She showed Nina into a cubicle, and five minutes later was back with a huge armful of clothes.

Nina eyed the assorted wisps of next-to-nothing with dismay. Was that what women on holidays wore these days? The last time she'd gone abroad she'd worn pretty, long floaty dresses, and she distinctly remembered her bikini had more than enough material to cover her modesty. The tiny triangles the assistant held up were barely large enough to hide her nipples, let alone the rest of her boobs.

Nina crossed her arms defensively, imagining how exposed she'd feel wearing so little. It was almost porno-graphic. The other tiny offerings the assistant showed her weren't any better; worse in fact, because one of them appeared to be made of some kind of loosely knitted wool, and she shuddered when she imagined the effect water would have on it.

'Er…' she said, 'have you got anything a little less revealing?' She didn't want to give any of the old folk in the hotel a heart attack. Nicely covered and modest would do. She guessed she'd stand out enough as it was, because she'd be younger than everyone else in the hotel, without drawing any more undue attention to herself. She suspected she'd feel self-conscious enough already.

'How about a one-piece? You're too small up top for the bikinis that really cover you up more. They're designed for the larger or older lady.'

Nina nodded weakly. 'A one-piece is fine.' Great, not only was she a prude, but she'd just been informed that she didn't possess enough in the breast department to be prudish about.

While she waited for her tormentor to return, Nina sifted through the rest of the clothes. Strappy, plunging necklines were complimented (if that was the right word) by hemlines short enough to reveal what she'd had for lunch. No thanks, but at least she now knew what she wanted – loose and floaty, preferably in cotton or linen, though linen did have a nasty tendency to crease.

She eventually left Debenhams with several bulging carrier bags and a seriously depleted bank balance. Who'd have thought such lightweight clothes would cost so much!

Flossie was already seated in a corner booth in Marks and Spencer's café, with a pot of tea in front of her. As soon as she saw Nina she called 'Coo-ee' to a waitress, who smiled and brought a coffee for the new arrival. Nina dumped her bags on the floor and dropped into a chair with a harried sigh.

'It's official,' she announced. 'I hate shopping.'

'Show me what you've bought,' Flossie said, and Nina bent down to retrieve the first thing which came to hand – a swimming costume.

She soon sat up straight again when Flossie produced a miniature bottle of vodka and poured it into her tea. 'Gran,' she hissed, 'what are you doing?'

'Drinking my tea,' the old lady said, a picture of wide-eyed innocence.

'Put it away, you'll get us thrown out!'

'Don't be such a wuss,' Flossie replied, sucking up her tea with relish and smacking her lips.

Nina had difficulty getting her head around the fact that her eighty-four-year-old, frail grandmother had just called her a wuss, *and* that she carried vodka in her handbag and was brazen enough to flash it in the middle of an M&S coffee shop, without even batting an eyelid.

Her grandmother was a secret lush.

'Want some?' Flossie asked, waving the half empty bottle.

'Put it away,' Nina repeated, scanning the café like a spy expecting an ambush. 'I'm sure they've got to have a license or something if they intend serving alcohol.'

'*They're* not serving alcohol,' Flossie pointed out. 'I'm serving myself.'

Nina sighed and looked away when a couple on a neighbouring table gave her a dagger-like stare. Anyone would think she had some control over what her grandmother did. She snorted and thought, 'I wish!'

She'd forgotten she was still holding her one-piece, until Flossie jabbed a finger at it and asked, 'What do you call that?'

'A swimming costume, Gran.'

'It looks roomy enough to fit a horse inside. Did you pick up the right size?'

'Yes, thank you.' Nina was indignant; there was nothing wrong with her costume.

'Bit old-ladyish, innit?' Flossie slipped the now-empty bottle into her voluminous bag.

'Not at all. I like it!' Nina changed the subject. 'Did you manage to alter the name on the booking, or do I have to take all this back for a refund?' Nina relaxed a little now the vodka was hidden away.

Flossie blinked owlishly. 'What name?'

'My name, remember? You were going into the travel agent to change the booking from Grandad's name to mine.' Please don't let her really be losing her marbles, Nina prayed silently.

Her grandmother looked relieved, as if her memory had suddenly come back. 'Oh that,' she waved a hand airily. 'All done. Nothing for you to worry about.'

'What about the rooms?'

'Booked. As I said, nothing to fret about, all sorted.'

'Shall I check the paperwork, just to make sure?'

'I'm perfectly capable of sorting it out myself,' Flossie said, sitting straighter in her seat and doing a Queen Victoria impression. Nina could tell she wasn't amused.

'Okay, if you're sure…?'

'I am. Now, let's not hear any more about it. Show me what else you bought, and I'll show you mine,' Flossie commanded.

Nina glanced around, not certain she wanted to drag any more of her purchases out, especially since Flossie had been so dismissive of her swimming costume. Her grandmother had no such qualms, producing a huge pair of knickers and holding them up for the whole world to see.

'Look, they've got a pretty bow on them,' Flossie announced.

Several titters from nearby tables had Nina wishing she could slide under her chair and hide.

'Lovely, Gran. Now put them away.' What on earth had gotten into the old woman, Nina wondered. She'd always been a bit odd, flighty some might say, but she never used to be as bad as this. Maybe it was grief; Nina had read it could do funny things to people. She just hoped it was nothing more sinister – like the start of dementia.

Her first phone call after she dropped her grandmother home was to the travel agent. Just to make sure.

'I'm ringing about a booking my grandmother, Florence Gibbins, made. She was in this morning, changing one of the names. You see, my grandfather, her husband, died and—'

'Florence Gibbins, you said? Yes, she was in this morning, booking an all-inclusive holiday for two people to Turkey, for two weeks, flying from Birmingham.'

'That's right, but I'm worried about the names. Did she manage to get one of them changed?'

'Mrs Florence Gibbins and Miss Nina Clarke are the names on the booking. Is one of them not correct?' The voice on the other end of the phone was rather impatient and Nina didn't blame him, not if he'd had to put up with her grandmother's peculiar brand of logic for an hour or so this morning.

'Yes, that's fine. That's what it should be. Thank you for sorting it out for her. She wouldn't let me help you see, she wanted to do it by herself and—'

'Is there anything else I can help you with?' he interjected, then maybe sensing the possibility of an add-on purchase, his tone became rather sweeter when he suggested, 'In-flight meal, additional luggage allowance, extra leg room?' The last was said with reverence.

'Er, no thanks. What about tickets?' she asked.

'Tickets are a thing of the past,' the man on the other end of the phone announced grandly. She used the term, "man", loosely – he sounded about twelve. 'It's all done via email now.'

'But my grandmother doesn't have email. She doesn't have a computer. I'd be surprised if she even knew what one was.'

'It's all sorted. I printed everything out for her before she left, and I've checked you in for both flights.'

Nina shook her head in consternation. 'How are people supposed to check in without tickets?'

'Mrs Gibbins knows what to do. Just turn up at the airport with your passports and a copy of your booking, which Mrs Gibbins already has, and everything will be taken care of by our excellent airport staff.'

'Oh. Good. That's it then, all sorted.'

'Precisely.'

Nina ended the call, relieved her grandmother seemed to have it all in hand, though she was still a little concerned about her gran's mental health. She phoned her mother, to put her own mind at rest – just to be sure.

'I'm a bit worried about Gran,' Nina said, as soon as her mother answered the phone. 'Oh, and by the way, thanks again for landing me with her.'

'You'll have a lovely time,' Alice said. 'Sun, sea, sand, sangria, and sexy waiters.'

'Sangria is Spanish isn't it? And I don't want a waiter, however sexy he might happen to be.'

'I'm sure Turkey has a sangria equivalent, just don't drink too much of it.'

'You should be giving that advice to your mother,' Nina replied dryly. 'She drank a whole bottle of vodka right in the middle of Marks and Sparks coffee shop.'

'A *whole* bottle? Is she alright? You didn't leave her on her own, did you? What if she vomits – she could choke.'

'A whole miniature bottle,' Nina amended, 'and you sound as if you're talking about a teenager, not an eighty-four-year-old woman.'

'I did think a whole bottle was a bit excessive,' her mother said, 'but there's not much in one of those little miniatures, is there?'

Nina rolled her eyes. She really did seem to be doing a lot of that lately. 'Anyway, the reason I rang, was to ask if Gran is alright.'

'She's fine. Missing your grandad of course, but this holiday is just what she needs to take her mind off it. They used to love their holidays. Always off gallivanting, they were. They used to call your gran Judith Chalmers down at the WI.'

'Who's Judith Chalmers?'

'She used to present a travel show on the BBC. Went all over the place, just like your grandparents and had more holidays than hot dinners.'

'So you think she's okay? Not forgetful or anything?' Nina persisted.

'She's fine. There's nothing wrong with her.' Alice was adamant, and Nina had to accept her verdict. After all, her mother spent more time with Gran than she did; if she said Gran was fine, then Gran was fine.

Chapter 3

Nina had been abroad before but Turkey was nothing like Majorca, or Paris, or Prague. It was hot (even at three-thirty in the morning) and the air outside the airport smelled different – exotic, strange, exciting, and definitely not English.

She was amazed at the amount of people around at such an early hour: tourists, reps, airport staff themselves, drivers, and other assorted men (they seemed to be mostly men), whose business she could not even begin to guess at, milled around the exits and spilled onto the concourse beyond.

Her grandmother was totally unfazed. Marching towards the bay where one of the tour reps had told them their bus was parked, as though she was the only person there, she forced people to move aside or risk getting trampled. Nina was left to manhandle both cases on her own. Her grandmother might be tiny and a bit on the scrawny side, but woe betide anyone who got in her way, or stopped her from doing something she had set her mind on doing. The fact that she'd drank several vodkas on the plane merely added to the old lady's determination. Nina wondered if her grandmother was as tipsy as Nina herself would have been under the same circumstances, and she suspected not.

Nearly two hours later, with Gran asleep in the seat next to her, the old lady's head lolling back and her mouth open, the coach dropped off the edge of the world.

Nina let out a gasp.

Spread out below was a glittering, illuminated resort, the flat silver light of dawn showcasing the steep, high sides of the mountains surrounding it, with the sea sprawling in front of her. They were so high up she felt as though she was on the aircraft again.

The coach, brakes squealing and with an alarming stench of burning rubber, descended the steep, winding road. A wall of rock rose above them on the right, and certain death lay on the left. She was pathetically glad Turks drove on the opposite side of the road to the Brits, because it meant there were at least a couple of lanes of tarmac between her and infinity. Then the horrible realisation that they would probably have to come back up this road on the return journey to the airport struck her. She closed her eyes, then opened them again in a hurry as an image of a moped with a goat riding on it flashed across her eyeballs.

She hastily twisted in her seat for a better look as the coach overtook the small vehicle, just in time to catch a glimpse of a man, a woman, three children, and a goat, all precariously perched on the too-small seat.

The boy clutching the resigned-looking goat gave Nina a big smile. Nina smiled back, with more of a sickly grimace than a grin. Dear lord, where were the traffic police? Had the moped's driver any concept of health and safety? What if they were to have an accident?

She was still shaking her head as the coach reached the bottom of the valley and manoeuvred its length through a narrow street, cars parked haphazardly on either side, before pulling up outside a grand building with *Aphrodite Hotel* emblazoned in enormous illuminated letters above the entrance. They'd arrived, thank goodness.

Nina roused her gently snoring grandmother, leaving her to light up a cigarette (she never knew her grandmother smoked until Gran had bought those cigarettes at the airport), while she supervised the unloading of their cases, checking carefully to ensure she'd been given the correct ones. The last thing she wanted was to get to her room to find she had the clothes belonging to one of the middle-aged women who'd been hogging the coveted front seats. Nina hated travelling by bus, and the journey would have been much more tolerable if she could have sat in the front, being able to see where she was going – or maybe not. Rock walls, steep drops, overloaded mopeds... Nina shuddered.

The hotel reception was a pleasant surprise, all marbled floor and walls, and polished wooden desk. And cool too. The air-con on the bus had been less than effective, and the flower-scented, slightly chilled reception area soothed her over-tired nerves and overly-sticky skin.

Her gran seemed none the worse for the journey, happily filling in the registration details and signing her name with a flourish. The staff, Nina saw, wore huge smiles, and everyone, including the cleaning ladies who were sweeping the floor with short-handled brushes, stopped to greet her grandmother. They mostly ignored Nina. She wasn't bothered; it was just refreshing to see a culture which seemed to revere the elderly. Britain could certainly take a leaf out of Turkey's book.

One of the reception staff handed Flossie a key. 'Room 216,' he said.

Nina waited to be given hers.

And waited.

'Is there something else I can help you with?' the man asked her.

'My key?' Nina looked at the array of pigeon-holes, wondering which one contained the key to her room. She hoped she'd be given a room close to her grandmother.

'I have given it to the other lady,' he said.

'My grandmother has my key as well as her own?'

'Your grandmother has the key, yes.'

'Oh, that's – hang on, did you say *the* key? There's only one key?' Nina was tired, but she was certain she heard him correctly.

The immaculately uniformed, professionally smiling young man replied slowly, as if she was as hard of hearing as her grandmother (though Gran's deafness tended to come and go when it suited her). 'There is only one key for each room, madam.'

Madam, he called me *madam*, was all Nina could think about. Since when had "miss" become "madam"? Surely, she wasn't that old! Mind you, she thought, the man in question was barely older than the kids in her A-level class, so anything over twenty was bound to appear old to him.

'Nina? What's the matter?' Flossie sounded impatient. Another equally young man waited next to her, their luggage at his feet.

'I need my key.'

'I've got it,' Flossie said and Nina tutted; something had obviously gotten lost in translation.

'*You've* got it?' she confirmed.

'I just said so. Come on, I want to get my head down for a couple of hours before breakfast.'

Nina let the bellboy lead the way. She would have preferred to wheel her own suitcase but was too tired to argue. He led them along well-tended twisting paths, and Nina quickly became disorientated, and was grateful for his guidance.

From what Nina could make out, the hotel consisted of a main building where reception was housed, a courtyard beyond which was filled with tinkling fountains, and a series of two-storey blocks of rooms. She spied other buildings through the bushes and trees dotting the hotel grounds, but had no idea what they were, and looked forward to finding out in the morning (this was technically the morning, but since she hadn't been to bed yet, it didn't count).

Flossie's room was on the top floor, and Nina hoped hers was close by so she could keep an eye on the old lady.

'216,' the young man said, in heavily accented English, and he opened the door with a flourish.

'It's lovely, Gran,' Nina said, following the bellboy and her grandmother inside.

Two single beds (towels in the shape of a bird artfully arranged on each of them), a TV, a couple of easy chairs, a bathroom with a walk-in shower, and a glimpse of the pool beyond the doors leading to the balcony – she hoped her own room would be as nice.

The boy dropped the cases on the floor, showed them how the air-con worked (Nina told Flossie to leave it on because the room was quite warm already – goodness knows what it would be like when the sun really came up), and waited while her gran dug in her purse for some Turkish money.

'Enjoy your stay,' the boy said, pocketing the note with alacrity, before disappearing out of the door with a big smile on his face. Nina wondered exactly how much Grannie had tipped him.

'Wait, what about my room?' Nina hissed after him, trying to keep her voice down, conscious of the sleeping occupants in neighbouring rooms. Too late. He had gone.

'What are you on about, dear?' Flossie demanded, throwing open the balcony doors and lighting another cigarette.

Nina waved at the air in front of her face and coughed dramatically.

'Oh, loosen up,' Flossie grumbled, stepping outside. 'Everyone smokes over here.'

Nina didn't care what everyone else got up to, she just wanted the key to her room. A cup of tea (she'd brought some Tetley tea bags with her), a quick shower and a sleep, that's what she needed.

'My key,' she prompted. 'He said you had it.'

Flossie gave her an exasperated look. 'It's there.' She pointed to the key sitting on top of a chest of drawers.

'Finally!' Nina scooped it up and looked at the number. '216,' she said. 'This is your key.'

'It's yours, too.'

'I want my own.'

Flossie stubbed her cigarette out in the ashtray on the little table on the balcony, and turned to her. 'Well, you can't have one,' she said. 'You heard what the man on reception said, one room, one key.'

It took some time for the penny to drop, and for an intelligent woman, Nina was aware she sometimes tended to miss the obvious.

'We're sharing, aren't we?' she said, closing her eyes when she realised. Mum, she thought, I'm going to kill you when I get home. 'I thought you said you'd sorted out separate rooms?'

'No. I forgot.' Flossie's eyes were wide and innocent. 'Look on the bright side, single rooms wouldn't be this nice, and you didn't think you were going to get a room like this all to yourself, did you, not with the prices they charge. Under-occupancy fee, my arse!'

That's exactly what Nina had thought. And that's exactly what she would have got if this was a Premier Inn. Premier Inns didn't expect people to share if they didn't want to. She knew she should have accompanied her gran when the old woman had gone to the travel agent to amend the booking.

At least there were single beds – the thought of being spooned by her inebriated grandmother made Nina wince.

'Come and look at the view,' Flossie commanded, and Nina let her change the subject. There was nothing to be done about it now, so she might as well make the best of it. Besides, her gran didn't need reminding the bed Nina was going to sleep in had been intended for Flossie's husband, and Nina felt a bit of a heel for making such a fuss.

Their balcony overlooked the pool, and what a lovely pool it was. Free-form was the description in the brochure, Nina recalled, staring at its curving lines and turquoise water. The pool was illuminated from below and there must be lights in the bottom, she surmised, hoping there were no sharp edges to scratch unwary feet.

The grounds, what she could see of them, appeared to be lovely too, with plenty of space between the sun loungers, and lots of umbrellas. Flowering trees and shrubs lined the paved walkways and grew against the white walls of the lower storeys. The grass was well-tended, and Nina noticed the sprinklers were on now.

The place seemed nice, she decided, glad her mother had talked her into coming. Sort of.

She remained on the balcony drinking in the sights and sounds of a foreign country, while Gran got ready for bed.

'Don't forget to set the alarm,' Flossie said, coming out of the bathroom with curlers in her hair and wearing a flannelette nightie. Thankfully she still had her false teeth in, so Nina wouldn't be faced with the sight of a pair of gnashers in a glass – not today, anyway, though tonight might be a different matter entirely. The only thing Nina wanted to see in a glass was a cocktail, and maybe a piece of fruit at a push.

'Don't forget Turkey is two hours ahead of us, so change the time on your watch,' Gran instructed.

'Why the alarm?' Nina asked, making sure both her phone and her watch had automatically picked up Turkish time (they had).

'I don't want to miss breakfast,' Flossie said.

'Snacks are available all day, aren't they?' Nina argued, looking longingly at the beds. Once she slipped inside those cool, cotton sheets she had no intention of crawling back out until she was good and ready.

'I *like* breakfast,' Flossie retorted. 'It's the most important meal of the day. Besides, if I don't eat regularly, I get constipated.'

Gross! TMI, Gran, Nina thought, TMI.

'Okay, I'll set the alarm on my phone,' Nina said, silently cursing the old woman. It was alright for Gran, who'd slept on the plane (only waking up when the drink trolley trundled past) and again on the coach. Nina had been awake since seven o'clock yesterday morning. Nearly twenty-four hours. It felt more like forty-eight; her eyes were gritty, her lids were heavy, and her brain was filled with cotton wool. She hoped if she slept for a couple of hours, it would tide her over until tonight. She'd go to bed about ten-ish – earlier if Gran couldn't stand the pace.

At least the hotel was lovely and quiet, so sleeping shouldn't be a problem, and she couldn't imagine a bunch of wrinklies staying up until the early hours whipping up a storm. I bet this place is dead by midnight, Nina thought happily. She had never been one for staying up late and partying, being too conscious of having to get up for school on a weekday and not wanting to waste a weekend by having a hangover or sleeping in late. And she didn't like to mess her routine up in the school holidays, because it was always difficult to get back into the rhythm of early rising once the new term started. She didn't often give in and let her hair down.

Anyway, maybe she could have a snooze on the sun-lounger, or nip back to their room for an afternoon nap. She suspected Gran would also give in to temptation and have a little sleep, too.

After she completed her own bedtime routine (quick shower, brush teeth, and not forgetting to cleanse, tone, and moisturise) Nina pulled the sheet back and clambered into bed. Her grandmother was already out for the count, snoring slightly, and Nina smiled at her before snuggling down.

'Hope you have a good time, Gran,' she whispered. After all, that's why they were here, wasn't it, because the old lady needed cheering up. Nina just hoped her grandmother wouldn't find her too young and lively, and she made a promise to the slumbering old lady to take it easy and to try not to forget how set in their ways elderly people could be.

Chapter 4

Loud Turkish voices dragged Nina from the depths of sleep. She turned over, pulled the pillow around her head, and grumbled, 'Turn it down, Gran.'

'I think it's the news. I always watch the news.'

Nina sat up reluctantly, rubbing her eyes. 'It's in Turkish,' she pointed out. 'You don't speak a word.'

'I can watch the pictures, can't I? I can get the gist of what they're saying from those. Ooh, look, they're talking about football. See?'

'Great.' Nina admitted defeat and got out of bed. 'What's the time?'

'Half past eight,' Gran said, her backside in the air and her head buried in her suitcase.

Nina groaned. They'd been asleep less than two hours. She blinked blearily and let out a huge yawn. 'You go. I'll have another hour in bed.'

'There's plenty of time for sleeping when you're dead,' Flossie announced. 'What do you think?'

'I think I need more sleep,' Nina replied, anxious to avoid the "D" word or anything associated with it. Her grandmother was so blasé about Grandad's death and her own mortality, but Nina felt uncomfortable talking about it. She didn't even want to think about it, yet it was one of Flossie's favourite topics of conversation. She was forever phoning Nina to tell her who had passed on.

'Guess who's died?' she'd ask with a dark, self-satisfied glee. Nina could only assume her grandmother was chuffed she'd managed to outlive the poor, unfortunate deceased.

'No idea,' Nina would say.

'Mrs Thingamy-bob from down the road. You know… her with the limp and a sister who lives in Cheshire,' Flossie would reply, leaving Nina none the wiser.

'I wasn't talking about more sleep. I was talking about this.' Flossie held up a fluorescent yellow tunic with tassels on the hem.

'What is it?' Nina squinted hard. It looked like some kind of hippy tablecloth.

'I bought it to slip on over my cozzie,' Gran said. 'I'll show you,' she added and reached for the hem of her nightie.

Nina dashed to the bathroom, making a grab for her own suitcase on the way past, and reached the door in three huge strides (faster than Usain Bolt on a really good day). There was no way on earth she wanted to see her grandmother naked.

'I'll have a quick shower and find my swimming costume. Then we'll go for breakfast, yeah? Will you be ready by the time I'm done?' Nina called through the firmly-closed bathroom door.

She turned the water on, pinned her short bob back as best she could, and stepped into the cubicle, not really needing another wash, since she'd only had one a couple of hours ago, but wanting to give her grandmother as much time as possible to get dressed.

She'd barely lathered up before Flossie banged on the door.

'Your phone is making a funny noise,' her grandmother yelled. 'I think there's something wrong with it. Shall I ask reception to find a man to come and fix it?'

'I'll get a man to come and fix *you*,' Nina muttered before calling back, 'I'll be out in a minute.'

'It sounds like someone's in pain. There's all this moaning coming from it.'

'It's whale song,' Nina shouted.

'I can't turn it off.'

'Press the button that says snooze, Gran.'

'Eh?'

'Press the – never mind, I'll be out in a second.'

She hastily rinsed off, grabbed a towel and wrapped it around her chest, tucking it in place under her armpits, and opened the door to see Flossie clutching the hotel phone in one hand and Nina's mobile in the other. Nina snatched the receiver out of her grandmother's hand and slammed it back on its base, hoping she hadn't cut anyone off mid-sentence. Whale song filled the room, but for once Nina failed to find it soothing. She grabbed her phone, stabbed at it, and was rewarded with silence.

'What was wrong with it?' Flossie demanded.

'Nothing,' Nina replied through a slightly clenched jaw. 'It was just my alarm, Gran. You told me to put it on, remember?'

'It didn't sound like an alarm,' the older woman grumbled.

'It's whale song,' Nina repeated.

'Never heard of 'em. In my day people sang proper songs – none of this rubbish you hear now-a-days. I couldn't understand a word they were saying, and they couldn't carry a tune either.'

Nina changed the subject. 'Nice tunic,' she said, thinking she should have put her sunglasses on before she looked at it. It was so bright it had probably damaged her corneas. The colour positively burned her eyeballs, but at least it covered her grandmother up, as did the very large, very floppy white hat and the oversized sunglasses. Flossie reminded Nina of an old, saggy Sophia Loren.

'I could murder a cuppa,' Flossie announced. 'Ready?'

Nina gave the old woman a disbelieving look. She still had a bath towel wrapped around her modesty and she hadn't even found her swimming costume yet. Did she look bloody ready?

'Hang on,' she said, resisting the urge to grit her teeth. She had a feeling this holiday was going to feel considerably longer than the fourteen days it professed to be. She'd need another holiday afterwards to recover from this one. Her grandmother was proving to be hard work already!

Back in the bathroom Nina found her costume and put it on. The black fabric looked a little stark against her too-pale skin but there hadn't been that many cozzies to choose from so late in the season. Especially since she had been searching for one which didn't make her seem as though she was about to take part in a fifty-metre free style competition, or one which was made for someone her Gran's age. It might be early August, but the shops were already selling off their summer stuff. The bright colours and light fabrics were now squashed together on the sale rails, like so many abandoned birds of paradise. Their uncoordinated, random-sized chaos made her feel slightly nauseous at the prospect of ploughing through them, whilst the rest of the shop sported pullovers in autumn colours and knee-high boots. They even had "return to school" stuff out, when the actual start of term wasn't for another four weeks and two days, if the teacher training days were included (not that she was counting).

It was lucky that, given a choice, Nina would have picked black anyway, and this one wasn't all pull-you-in and push-you-up, but neither was it too revealing. She'd bought another very similar one, but it was lower cut at the back and she wasn't sure she was ready to bare that much white skin just yet.

A pair of shorts, a T-shirt, and flip flops completed her outfit – she was good to go.

She stopped dead when she opened the bathroom door to see the four inch, gold coloured, wedged sandals on Flossie's gnarled feet.

'You're not wearing those,' she protested. 'Are you?'

'Why not?' Flossie shoved her sunglasses to the top of her head and peered down at her feet. 'What's wrong with them?'

'They're too high! You'll fall and break a hip.'

'Listen, young lady, I've been wearing heels higher than this since before your mother was born. Worry about your own hips.'

'Yes, but you weren't eighty-four then.'

'I'm not eighty-four now,' came the indignant reply.

'Yes, you are. Hang on.' Nina counted back on her fingers, her face screwed up in concentration. 'We celebrated your eightieth birthday when I was twenty-four. I'm now twenty-eight. That makes you eighty-four.'

'No, it doesn't,' Flossie retorted.

Nina blinked, confused. Maths might not be her specialist subject, but adding and subtracting had never been an issue for her.

'It wasn't my eightieth birthday,' Flossie said. 'It was my seventy-ninth.'

'Your seventy-ninth? But there were balloons with eighty on, and cards saying "Happy 80th Birthday", and a banner. You even had a cake.' Dear lord, the old lady really was losing it. Poor old thing. Nina prayed her grandmother wouldn't deteriorate too much before she got Flossie safely back home.

'Yes, that's right, dear, I did,' Gran said. 'Lovely cake it was, too.'

'But if it wasn't your eightieth birthday, why did we all…? Forget it, it doesn't matter.' Her grandmother's logic often confounded Nina, and her mother had long ago given up trying to make sense of it all.

And with that Nina escorted her grandmother to breakfast.

Chapter 5

The hotel was still nice and quiet. A few people sat at tables and there were one or two more at the buffet, but that was all. Nina thought there might have been some children up and about but... Hang on, Nina gave herself a mental slap on her forehead. Of course! This hotel was probably aimed at the elderly. They weren't travelling with *Saga*, the most well-known of the holiday companies for the over fifties, but she guessed this was similar. Ergo, no children.

Her theory was shot out of the water when she got a good look at the other breakfast eaters. They all seemed to be around her age, or a little older, and certainly not in the retired league.

She settled Flossie at a table, and went off to forage, coming back with a heaped bowl of fruit salad topped with creamy yoghurt. Yum. Whilst she was gone, two cups of coffee had been placed on the table.

'They've got three different kinds of muesli,' Nina enthused, tucking into her fruit with gusto. She'd almost finished when her grandmother returned with a plate piled high with pancakes and syrup, with a selection of pastries on the side.

'Want one?' Gran offered.

'No, thanks. I only usually have a smoothie, so this is a treat for me.'

'Hmmph. We're at an all-you-can-eat buffet and you stick to rabbit food. Live a little.'

'I don't call eating sugar-laden pastries living a little,' Nina retorted as her grandmother stuffed a huge forkful of dripping pancake into her mouth and chewed enthusiastically.

'Let your hair down for once,' Flossie said. 'Have some.' She picked up the plate of pastries and thrust it in Nina's direction.

Nina shuddered. 'Maybe later,' she said, trying to placate the old woman, who seemed intent on getting her fat. Nina knew she'd have to be careful on the food front, else she'd return home the size of an elephant. And she'd probably break out in spots too, if she ate too much rich food.

Breakfast done, Flossie headed off towards the pool, Nina trailing behind. Flossie, after much dithering, decided on a spot halfway between the poolside bar and the pool itself. Several sunbeds had towels draped over them, but there were plenty to choose from. Nina, after checking where the sun was (it was just peeping over the top of the rather high mountain and already the temperature had started to rise) angled hers so it was in the shade of two umbrellas.

She wished Flossie hadn't rushed her out of the room – she'd intended to lather herself with factor fifty before she staked her body out on a lounger to bake. Once she'd stripped off down to her swimming costume, she made do with lifting straps and moving the edges of the material aside to make sure she coated every inch of exposed skin. She had no intention of burning.

Her grandmother, on the other hand, dragged her tunic over her head, and flopped down on her sunbed with a grunt.

Nina stared at her in horror.

'What?' Flossie looked down at her wrinkled, sagging body and gave Nina a defiant look. 'You'll be old one day,' she warned.

'You're not seriously going to wear that?' Nina exclaimed.

'I've got it on, haven't I?'

The *it* was one of the tiniest bikinis Nina had ever seen, and not only was it almost indecently skimpy, it was also neon pink, a pink so bright it could bring down passing aircraft.

Nina's mouth was open as she stared in disbelief.

'And *you're* not seriously going to wear *that*, are you?' her grandmother retorted, peering over the top of her sunglasses, her mouth screwed up like a drawstring bag. 'You look like an old woman.'

At least I don't look like mutton dressed up as lamb, Nina thought, before replying with, 'There's nothing wrong with my swimming costume – it's a perfectly acceptable one-piece. In fact, I've brought another one very similar. Sorry Gran, but a *bikini*, at *your* age?'

'*My* age is the best time to wear one, when nobody cares what I look like, least of all me. I wish I'd had the guts to wear something like this when I was a young woman and could have done it justice.'

'But, Gran, you're showing practically everything you've got.'

'My nipples are covered, I'm not flashing my tuppence, and there's enough material to cover my backside, so what's your objection?'

Your age, that's my objection, Nina wanted to say. It simply wasn't seemly for a woman of her grandmother's advanced years to be exposing so much flesh. She hoped the rest of the clientele were better covered up.

'Morning.'

Nina glanced up, and found herself staring a pair of budgie-smugglers in the eye. The white swimming trunks were so tiny and tight, she could see exactly how well-endowed (or not) the man who wore them was.

She gulped, and hastily dragged her eyes away from his pride and joy and up to his face. In between, she caught a glimpse of a hairless chest and a slight pot-belly.

'Good morning,' she replied, a little haughtily.

'Are you going to the bar?' her gran asked. 'I could murder a vodka.'

'Gran! It's only nine-thirty.'

'So? I'm on holiday.'

The stranger laughed, and Nina squinted up at him. She couldn't see his face clearly because the sun chose that moment to rear its head above the parapet of the mountain and try to blind her. The sudden rise in temperature as the rays hit her exposed flesh made her wince.

'They don't serve alcohol until ten,' the man said to her grandmother, then, much to her chagrin, he addressed Nina. 'It gets much hotter than this in the afternoon. I guess this is your first day?'

She nodded, not wanting to encourage him, but not wanting to appear rude, either.

He squatted down in front of their sunbeds, his knees spread wide, and Nina had a close-up of his manhood as everything bulged against the thin fabric, fighting for space.

Please put it away, she begged silently, trying not to look.

'We arrived this morning,' Flossie said, lying back on her sun lounger, before sitting up sharply again to remove a forgotten curler from the back of her hair.

'Thought so. You can always tell the new arrivals by the colour of their skin. Or lack if it!' He laughed heartily at his own joke. 'I'm Carl,' he said. 'Got another three days to go. Maybe I'll see you later?'

This last comment was aimed at Nina and she managed to produce a weak smile. He waited expectantly until she said, 'I'm Nina, and this is my grandmother, Flossie.'

'Nice to meet you.' He held out a hand, and Nina shook it reluctantly. His grip was flaccid and clammy (flaccid wasn't a word she wanted to think about right now, not when she was in such close proximity to the contents of his budgie-smugglers, but she couldn't help herself), and he held her hand a little too long, stroking a finger across her knuckles.

She snatched her arm back and tried to resist the urge to wipe her hand on her towel.

'If you don't mind me asking,' Carl said, looking at Flossie, 'but how did you manage to get a room here?'

'Excuse me!' Nina was incredulous at his rudeness. How dare he! Her grandmother had as much right to be here as he did. Just because she was old didn't mean she shouldn't be able to go on holiday.

'I told the travel agent I'd sue them for being ageist,' Flossie said, her expression deadpan.

'Nice one!' Carl chortled, 'though I don't think there's anyone else in your age group here. Trying to bag yourself a toy-boy, are you? Go for it, I say.' He stood, and Nina kept her attention firmly on the ground, so as not to risk getting another eye-full. 'See you later, I hope.'

He sloped off. Nina let out a sigh of relief. 'What an obnoxious man,' she said, 'suggesting old people shouldn't be allowed to go on holiday.'

'I'm not old,' Flossie replied, reclining back on her lounger. 'I thought he was quite nice. Very friendly.'

'Perhaps he can be your "toy-boy",' Nina retorted, sarcastically.

'I think he fancied you, dear, not me.'

'Yuck. Did you see the budgie smugglers he was wearing – or barely wearing, I should say.'

'He had a nice physique,' her grandmother replied, then did a double-take. 'What budgie?'

'Not a real budgie, Gran. It's what they call those tiny, tight swimming trunks, where it looks like the wearer has a small bird stuffed down them.'

'How ridiculous! He was simply proud of his assets.'

'But he was so rude,' Nina persisted, trying to push the memory of those "assets" firmly to the back of her mind.

'I didn't think so. I thought he was lovely.'

'He more or less inferred you shouldn't be here!' Nina's indignation was getting the better of her. She was becoming all hot and bothered, and a trickle of sweat ran down her back.

'He's right, I shouldn't.'

'What do you mean?' Oh god, don't tell me Gran had thought about topping herself now she no longer had Grandad.

'I'm the wrong age to be on this sort of holiday,' Flossie said, 'but then, so are you.'

Nina was flummoxed. It wasn't a word she often used, but it suited this occasion perfectly. She was totally

41

and utterly flummoxed – her grandmother was either speaking in riddles or was showing ever increasing signs of dementia.

'Gran,' she began cautiously, wondering how to broach the subject. Flossie had been acting a little strange of late, and this wasn't the first time the D-word had flashed through Nina's mind. Her grandmother had always been a little, what was the word? Strange, odd, a law-unto-herself? But what with smoking (Nina had never seen Flossie smoke before), the insistence on drinking alcohol at each and every opportunity, and the totally inappropriate bikini, Nina was becoming seriously worried about the old lady's mental health.

'It's a thirty-to-forty-five hotel,' Flossie said, before Nina could gather her thoughts together enough to say anything.

'A what?'

'This hotel is for people between the ages of thirty to forty-five.'

'But what about *Saga*?'

'Eh? *Saga*? No thanks! That's a travel company for old people.'

'You are old, Gran,' Nina replied, automatically as she struggled to digest the information.

Flossie lit one of her vile cigarettes and blew out a contented plume of smoke. Nina waved a hand in front of her face and coughed, with some exaggeration.

'Oh, get used to it!' Flossie said. 'And if you're that bothered about it, take a walk over to the bar and see if they're serving yet. I'm parched.' She licked her lips in anticipation.

'Let me see if I understand you correctly,' Nina said slowly. 'You've booked us into a hotel which caters solely for people between the ages of thirty and forty-five?'

'Give the girl a gold star,' was the sarcastic reply.

'And the travel agent was happy to do that, despite the fact neither of us fall into that category?'

'Not really. I already told you, I threatened to sue them.'

'I thought you were joking.' Nina let out a long sigh. 'Can you sue over something like that?'

'No idea, but it worked. "*Athena Holidays — For the More Discerning Travel Lover*",' Flossie quoted. 'I thought it was more suitable than an *18–30* holiday. You're a bit long in the tooth for that.'

'Gran, an *18–30* holiday is a party type of hotel, where people go to drink and have… you know…'

'Sex?' Flossie interrupted loudly, and Nina cringed, hoping no one else had heard. 'Yes, well, this is an older version, a more sophisticated version,' the old woman said.

Great, that Carl bloke thought she looked at least thirty, when she was only twenty-eight! Nina closed her eyes and took a deep breath as another thought occurred to her. 'Don't tell me everyone here is single,' she begged, opening them again and giving the pensioner a steely stare.

'Okay, then I won't.' Flossie stubbed her cigarette out and sat up.

'Thank god for that,' Nina started to say, then paused. Her gran could be sneaky, so she aimed for clarification. 'They aren't single, or you won't tell me?'

'Yes.'

'Which one, Gran?' Nina's patience was starting to wear very, very thin.

'The last one.'

'They *are* all single!'

'I expect so.'

'Why—? No, don't bother, I'm not sure I want to know.'

Dear god – Gran and Grandad had deliberately booked a hotel where everyone was at least half their age and unattached, and where the sole purpose of that type of holiday was to hook up with as many people as possible, to have as much sex as possible. Wasn't it? What did that make her grandparents? Voyeurs? The oldest swingers in town? Incredibly hopeful?

Nina sank back onto her sunbed with a groan. No wonder there'd not been any children at breakfast. She supposed it might be a tick in the plus box, as she searched for the positives. Being around children all day meant that by home-time she was heartily sick of the sight and the sound of them. Perhaps this mightn't be so bad after all. It's not as if she had to join in, or was obliged to have a holiday fling, was it?

Besides, she had Flossie with her as a chaperone; her grandmother would put even the most ardent admirer off.

As long as Nina kept herself to herself, nothing would go wrong.

Chapter 6

Someone was holding a match to Nina's ankles and the tops of her feet. She shifted uncomfortably, coming awake with reluctance but unable to remain in the depths of slumber with a blowtorch aimed at her legs.

It took her a moment to realise the bed she was lying on was of the sun-lounger variety. The heat came from the sun itself, which had sneakily moved across the sky with the express purpose of seeking out any bit of exposed flesh it could find and burning it off her bones. Sweat trickled unpleasantly down her back, and her hair clung stickily to her neck.

It was the loud music coming from the bar on the other side of the pool which had woken her, and she lay there for a minute wishing they'd turn it down. She'd never much liked pseudo-rap (or any other kind of rap, for that matter), Adele being more to her taste, even though most of those songs were all aching hearts and lost love, and that one song, *Someone Like You*, was actually a bit stalkerish when you listened to the lyrics. The poor bloke she was obsessing over clearly didn't want anything to do with her – take a hint, why don't you.

It wasn't just music Nina heard, there was chanting too, and it took a second for the actual word which was being shouted to sink in – FLOSS*IE*! FLOSS*IE*! FLOSS*IE*!

It couldn't be! Nina sat up, adjusted her wonky sunglasses, and peered across the sun-sparkling pool. A crowd had gathered around the pool bar, clapping in time to the chanting. In between the swaying, half-dancing bodies, Nina spotted a large, cardboard cut-out of a naked man. And there was something else, something which made her heart plummet to her feet.

Flossie was in the centre of the group, wearing a blind-fold and groping around with one hand, whilst clutching an overly-large, erect, cardboard penis in the other.

Nina leapt to her feet, trying to angle her toes at her flip flops, stuff her legs into her shorts, and yank a T-shirt over her head all at the same time, as she staggered around the pool to the bar to rescue her grandmother. Lord knew what these people were doing to her!

She arrived in time to see Flossie stab the penis in the naked, hairless juncture of the cut-out's thighs where it hung at an eye-watering angle, whip the blindfold off, and turn to her audience with a triumphant smile on her caved-in face.

Somewhere along the way, the old woman had lost her teeth.

Nina reached her grandmother's side, just as a drink was thrust into Flossie's hand. And it wasn't any old drink – this one was in a glass larger than a washing up bowl, and filled to its umbrella-ed brim with lurid green liquid. Chunks of fruit swam in it like sharks in a too-small pool.

Flossie, maybe sensing her granddaughter's intent, gulped down half the contents before Nina had a chance to take it away from her. She sidled around the back of a maniacally grinning bloke who was all teeth and bronzed skin, wearing a white polo shirt with Aphrodite Hotel Entertainment Team and his name, Mohammed, emblazoned across the front, and the old lady defiantly polished off the rest of the concoction.

'Bloody hell, she's a game old bird, ain't she?' a man standing next to Nina said.

Nina drew herself up to her full height of five foot four, and gave him a haughty glance.

'That "old bird" is my grandmother,' she declared, at that moment wishing she was no relation whatsoever to the little woman who was trying to hook out an alcohol-soaked piece of fruit from the bottom of her glass with a stick-like, knobbly finger.

'Wish my grannie was like her. All mine does is sit in her chair and drool, poor bugger. Dementia, see? You're lucky your gran has got all her marbles.'

Nina supposed she was lucky, though right now she was wishing Flossie's marbles weren't quite so lively, or embarrassing.

Drink finished, Flossie wiped her mouth with the back of her hand, plonked the glass down on the bar, and fished in her pocket, drawing out her false teeth. She wiped them on the hem of her neon-yellow tunic and popped them back in, her cheeks filling out like a squirrel with a mouthful of nuts.

'More games in the pool bar, laters,' Mohammed said. 'And do not forget the party tonight after the entertainment in Billy's Bar. Thank you for playing Pin the Prick on Rick with me,' he continued to a round of applause. 'And I hope you come to play with Rick's Prick tomorrow. The winner gets a Jolly Green Giant, on the house.'

Goody, she thought, more silly, suggestive drinking games, and speaking of drinking, she asked Flossie, 'What was in that glass?'

'My prize,' Flossie said. 'A cocktail. They're not part of the all-inclusive. I won it,' she added, sounding tremendously pleased with herself.

'Do you have any idea what was in it?' she asked her grandmother, hoping it wasn't too alcoholic. They hadn't even had lunch yet, and the old lady was well on her way to being four sheets to the wind.

'Vodka, rum, and green stuff,' Flossie waved a hand in the air, not in the least bit concerned.

The assorted watchers had started to drift away, many towards the restaurant, and Nina said, 'Lunch?' hoping food would help soak up the booze.

Her grandmother's face lit up. 'Is it that time already? Good, I'm famished.'

Nina was a bit peckish too, the fruit and yoghurt having failed to fill her up. A nice salad would tide her over until dinner, then she could let her hair down a bit and have whatever she fancied. She liked to keep to the routine of eating lightly during the day (sometimes she didn't manage to eat at all in work, if she had a lunchtime revision class or a meeting), and having a more substantial meal in the evening. She made a habit of cooking several meals at once on the weekend and storing them in the freezer, bringing one out in the morning to defrost in time for her tea.

'Would you ladies like me to escort you to lunch?' a voice said, and Nina's mood, which was slowly clambering its way up from her feet, where it had sunk to a few minutes earlier, now plummeted back down with the speed of a stone dropped down a well.

Carl stood at Nina's side with a sleazy grin on his face. At least he had a shirt on and a pair of shorts, she saw. She didn't think she could face those tighty-whitey swimming trunks over a tomato and cucumber salad.

She was about to refuse when Flossie took his arm, letting him lead her towards the restaurant. Nina had no choice but to follow reluctantly, her eyes rolling yet again when Flossie looked back over her shoulder and mouthed 'nice' at her.

No, he wasn't nice. He was slimy, too full of himself, and at least ten years too old for her. She guessed him to be at the top end of the thirty to forty-five age bracket the hotel guests were supposed to be in, when Nina wasn't even out of her twenties yet! What was her gran playing at anyway – was she trying to set Nina up with the first guy to show an interest in her?

Nina definitely didn't want to be set up with anyone, especially not a man on a singles holiday who was only after a quick shag.

Oh dear! She hoped he didn't assume that was the reason she was here. Bet he did. Bet *everyone* did. What other reason was there to go on this type of holiday?

As Nina trawled grumpily along the salad display, grabbing a bit of this and a bit of that, and looking longingly at a pile of roast chicken and chips on a passing woman's plate, she had an idea.

Flossie and Carl were already tucking into their meals when Nina sat down, but before she started on hers, she dug around in her bag.

Got it!

'We've been invited to a welcome party this afternoon,' she announced, waiving the leaflet under her grandmother's nose.

'Ooh, I like a party,' Flossie said.

'It's not that kind of party, Gran,' Nina clarified, scanning the page. 'It's more like a meeting where the rep tells guests all about the area, where to go, and what to see.'

'And persuade people to buy expensive trips,' Carl interjected, pointing at the sheet of paper with a fully loaded fork.

Nina winced as a dollop of mashed potato fell off and plopped onto the white tablecloth. She positively grimaced when Carl said 'Oops', then scooped it up and popped it in his mouth.

'What sort of trips?' she asked, trying to keep her mind off his table-manners, and pushing her own plate away, appetite gone.

'Oh, you know, the usual.'

No, Nina didn't know. She'd never been on a package holiday before, not like Flossie, who had seemed to go on three or four a year when Grandad was alive.

'Boat trips (there are lots of those), trips to markets, a couple of excursions to some ruins, other stuff,' he explained.

Ruins? Nina's ears pricked up. She liked a nice ruin, and she'd read that Turkey was full of them, steeped in history going back thousands of years. Turkey was where the Ark came to rest, on Mount Ararat (though she was fairly sure the mountain was nowhere near the coast). Nina taught post-twentieth century, but at university she'd specialised in the Tudor and Jacobean eras, and she was positively fascinated by ancient history.

Maybe she could book them on a trip to go and see some historic places. If nothing else, it would be a day out, and they'd get to see a bit of the countryside. It would be a shame to come all this way to see nothing except the hotel and the beach.

Even the thought of travelling back up the impossibly steep road didn't put Nina off, not when there were some ancient monuments on offer.

Chapter 7

Thankfully, Carl left them to attend the welcome meeting on their own, more interested in a post-lunch drink and a bake in the sun (his words), so Nina and Flossie made their way down into the relatively cool depths of the hotel, into a large room with chairs laid out conference style.

A uniformed rep greeted them at the door, and handed them a drink each and a glossy leaflet. Flossie downed her drink before they'd taken their seats. It was some kind of pink, cloudy concoction which, to Nina, tasted of slightly gone-off cherries. She took a sip, grimaced, and placed the glass on the floor beside her chair, where it remained for the duration of the meeting. Flossie went to fetch another one, returning with a glass in each hand and a grin on her face.

'Told them I was dehydrated,' she said. 'The cheeky buggers tried to palm me off with a bottle of water! I said I needed the sugar.'

Nina tried to let her grandmother's seemingly insatiable appetite for anything remotely alcoholic wash over her, and concentrated on the leaflet, instead. Carl was right, there were quite a few boat trips. Some of them sounded rather intriguing. The occasional one appeared downright romantic. On the "Six Island Tour" you could see St Nicolas Island, where Santa Claus used to live (or so the leaflet claimed). The leaflet went on to say that

Saint Nicolas was where the story about Father Christmas originated. The "Twelve Island Tour" claimed visitors could bathe in Cleopatra's Pool, the hype being that bathers would come out looking ten years younger. The tour to Dalyan suggested travellers immerse themselves in mud baths, where a similar claim to knock ten years off one's age was also made. Nina wondered if there was a cumulative effect if you visited both – she'd be down to about eight years old.

The Dalyan excursion sounded lovely actually, for along with the mud baths (she wasn't entirely sure she liked the sound of those, if she was honest), there was a boat trip down the river, where ancient tombs which had been carved out of the hillside above were visible, and the river itself navigated through huge reed beds. A promise of a pristine beach with the possibility of seeing turtles clinched it for Nina. This was one trip she wanted to go on.

Another page caught her eye. Tlos, an ancient city over four thousand years old and rumoured to hold the tomb of Bellerophon, of the Pegasus fame. Ooh, that one sounded good. It was teamed with a visit to Saklikent Gorge, where the brave could wade through the icy, waist-high waters of the Xanthos River, or alternatively enjoy a cool drink lazing on one of the floating pontoons (that sounded more like it!).

Wait. When she looked at the next page her heart nearly stopped.

Ephesus, where the Temple of Artemis lay, one of the Seven Wonders of the Ancient World, and Nina had a chance of visiting it!

The historian in her leapt up and did a little excited jig. She squirmed so much Flossie asked her if she needed to go to the lavatory.

'You should have gone before this started,' her grand-mother said, and Nina hid a smile. Flossie sounded as though she was speaking to a child, and Nina supposed, from her grandmother's advanced years, anyone below sixty was probably a mere youngster.

'Is there anything you fancy?' Nina kept her voice to a whisper because one of the travel company reps was in full flow about the fun of a jeep safari, where the recommended accessory for the day was a very large water-pistol. It sounded far too rowdy for Nina's liking.

'Shh, I'm listening,' Flossie hissed, so Nina let her get on with it, whilst she scoured the leaflet for every little detail regarding Ephesus. Fancy that, a Roman city within travelling distance – Nina had always wanted to visit Italy, Rome especially with its famous colosseum. So far she'd not got around to it, but one day she would. She just didn't fancy going on her own. A place like Rome was meant to be shared with loved ones (or loved *one*, though she'd yet to find a lukewarm one who she cared enough about to go on a romantic holiday with). The nearest Nina had come to Roman ruins was a day trip to the ancient baths in Bath. Excitement fluttered through her at the thought of Ephesus. Yes, it was rather a long excursion (a two-day trip, to be exact), but Nina was unlikely to return to Turkey. It felt like a sort of sacrilege not to see as much of the country as she could.

The presentation drew to a close, with final reminders to not drink the tap water (high mineral content appar-ently), to take care in the sun (Nina had brought three bottles of factor thirty with her, and one bottle of factor fifty just in case), and to not flush toilet paper down the toilet but to use the bin provided (yuk), 'and don't forget to book your excursions before places sell out.'

'Right,' Flossie said, getting to her feet, and stomping over to the nearest rep.

Nina watched her go for a second, wondering what her grandmother wanted, before hastily following her when she saw the old woman get her credit card out.

'What are you doing, Gran?' Hope flared in Nina's chest. She hadn't been looking forward to trying to persuade Flossie to go on such a long trip.

'Booking us on that.' Flossie stabbed a finger at her leaflet. She'd opened it at the "Sunset Cruise" page. Nina had barely given it a first glance, let alone a second. 'And that.' Flossie turned over to the "Jeep Safari" page.

'Gran...' Nina began. Okay, maybe she could tolerate the cruise, but there was no way on this earth she was going to allow her eighty-four-three-something-year-old grandmother (Nina hadn't yet clarified Flossie's true age) to be rattled and bounced to death in a jeep, and squirted with water every five minutes. She'd be taking the old woman back to the UK in a box.

'Don't "Gran" me, young lady. You can't tell me what to do. You're not my mother.'

'Carer, more like,' Nina muttered.

'I heard that!' Flossie retorted sharply.

Yeah, amazing how Grannie heard a mutter like that, yet you could shout right in her ear and she'd say "pardon", Nina thought.

'Listen here, Nina, and listen good,' Flossie said in a low voice. 'I didn't bring you here to grannie-sit, I brought you here to... because...' She shook her head. 'Never mind. I just want us to have a good time, and

54

sometimes that might involve doing things you've never done before. What do you young 'uns call it, being outside your comfort zone? I'm old, so my comfort zone is very, very narrow, but if I stayed in it I would fossilize. Old people tend to get stuck in their ways, and the more stuck they get, the more reluctant and frightened they are to try anything new. I don't want to spend the rest of my days sitting in a chair, drinking endless cups of tea and watching rubbish on TV. Your grandad wouldn't have wanted me to do that either – he made me promise I wouldn't.'

Nina, tears in her eyes, could think of only one reply. 'I thought you said you weren't old.'

'I'm not. Now, are you coming with me, or do I have to go on my own?'

'I'll come with you. Somebody's got to make sure you don't break a hip.'

'Will you shut up about breaking hips? I keep telling you to worry about your own hips,' Flossie retorted. 'They could do with seeing a bit more action.'

'Gran!'

'Two for the Sunset Cruise, the Jeep Safari, and the diving, please.'

'Hang on a minute, what diving?' Nina asked.

'It's only ten feet down. Easy peasy.'

'Surely they won't let you dive at your age?' Nina turned to the bemused looking rep. 'Will you?'

'As long as your grandmother is fit and healthy, I don't see why not. It's very safe, and the instructors are excellent.'

'Oh. Okay, I'll go on a trip with you, but only,' Nina said to Flossie, seizing her chance, '*only* if you come on one with me.' I'll pick the Sunset Cruise, Nina decided, it sounded the safest and the shortest.

'Which one? Please don't say the market, I hate markets. Old people go to markets to buy tablecloths and new purses.'

Nina smiled. 'Not a market. Ephesus.'

'Elephant? I didn't know they had elephants in Turkey.'

'Ephesus!' Nina said, louder. 'It's a Roman city.'

'Elephant is a Roman city?'

'Eff-ess-uss,' Nina enunciated clearly.

'Effy-what.'

Nina gave up. 'Okay, Elephant,' she said with a sigh, sure her grandmother was being deliberately awkward; she wasn't usually this deaf.

'That's what I thought you said the first time,' Flossie said, 'but I already said I don't want to go shopping.'

'Not that type of city. Elephant,' (now her grand-mother had got her saying it) 'is an ancient ruin.'

'I can see plenty of those down the Old Age Pensioners' hall every Wednesday afternoon,' Flossie cackled.

'Please, Gran, I really want to see this.'

Flossie had a shrewd, cunning glint in her eye, and Nina had the feeling she was being set up.

'Tit for tat – you do *all* the things I want to do, and I'll go to Elephant with you,' the old lady said.

'But that's not fair! You want to go on that jeep safari thing. Can I just say, I think it's far too dangerous. You also want to go on a boat trip in the middle of the night, and you want to go diving. At your age! I'll go on the boat trip, but as for the others...'

'I told you before, dearie, age doesn't matter. As long as I'm not nailed down in a box, I'll do what I bloody well like! And anyway, your trip takes two whole days out of our holiday. The Jeep Safari and the diving work out about the same time-wise.'

Sensing her commission slipping away, the rep said to Nina, 'The Jeep Safari takes you to Tlos first, then Saklikent Gorge, the second largest gorge in Europe, then on to Patara Beach. There's something for everyone really.'

'I didn't realise that was part of the Jeep Safari,' Nina said.

'Oh yes,' the rep said as she got into her stride. 'We do a more sedate coach version, or we go by jeep. The jeep is loads of fun and not at all dangerous. You'll love it!'

Nina still wasn't convinced but before she could raise any more objections, the rep turned to Flossie with a professional smile. 'The excursion to Ephesus is a long way, but it's well worth a visit. We put you up in a great hotel. All your meals are included, and we don't just visit Ephesus, we also get a chance to see Pamukkale, and bathe in the thermal springs.'

'Pinky-what? Moon, did you say?'

'Pamukkale, Gran,' Nina said. 'It's some kind of natural limestone spring.' Nina wasn't bothered about visiting it, but if it helped persuade her grandmother…

Flossie's eyes narrowed, 'Do we have a deal? You go on my three and I'll come with you to this Elephant and Pinky Moon place?'

What could be the harm in it, Nina thought and, as lovely as their hotel was, she really did want to explore the country a bit.

'Deal!'

Chapter 8

Nina and her grandmother looked like a pair of bookends, or a couple of teenagers who had been on the phone to each other before a night out, demanding to know what the other was going to wear so they could synchronise outfits.

A white linen skirt with a pretty floral top seemed to be the uniform for tonight. The only difference between them was that Nina's skirt didn't have an elasticated waist and her top was slightly strappier, though not as low cut. Flossie's revealed rather more cleavage than Nina deemed appropriate for a woman of her grandmother's age. It didn't help that Flossie wore an industrial-sized bra, designed to keep her saggy boobs firmly in their place, which could clearly be seen poking above the neckline of her top.

'Ooh, you look lovely,' Flossie said. 'Just like me.'

Nina gave her a narrow-eyed look and rummaged about in her half of the wardrobe. She suspected her grandmother might have chosen her own outfit deliberately, because Flossie had seen the skirt in Nina's hand when she'd escaped to the bathroom to shower and get dressed.

'I think I'll wear these,' Nina said, fishing out a light-weight pair of stretchy trousers. 'Especially if there's dancing.' Nina had absolutely no intention of dancing with her grandmother; she didn't think a waltz or a foxtrot would go down too well to DNCE's *Cake by the Ocean*, which had been blasted through the speakers approximately every other song that afternoon as they'd sunbathed by the pool. Actually, Flossie had staked herself out in the sun like a cat on a sunny windowsill, whilst Nina had smothered herself in factor thirty (factor fifty on her nose and collarbone) and waged a silent war with the ever-moving sun, using two strategically angled canvas umbrellas. When she couldn't stand any more DNCE, she'd eventually given up trying to read the latest hardback about Elizabeth Tudor, and had rammed her earbuds in her ears, listening to her gym playlist instead.

Still, it had been an enjoyable first day, and she felt relatively relaxed, though she wasn't particularly looking forward to the party later. Her bed was calling to her, the little nap she'd taken before lunch nowhere near making up for an almost complete loss of a night's sleep.

Finally ready (she would have been ready much sooner if her grandmother hadn't tried to dress like her twin), Nina followed Flossie to the restaurant. Her stomach gurgled loudly as the enticing smells of roasted meats and bubbling sauces reached her nose.

They chose a table on the terrace. Nina ordered a soft drink from one of the attentive waiters and Flossie asked for a glass of white wine. There's a surprise, Nina thought somewhat sarcastically.

'Go wild, have a glass of wine, or a beer,' Flossie suggested, but Nina was having none of it. One of them had to stay sober, and it looked like it wasn't going to be her grannie. Anyway, if Flossie kept drinking like this (she'd already emptied her glass and was waving it at the waiter for a refill), the old lady wasn't going to be long out of bed, which suited Nina just fine.

They took their time over dinner. When they'd finished Nina wished she was the one wearing the elasticated waist; her food-baby of a stomach was positively obscene and slightly uncomfortable. She made a mental note to explore the hotel's gym tomorrow. At this rate, if she didn't keep things in check, she'd be going home two sizes larger.

Flossie, for all her apparently old lady frailness, couldn't half pack her food away. She'd already had two large meals earlier in the day, then a couple of slices of odd-looking cake and some strange pastry-type biscuits in the afternoon, she had then eaten her way through a piled-high plate of spaghetti with a tomato sauce, followed by mashed potato and a lamb (probably goat, Nina thought cynically) casserole. After that, she'd had some curry and rice, a wobbly pink and green jelly-like dessert, some baklava, and a slice of gateau. All washed down with what was probably the best part of a whole bottle of wine. At least the old woman had something inside her to soak up the alcohol.

Later, sitting in the larger of the hotel's three bars – Flossie had insisted on this one because it was where the party was being held later – Nina surreptitiously undid the button on her trousers and relaxed back into her seat, with a glass of cool white wine in her hand. She took a cautious sip, realised it was in fact quite drinkable, and took another. She wouldn't have more than a couple of glasses though, because she hated that not-in-control feeling, and besides, her nose and lips went numb when she'd had too much to drink, and so did her brain.

The tables around them quickly filled up. Nina noticed there was a variety of mixtures – couples, same gender groups, mixed-sex groups. Knowing everyone had come here as a singleton, she spent the next half-hour people watching, trying to guess which ones were after a quick shag, and which ones might actually have the beginnings of a burgeoning relationship.

Her game was interrupted by a man, but thankfully it wasn't Carl, The Budgie Smuggler.

'Mind if we sit here?' A tall bloke in a white button-down shirt and a pair of jeans indicated the two empty chairs at their table.

Nina did mind, but considering the bar was full and there weren't many free seats, she could hardly say no. Then she felt slightly hurt when she realised their table did in fact have the only two unoccupied seats in the room – her grannie was obviously putting people (men and women alike) off.

Chagrined at her uncharitable and downright nasty thoughts, Nina smiled. 'Help yourself.'

The man and his friend pulled out a chair each and sat down. The friend looked around for a waiter, whilst the one who'd spoken kept shooting little glances in her direction.

'Put a smile on it,' Flossie leaned in close and hissed. 'You're enough to scare a corpse.'

'Gran!'

'Well you are. You've got a face on you like a bulldog chewing a wasp.'

Nina had to laugh; some of her grandmother's sayings were quite funny. Then she realised the reason those seats were free wasn't because of her grandmother – it was because of her own expression. They must look a right pair. Nina was wrapped up in her own world, trying subconsciously to pretend her grandmother wasn't sitting next to her in a crowded bar, whilst the old lady tapped her feet and bobbed her head to whatever loud music was blasting out from the speakers, and downing drinks at the same rate as a kid with a bag of sweets whose mother was threatening to take them away. Nina, on the other hand, sipped hers like it was poisonous and stared enviously at the people around her who were clearly having fun.

At least she recognised her own emotion. It wasn't a slight disdain (though at first, she'd convinced herself that's what it was), or a superiority (she'd never lower herself to go on a singles holiday – this was like a dating site with sun), but a twinge of envy at the smiles and laughter all around her. And there she was, sitting in a bubble of 'don't-talk-to-me', and giving off sour vibes. She was on holiday; it might not be the sort of holiday she would have chosen for herself, but it was the only one she was going to get this year, so Nina decided to make the most of it. It wouldn't hurt her to be friendly and to join in (within reason).

'Hi,' she said, leaning forward and holding out her hand to the man who had asked if the seats were taken. 'I'm Nina, and this is my grandmother, Flossie.'

He stared at her hand for a second too long before shaking it. 'Ben. He's Jerry.'

It was Nina's turn to pause, then she burst out laughing. 'You're joking, right?'

Ben looked rather put out. 'No, my name really is Ben.'

'And he's Jerry?'

'Jeremy, actually,' Jerry said. 'I prefer people to call me Jezza, but Jeremy Clarkson got there first, so Jeremy will do.'

He had a point, Nina conceded. Not that she was a *Top Gear* fan, but the name "Jezza" was synonymous with the famous car show. Even *she* knew that. But Ben and Jerry? Honestly?

A waiter appeared and as the two men placed their order, Nina examined them out of the corner of her eye. Ben was tall, well-built like a rugby player, with big shoulders and chunky thighs. Not bad looking, either – straight, sandy hair, cut short at the back and sides, a little longer on the top, causing a bit of the front of it to flop over his forehead. She guestimated him to be in his early thirties. Jerry (she resisted the urge to snigger) was a couple of inches shorter, thinner, with dark hair and freckles spattered over his round face. He had a nice, wonky-toothed smile, and reminded her of a little boy she taught a couple of years ago. If she compared them to ice cream (and once the ice cream idea was in her head, she couldn't shift it), Ben was fudge with chunks in, and Jerry was vanilla.

'Been here long?' Ben asked, using the standard holiday line.

'This is technically our first day. We arrived very, very early this morning,' Nina said.

'No wonder you look tired,' Ben replied.

Charming! That's what you get for trying to be nice. Nina frowned at him, before deciding that "tired" was better than "miserable" or "grumpy".

'Travelling does take it out of you,' she agreed, wincing when she heard her mother's voice coming out of her mouth.

'I hate night flights,' Jeremy said, 'but that's all we could get. Are you here for a week?'

'No, a fortnight.' She winced again. Did anyone below the age of fifty actually *say* "fortnight"?

'Sweet. We've been here a week already, haven't we, Ben?' Jeremy nudged his friend with his elbow, bringing the other man back into the conversation. Ben had been busy eyeing up a gaggle of women on the next table, with their short, short skirts, and their cleavages hanging out. They were loud too, all screeching laughter and innuendoes, and more hair than you could shake a can of hairspray at.

Nina smoothed her own neat bob with her free hand. The other clutched her wine glass tightly.

Flossie was uncharacteristically silent and Nina shot her a concerned glance, relieved to see her grandmother still awake and still with it. The old lady was staring intently at the two men opposite, her gaze going from one to the other and back again.

'I prefer the smaller one,' Flossie said, far too loudly.

The larger one smiled, a wolfish grin. 'That's you sorted tonight, Jerry,' he said. 'You've pulled.'

'Not for me, stupid,' Flossie said to Ben. 'For her!' She pointed in Nina's direction. 'You're too full of yourself for my liking, young man. *He* seems much nicer.' The knobbly finger was now aimed at Jeremy and it was his turn to smile, but Jerry's small uplifting of the mouth looked a bit strained, Nina thought. In fact, he appeared rather put out.

'Gran!' Nina hissed. It seemed eye rolling and hissing were going to be featuring quite a lot on this holiday. Mortified at her grandmother's rudeness (and that the old lady had given the men the impression Nina was in the market for a holiday romance and her grandmother was touting for business on her behalf), she smiled apologetically.

'It's okay, I love old people; they call a spade a spade,' Ben said, shrugging his huge shoulders. 'But you're barking up the wrong tree with Jerry – he's got a girlfriend, or rather, he did have a girlfriend. Still pining over her, aren't you, Jer?'

Jerry's smile was decidedly forced.

'I had to practically man-handle him onto the plane,' Ben carried on, oblivious of his friend's mortified expression. 'He didn't want to come, but I told him this holiday was just what he needed to forget all about Sally. Plenty more fish in the sea, eh?' Ben jostled Jerry with his elbow and Jerry fought to save his drink, narrowly avoiding spilling some down his blue-checked shirt.

Nina (and Jerry by the look of it) was relieved when Ben announced his need to 'have a whazz' (why announce it, eh? There was absolutely no need; loo or toilet would do. Better still was a simple "excuse me, I'll be back in a minute"). She watched him swagger off in the direction of the toilets, and hoped he'd fall in. So far, her impression of the type of men who came on this kind of holiday wasn't good, though Jerry seemed okay, if a little overwhelmed by his louder, brasher friend.

'Were you together long?' Nina asked.

'Eh?'

'You and your girlfriend.'

'Only all our lives,' Jerry said, his gaze dropping to his glass. 'Our mothers used to take us to the same baby play group.'

'I'm sorry,' Nina said.

'She said she needed to stretch her wings, whatever that means.' He swirled the last of his beer, the liquid coating the sides of the glass. 'I'd asked her to marry me.'

'Oh, that's awful.'

'She said yes.'

'Oh? Er… good?'

'But she said she wanted to see a bit of the world first, meet new people.'

'Um…'

'She's backpacking round Australia with a mate. I reckon it's an early mid-life crisis.'

Jerry had to be at least thirty, and if they'd met at a playgroup it meant Sally must be roughly the same age, so it had certainly taken Jerry long enough to pop the question. Maybe him asking had been a wake-up call for this unknown woman and—

Nina gave herself a mental shake. She had a habit of making up stories about people she'd only just met. Or even people in the street, or at the supermarket. Everyone had a story, everyone had more to them than they showed the world.

Take Flossie, for instance; on the outside she appeared to be a typical little old lady, but Nina was starting to realise there was nothing old-ladyish or typical about her grandmother. Especially now, when the old lady in question was flirting outrageously with a bloke on the next table.

'I like proper knickers myself,' Nina heard Flossie say. 'Want to see?'

'Gran! No, he doesn't want to see your knickers.'

Flossie sat up straighter in her chair and gave Nina a superior look. 'We were talking about cheese graters,' she said, shaking her head when Nina stared at her blankly because she was wondering what "cheese graters" were.

'Thongs,' Flossie explained. 'He says every girl he's been with wears 'em. I can't understand why – they look bloody uncomfortable, splitting your difference like that.'

Nina's mouth opened and shut, and opened and shut again. She seemed to have no control over it. How Flossie and this guy had got onto the subject of women's under-wear, Nina had no idea, and she had no intention of asking. And then there was Flossie's turn of phrase – cheese graters (she guessed Gran meant cheese wire; no wonder Nina had trouble keeping up with her gran's conversation – it had taken her a moment to realise they weren't discussing kitchen implements). Then there was splitting one's difference indeed! The woman was a law unto herself.

She shot the poor man an apologetic look. The "poor man" seemed rather amused. He gave Nina a wide smile, then turned his attention to Flossie.

'It was nice talking with you,' he said. 'You've given me a lot to think about in the women's underwear depart-ment.' He stopped, and blushed. 'Not that I spend any time in women's underwear departments,' he stammered. 'I mean… oh heck.'

Welcome to my world, Nina thought, as Flossie chuckled and said with a wink, 'Bet you do!'

Oh dear, this was going to be a long night.

Chapter 9

Parrots. Not what Nina had expected as part of the hotel entertainment. Dancing, a magician maybe, and after this afternoon's performance, games full of innuendo and thrusting hips wouldn't have been out of place – but *parrots*?

Nina had nothing against parrots, in fact these were quite charming, especially the little green one who said "fuck off" a lot, but she'd not anticipated seeing them on centre stage at her hotel.

The audience were lapping it up. Amused, Nina spent more time watching her fellow tourists than she did the antics of the exotic birds in front of her. Most of the women vied for the chance to be chosen to go up on stage, to be verbally and physically abused by a bird, the rest of the audience egging them on. The parrot-handler picked a couple and invited them onto the stage.

'Too dark,' one parrot announced, after disappearing down one of the women's very ample cleavage, and popping back up again.

'Too light,' it said, after investigating the chest of a lady who had much less up top.

The parrot-trainer scoured the audience for his next victim, opening his eyes a little wider when they skimmed over Flossie. His gaze came back to her in a hurry, as if he couldn't quite believe what he saw.

Flossie, aware of the attention and loving it, stuck out her bosoms and put her hands on her hips.

'Come,' he gestured to her, holding out a hand.

Flossie scrambled out of her chair, hauling her body onto the little stage with a bit of difficulty (the other ladies had hopped up – well they would, wouldn't they, being fifty years younger an' all, Nina thought meanly). A man sitting nearby was forced to place his hands on the old lady's backside and push.

It all made for hilarious viewing, and even Nina might have found it amusing if it hadn't been her grandmother up there, making a show of herself.

'What's your name, sexy?' Parrot-Man said.

Flossie, deadpan, replied, 'Sexy.'

She went down a storm. The man who'd manhandled her backside, shoved two fingers in his mouth and whistled, stamping his feet.

'Your name is "sexy"?' Parrot-Man said, and Flossie played to the crowd, waggling her hips and doing a little dance. Is this the sort of thing they got up to at the Salvation Army, Nina wondered. Was this kind of behaviour considered normal in geriatric circles?

'Don't you believe me? Are you saying you don't think I'm sexy?' Flossie cried, exaggerating a hurt look.

'You are the most sexy woman I see in all my life,' Parrot-Man said, knowing he was onto a good thing. Nina wondered if she could rent Flossie out to him for the duration of their stay, so Nina could find a nice, quiet corner and not have to endure many more evenings like this. She sincerely hoped the hotel hadn't booked a fire eater…

He sent the parrot down Flossie's cleavage.

It took a while to come back out, Gran chortling all the while, wriggling like a kid needing a wee, at the sensation of having a bird down her bra. When it eventually emerged, the poor thing looked rather ruffled.

'Just right,' it screeched. 'Goldilocks tits.'

The crowd went wild.

Nina wished she was anywhere but here – in a boring meeting, at the dentist, being chased by wild animals...

When she was tapped on the shoulder from behind, Nina turned to see a red-faced woman, wearing far too much make-up and little else, smiling at her. 'Bless her, she's a scream,' the woman declared. 'You must be so proud.'

Yeah, right; proud wasn't the first word which popped into Nina's mind when she thought of what her grandmother had got up to lately.

'Come and join us,' the woman offered, and her two friends nodded.

To be polite, Nina inched her chair backwards a little, as a token gesture, only to have it dragged almost out from underneath her until she was in the thick of them, like a boring sandwich filling between two flamboyant pieces of bread.

'You, too,' the woman said to Ben and Jerry, and Nina noticed how the woman batted her false eyelashes at Ben, pouting seductively. Nina realised why the woman had been so friendly to her, as a way to get into Ben's pants. Ben, recognising a fellow party-goer when he saw one, obligingly pulled up his chair, trailing Jerry behind him with all the force of a yacht towing a dingy.

Trapped, Nina sent dagger-eyed glowers at her grandmother, but Flossie was oblivious, prancing around the stage with a parrot on her head. Hope it poops on her,

Nina thought, trying to send pooping vibes in the parrot's direction via the power of her mind.

At this time of night, her mind had about as much power as one of those wishy-washy hand-held fan things you can buy from the Pound Shop. She was exhausted, fed up with the raucous laughter, and definitely not in the mood for a party.

'Here, try this.' The woman who'd invited Nina to share their table put a drink in front of her. 'I'm Lauren, this is Mandy and Rhian. And who are you two gorgeous fellas?'

Nina sniffed the drink and took a miniscule sip, whilst she waited for the inevitable screams of laughter when Ben introduced himself and Jerry.

Wincing at the noise, Nina took another mouthful; the drink wasn't half bad. In fact, it was quite nice. She couldn't taste any alcohol at all, so she finished the lot and gestured to a waiter. Being continually embarrassed was thirsty work.

'Another one of these… what was it?' Nina asked Lauren.

'A Raunchy Cowboy. Make it two,' she said.

By the time Flossie was evicted off the stage, Nina had polished off both drinks, and realised there was alcohol in them after all. She felt a bit tipsy and the lack of sleep last night was really getting to her. She could hardly keep her eyes open.

Flossie, however was raring to go. 'What time does this party kick off?' she asked, dancing in her chair and waving her arms about, nearly knocking a tray out of a waiter's hand.

'Any minute now, though I don't think the foam starts until later,' the one called Rhian said.

How much later is later, Nina wondered; it was late enough already. She checked her watch – ten o'clock – and stifled a yawn.

Trust Flossie to notice. 'You youngsters haven't got any stamina,' she said, proving she had lots of it by jigging up and down in her seat, whilst Nina slumped in hers.

'*I've* got plenty of stamina,' Lauren said to Ben, her eyelashes flapping about like washing on a line. Nina almost gagged on the innuendo.

'You're no spring chicken though, are you?' Flossie pointed out to Lauren. 'Not like her.' She jerked her head in Nina's direction. 'She's years younger than you.'

Lauren looked quite indignant. 'She can't be that many; I'm only thirty-three.'

'Aye, and the rest. Our Nina's only twenty-eight. Just the right age for having babies.'

Nina pursed her lips. Thanks, Gran – you've insulted a total stranger and you've let everyone believe I'm only here to bag myself a husband.

'I want kids one day,' Jeremy piped up. 'I thought I'd have them with Sally—' he broke off.

See? That there, him, Jeremy – he was a walking talking advert for not falling in love, Nina thought. There he was, two thousand miles away from home, missing his ex, being forced to watch a parrot show, with his best mate who was not being at all best-matey, and probably wishing he was tucked up in his own little bed with a mug of cocoa and a re-run of Downton Abbey on the telly. She knew that was what she would like to be doing right now, but not necessarily watching Downton Abbey, not that she had anything against the show (she didn't), but that book she'd got out of the library on Greek myths and legends was calling to her. She'd been too frightened to bring it on holiday, in case it got lost or damaged.

Flossie elbowed her in the ribs.

'Ow! What did you do that for?' Nina cried.

'Because you've got a face like a slapped arse. Stop being so miserable; no wonder you haven't got a fella if you go around looking like that all the time.'

'We're all here because we haven't got fellas, my love,' Lauren said. 'But that's about to change, isn't it?' More eyelash fluttering in Ben's direction, followed by a seductive pout.

Oh, give it a rest, Nina thought, and wished they'd bring the parrots back on – anything was better than watching these two playing the mating game.

Ew!

Chapter 10

A huge yawn split Nina's face and she couldn't help giggling as she ran through the evening in her head. She'd enjoyed herself, despite being propositioned by several hopeful males (Nina had quickly put them in their place), and watching Lauren and Ben getting increasingly loved-up as the night wore on. It hadn't been too bad, as she'd been able to ignore it most of the time. Her grandmother had made her laugh (had made her cringe too, but Nina chose to try to forget that).

'Split your difference,' she chuckled, remembering. 'Where *do* you get your sayings from, Grannie?'

'My mother, my own grandmother, TV.' Flossie was stripping off with abandon, and Nina averted her eyes from her gran's naked backside. She'd already de-robed in the privacy of the bathroom, and she wished Flossie would follow her example and do the same.

'It's been nice,' Nina said, suddenly. 'Spending time together, I mean.'

'You used to spend a lot of time with me when you were little,' Flossie replied, pulling her voluminous night-dress over her head.

'We had a laugh tonight, didn't we? What with Ben and Jerry' (Flossie still didn't get why Nina sniggered every time their names were mentioned together, despite Nina explaining it to her twice), 'and that guy you offered to

74

show your knickers to. Then there was that man who kept telling you he missed his Nonnie, and stroking your cheek. What was all that about?'

'Bless him. His grandmother died when he was in teens and he doesn't appear to have got over it. I think he was a bit tiddly.'

'A bit! He was totally wasted.'

'I would have liked to have stayed for the foam,' Flossie said, wistfully. 'I've never been to a foam party before.'

'We're both dead on our feet,' Nina argued. 'We can hardly keep our eyes open.' As if to prove a point, she was overtaken by an enormous yawn. 'We'll have another quiet day tomorrow,' she suggested. 'Maybe lie on the beach rather than by the pool; then we're off on that jeep safari the day after. You need to conserve your energy for that.'

'I need to buy a water gun, that's what I really need,' Flossie declared. 'The biggest one I can get.' Her smile was on the evil side of naughty. 'You should get one too.'

'Oh, I don't know. I don't like violence and—'

'It's a *water* gun, it's not exactly a Kalashnikov. Get over yourself.' Flossie clambered onto her bed and slid under the sheet.

The air-con was loud in the ensuing silence. Get over myself indeed! Nina huffed as she turned over to get comfy. She spent half her teaching-day trying to keep the peace and stop a teenage version of World War Three breaking out in her classroom, and the other half persuading pupils to try mediation when they had issues with their peers. And here was her grandmother positively relishing the thought of blasting complete strangers with the holiday equivalent of a water cannon. Surely it should be the other way around – her gran warning her about such things? Had her grannie always been this feisty? Or should she say "reckless"? Nina was ninety-nine percent certain Flossie had been more like a normal grandmother before Grandad died – into baking cakes for the church fete, rather than getting drunk and pinning cardboard penises on cardboard men. Okay, she'd always been a little off the wall, but not this much.

Maybe this was her gran's way of dealing with Grandad's loss. Nina had read somewhere that grief could do strange things to a person, making them act in unusual ways, and the images of Gran holding an oversized cardboard penis chased her down into sleep, accompanied by the old lady's heavy breathing.

She had no idea what woke her: late night revellers returning to their rooms, the ceaseless hum of the air-con, or her grandmother snoring in the next bed?

Whatever it was, she couldn't hear anything now, apart from muted music coming from one of the hotel's bars and the distant peal of laughter and voices. With the balcony doors shut and the air-con burbling away, not much outside noise penetrated their dark room, unless it was someone right outside their door who had disturbed her.

Nina was just grateful the noise hadn't woken her gran. Flossie claimed to be a light sleeper, and maybe she did have a tendency to wake up in the middle of the night and find it hard to drop back off to sleep again; but she had fallen asleep quickly enough tonight and was fast asleep still.

Fully awake now and cross because of it, Nina quietly got out of bed and went to the bathroom. Blackout curtains ensured the room was almost completely dark, and she felt her way along the wall until she reached the bathroom door. Business taken care of, she rinsed her hands, wincing as the water splashed loudly into the basin, and made her way back to her bed, pulling the sheet up to her chin, thankful not to have disturbed the old lady.

Her grandmother hadn't stirred; not a snore, or a sigh. Or the sound of breathing. Nothing.

Nina pushed the sheet down to her waist and sat up; then leaned as far across the gap dividing the two beds as she dared, without risking falling out, and stared intently, ears straining.

Flossie's bed was nearest the balcony doors and by the tiny amount of light seeping in through a chink in the curtains, Nina made out a lump.

She concentrated on it, willing it to move.

Nothing.

She swung her feet out of bed and perched on the edge of the mattress, holding her own breath as a terrible, horrible thought occurred to her.

What if…?

No. Gran couldn't be.

But…?

Stop it! You're being silly, she told herself, arguing against the insidious internal voice which, once it had started talking, simply wouldn't shut up.

It was no good; she'd have to check. Not that there was any possibility, but just to reassure herself. She knew she was being daft – of course Gran was still breathing, it was just that the hum from the air con masked the noise. There was nothing to worry about, but she had to check, all the same. Just to make sure.

A bedside table separated the two single beds, forcing Nina to lean across the divide. For some inexplicable reason she was reluctant to actually leave her own bed, as if the flimsy sheet she was hanging onto with one hand could protect her from the aftermath of a visit from the Grim Reaper. There, she'd said it. Not out loud, but she'd thought it. She'd acknowledged the possibility that her grandmother might have moved on.

An old *Monty Python* sketch popped unbidden into her head – the one with the dead parrot (how fitting!) – and she had to stamp down hard on an urge to laugh. Or cry. Or was it, scream? Because she'd never seen a dead body before, and had certainly not been in the same room as one, at night, alone, in the dark.

Nina let out a yelp. It had moved! The body had twitched, she was certain of it. Eyes wide with fear, she paused, her hand outstretched, waiting for her dead grandmother to turn over and reach towards her with grasping fingers.

Nerves shot to pieces, Nina lunged for the switches on the wooden headboard and slapped on the light. She didn't care if Gran was really asleep and she woke the old lady up – the not-knowing was killing her. She'd be the one they'd be grieving over if she had to spend another second in a room with a corpse!

Bright yellow light flooded the room and Nina had to blink several times before she became accustomed enough to see properly.

Flossie hadn't moved so much as a hair. She lay under the sheet, still, lifeless, and very, very small.

Wait a minute. The mound in the other bed was too small. At least two feet or more, shorter than it should be, even accounting for old lady shrinkage.

And her head was missing.

Nina leapt across the space between the two beds.

Flossie's bed was empty, apart from a pillow strategically placed lengthwise down the centre.

Her grandmother had gone.

'I'm gonna kill her when I find her,' Nina muttered, dragging on a pair of trousers and the first top she laid her hands on. As she wrangled her big toes through the loop in her sandals, hopping first on one foot then the other, she hunted around for the key to the room. Gone, like her grandmother. Why didn't that surprise her?

Wondering if she should grab their passports (just in case, but of what, she wasn't entirely certain), Nina stuffed some money in her pocket and slammed the door shut behind her.

'Sorry,' she mouthed at the closed doors to either side of her own, hoping she hadn't woken anyone in her haste. If she had, then Flossie could jolly well apologise in the morning, because it was all her fault.

What was the time anyway? It couldn't be too late because noise from the bar still drifted across the well-tended gardens, and it sounded as if quite a few people were still up.

She set off down the path, music and voices getting closer. Stumbling slightly on the cobbles, she hurried towards the first people she saw, a couple weaving rather unsteadily away from the bar. They had their arms wrapped so tightly around each other, that in the softly-lit darkness Nina couldn't tell where the one ended and the other began. When she drew level with them, she noticed the bloke had his tongue shoved firmly in the woman's ear as his beau giggled and squirmed against him.

Maybe Nina would give these two a miss. They were so engrossed in each other it was doubtful whether they would have noticed a little old lady anyway. Instead, she pattered up the steps to the bar area and made a beeline for the nearest occupied table.

'Excuse me, have you seen an old woman? She's about this tall,' Nina held a hand up to her shoulder, 'and she's got white hair and false teeth.' Why did she feel the need to mention Flossie's teeth, or lack of them? It wasn't as though false teeth would be the first thing someone would notice.

She received some blank looks and one bloke shook his head.

Nina moved on to the next table, and the next.

'You are looking for Flossie, yes?'

'Yes!' Nina, could have hugged the man who'd spoken. He wore a polo shirt with a "Bar Staff" logo on his chest. 'Do you know where she is?'

'The free drinks ends at two o'clock. No more all-inclusive, so the bar is closed. The lady, she is going with other guests to *Talk of the Town*.'

'What... where?' Nina ground to a halt. Was it another hotel?

'On the main street,' he said. He turned to point at the promenade-side exit. 'Leave the hotel here, walk to the right and in a few minutes you will see the main street. Many bars and restaurants are there. Shops too.'

'Okay, thanks.' She offered him a grateful smile and trotted towards the exit.

Having not yet explored outside the hotel, she was rather nervous. What if she got lost? Or propositioned? Or worse?

Stopping to get her bearings, she knew the hotel's main bar was situated right on the promenade with a view over a grassy strip where paragliders landed (she'd watched them come down and had shuddered at the very idea), with the even-wider beach and the sea beyond. It was a prime spot with a beautiful view, and Nina and Flossie had watched the sun dip down over the mountains, with a drink in one hand and a fag in the other before dinner (Flossie had the cigarette, not Nina – she still couldn't get over the fact that her grandmother smoked!), and they'd people-watched for a while until the evening's entertainment started.

She turned right, following the instructions, and walked swiftly, passing shops and restaurant, many of which were closed for the night. There were a surprising number of people around, tourists and locals alike. Most tourists were strolling or staggering, probably back to their hotels, while the locals were engaged in an array of activities, from sweeping the pathway to smoking pungent cigarettes and drinking tea out of tiny glasses. Some lay under the trees which dotted the grass, fast asleep, and others slept curled up amongst the various goods displayed outside their shops.

When she came to the main street which ran at right angles to the beach front, she paused. Music bellowed from several different places, and lights flashed and sparkled for about half a mile. She peered at the first two signs, but neither of them said *Talk of the Town*, so she ventured further on, not liking what she saw. Most places were closed, lights off, and battened down for the night, but the bars which were still open seemed to be competing to see which one could play the loudest, raunchiest music. And none of the places, not even the shops were like those back home – they were all open-fronted, encroaching onto the road. Thankfully the street itself appeared to be pedestrianised, though a man on a pedal bike dodged drunken revellers with wobbling caution.

There it was! The neon sign was huge, the words an incandescent purple with white stars flashing so fast the whole thing should have carried a warning for anyone suffering from epilepsy. She recognised the music – she'd caught one of her pupils listening to it on his phone when he should have been listening to her explain how best to answer a question on the rise of fascism in Europe. He had been so pleased with his "toon" he wanted to let the whole class have a listen to the song because it was "sick", though Nina didn't consider it a song suitable for anyone his age.

Nina caught a brief glimpse of figures hopping and bopping on top of the actual bar itself, before she turned her attention to the tables. All were occupied. As she wove her way in between them she realised Flossie wasn't seated at any of them.

She might be in the loo, Nina thought, trying to make out any signs for the toilets through the frantic pulsing, flashing lights (was that a disco ball?), the smoke, and several gyrating bodies on the dance floor. No use – either she'd have to wait and hope Gran would appear, or she could ask at the bar.

Not wanting to be in the place a minute longer than she had to, she opted for asking the bar staff, though most of them appeared to be bopping about on top of the bar, rather than serving behind it. Five men with gleaming bare chests, wearing black jeans and cowboy hats, strutted and preened, gathering yells and whistles, whilst several female party-goers in assorted very short dresses danced alongside them.

And one old pensioner.

Nina stopped, mid-step, and her mouth dropped open.

Flossie fist-pumped the air, holding her skirt up over her bony knees with her other hand and shook her skinny backside from side to side, laughing like a loon.

'Gran!' Nina yelled, shock abruptly replaced by fear. What if Flossie fell? She could break something, and at her age it might be the end of her. 'Get down!'

She looked around for someone to help her lift her grandmother off the treacherously shiny bar. If she slipped on one of those wet patches, it didn't bear thinking about…

She liked to think no one heard her, rather than everyone was ignoring her, so she tried again. 'Gran! You'll hurt yourself.' Still no reaction from anyone. Nina might as well be invisible.

She stood, mouth open, eyes wide, watching her grandmother shake her skinny hips. The old woman's false teeth glowed eerily white in the UV glare as she grinned widely, stomping her feet and twirling around so her back was to the room and wobbling precariously on the slick wood; then she bent over, flipped up her skirt, and wiggled her bottom at the delighted audience, displaying the biggest pair of knickers Nina had ever seen.

The only thing running through Nina's shocked mind was, 'Thank god she was wearing some!'

Chapter 11

Where could they have possibly gone? Nina checked the little dryer on the balcony. Nope, neither of them, though she had expected to see the costume she had worn yesterday, which she'd rinsed out and hung up to dry. The other one should be in a drawer, ready for her to put on today. But neither of them were anywhere to be found. Strange, considering nothing else appeared to be missing.

'What are you looking for?' Flossie was dressed for the beach in a more sedate one-piece and was perched on one of the room's two chairs, ready to walk to the restaurant and tackle her breakfast. The old lady had gone from one extreme to the other, and rather than four pieces of small triangles trying vainly to cover her elderly assets, this morning Flossie sported a more age-appropriate costume with built-in cups which made her flabby boobs look like a shelf, and had more support in it than the scaffolding supplied by a builder on a two-up, two-down extension. It even had a skirt around the bottom. Now she really did look like a grannie.

'Nothing,' Nina said, opening a drawer she'd already looked in three times. Her swimming cozzies still weren't there.

'Clearly it's something.'

'My swimming costume.' Nina forced the words out. After last night, her grandmother should consider herself lucky Nina was speaking to her at all.

'You can borrow this.' Flossie struggled to her feet and brought forth the neon pink monstrosity she'd worn yesterday.

'No, thank you. I'll find one of mine in a minute.' There was no way Nina would even consider wearing anything which had been so close to her gran's under-carriage.

'How about this? It's still got the tags on.' Her grand-mother held up another bikini, this one in an eye-watering turquoise, though the colour was preferable to the Barbie pink.

Giving up and vowing to have a word with reception about swimming costume thieves, Nina almost snatched it out of the old lady's hand and marched off to the bath-room to get dressed. She emerged with far more flesh on show than she was comfortable with, pulling at the strings holding the scraps of material together, while being careful not to take too deep a breath in case the whole thing decided to fall apart, leaving her standing in the buff.

Flossie whistled wheezily through her teeth. 'You look hot.'

Nina caught an unwelcome glance of herself in the mirror. She didn't look hot (and what did her grand-mother know about hot anyway?), she looked downright awkward, and she didn't feel much better when she'd put on a T-shirt and a pair of shorts over the top. She'd go straight to the nearest shop after breakfast and buy a proper costume.

–

'Well that wasn't very successful, was it?' Nina said, forgetting she was supposed to be giving Flossie the silent treatment. Disappointment at discovering none of the local shops sold what Nina would call a "real" cozzie must have thrown her off course. At least Flossie was happy, having gone into raptures of delight at the huge array of water pistols on display. She'd come away with a huge carrier bag and a smug expression. Nina had come away with a bikini not much more substantial than the one her gran had loaned her, but at least it was hers and hadn't been exposed to her gran's wrinkly backside.

'Ow!' Nina cried.

How was it possible for sand to get so hot? Nina had wanted to feel warm sand between her toes and as the pair of them had stepped off the promenade and onto the beach, Nina had kicked her flip flops off. Hastily, she put them back on again; it wasn't even midday yet, and already the sand was hot enough to give the unwary third degree burns. She was relieved when it gave way to pebbles nearer the water's edge, but it wasn't until they'd chosen a couple of sunbeds and Nina had wrestled another umbrella away from some nearby unoccupied beds, she discovered the pebbles were equally as hot. Already beads of sweat had joined together and trickled between her shoulder blades, making her feel like a ready meal in a microwave.

She made a mad scramble to dive under the parasol, and hunted frantically for the factor fifty, lathering on several layers. Flossie, as usual, sat back and cooked, not bothering with hat, glasses, or sun tan lotion. It was a wonder the pensioner hadn't burned to a crisp already.

'Look at those,' Flossie said, pointing skywards.

Nina paused, her palm full of white goo, and lifted her head.

Paragliders, tens of them, swirling and turning in the cloudless sky. One was doing some kind of looping thing. The screams issuing from the poor unfortunate person suspended on a couple of ropes from a sheet of nylon, made Nina shudder.

'These lot are tandem flyers,' Flossie said, sounding as if she knew what she was talking about. 'You can pay to go up and one of them will bring you down.'

'*You* can pay for it. *I'm* not,' Nina retorted crossly, then realised what she'd inadvertently implied. 'I mean, other people can pay for it. Not you. You can't do something so dangerous.'

'Can, too.'

'Gran, you're too old. They won't take you.'

'They will. They said.'

Nina sighed, wondering when her gran had managed to find the time to talk to a paraglider. Oh yeah, possibly when she was playing drunken pin the cock on the human donkey, or when she'd slipped out last night like a fifteen-year-old scaling a drainpipe to go to a rave, or wherever it was teenagers slipped out to go to these days.

'They take kids as young as five, and adults as old as… well, whatever. They said they'll take me. It's about sixty pounds for a flight. Why don't you have a go? Live a little – what have you got to lose?'

'My life?'

'It's as safe as houses.'

'Yeah, right. And no, you can't have a go.'

'Try stopping me.' Flossie lay down on her sunbed with a huff, and muttered, 'It's worse than being on holiday with an old fogey.'

'I'm not an old fogey,' Nina protested. 'I'm simply trying to make sure you don't injure yourself. Look at last night, disappearing off without a word. I was worried sick about you. Anything could have happened.'

'It did – *you* showed up.'

'You're more trouble than twenty teenagers on a school trip!'

'No one asked you to come.'

'Yes they did! *You* did.'

'I didn't. It was your mother's idea. I told her it wouldn't work. You're too anal.'

'Anal?' Nina screeched. 'I've never been anal in my life!'

'You wanna try loosening up a bit before you give yourself an ulcer. You act like you're seventy already.'

'And you act like a thirteen-year-old.'

'Better young than dead, my girl. The way you're going, you'll be old before you know it and all you'll have to show for your life is a watch off the school for long service and a couple of cats.'

'I don't like cats.'

'You know what I mean. You never go anywhere, or do anything. When was the last time you had sex?'

'Gran!'

'Well?'

'It's none of your business.'

'I'm making it my business. Go get yourself laid. It might make you smile for once. Oh, stop frowning – if the wind blows the wrong way your face will stay like that.'

'Ha ha.'

'Your grandad and I had a wonderful sex life. At it like rabbits we were – right up to the day he died, more or less. I miss sex.'

'Ew. No. I don't want to hear about it'. Nina stuck her fingers in her ears, then took them out again. 'For your information, I had sex last year.'

Flossie turned to look at her, interest sparking in her eyes. 'Who with?'

'A bloke from work.'

'What happened?'

'His wife.'

'Okay.' Flossie shrugged. 'No strings sex can sometimes be the best.'

'It wasn't okay. His wife found out about the string and I didn't know he was married. Anyway, how do you know about stuff like that?'

'I wasn't born eighty-four, you know.'

'According to you, you're not eighty-four now.'

Flossie stood up, with a great deal of groaning. 'I'm going in the sea.'

'Those waves look a bit rough, and the beach is pebbly,' Nina pointed out.

'So what?'

'You might get… never mind.'

'Good. I'm old enough and ugly enough to look after myself. I don't need you doing it for me.'

'I thought that's why I was here,' Nina muttered, watching her grandmother scramble gingerly down the beach, and almost get bowled over by a wave.

By the time Flossie had bunny hopped out of the sea and up the treacherously pebbly beach, Nina had come to a decision. The hotel was a stone's throw away (admittedly, you'd need to be of the standard of a Russian shot-putter to hit it), and she'd only be gone a few minutes.

'I'm popping back to the hotel for a wee,' she said when Flossie dropped onto her sunbed with all the grace of a sack of spuds.

'Pee in the sea. I just did.'

'Yuck. Remind me never to go in there.'

'Fish pee in the sea, what's the difference?'

'You've told me about it, that's the difference. Will you be alright on your own for a bit? I won't be long.'

'I'll be fine.' Flossie got out a book of crosswords and a pen. She clipped on a pair of tinted over-glasses onto her reading glasses and shoved them on her nose. 'Go on then, what are you waiting for?'

She'll be fine, Nina convinced herself as she winced all the way up the beach, scalding sand spraying the back of her legs; the heat was even noticeable through the bottom of her flip flops. She was glad to step onto the promenade.

'Move! Move!' a voice yelled at her.

A faint whooshing came from almost directly over-head. Nina looked up, screamed and lunged to the side.

An incoming paraglider and passenger missed her by inches.

'You okay?'

'Er… yeah… I think.' She checked herself over.

The man who had shouted pointed to a sign. *Paragliders landing. Caution.* She'd seen it, and she'd noticed some of them landing along the front, but it hadn't really registered until she'd almost been flattened by one. Unnerved, she did a meerkat impression, checking the sky for danger as she scuttled across the open area to the safety of the hotel.

What a stupid place for a landing site, people walked across there for goodness sake, children, old people, and the disabled. In Britain, there would be a dedicated, cordoned-off area, with the St Johns Ambulance volunteers standing by, and marshals in hi-viz jackets to make sure the public stayed out of the danger zone, not parachutes randomly falling out of the sky wherever they felt like, not caring who they landed on. Nina was flabbergasted at the speed of their descent as she scanned the sky one final time before ducking into the relative cool of the hotel's interior.

'What can I help you with today?' The rep sat in the courtyard with an empty cup on a table in front of her and paperwork strewn over a wicker sofa.

'I don't think this hotel is for us. We need to move,' Nina said.

'Is there a problem?'

'Not with the hotel as such, but with the guests.'

'Some of them can be a bit boisterous,' the rep said with a smile. 'But that's part of the charm of this type of holiday.'

'I think my grandmother booked it by mistake.'

'Your grandmother.' This was said in a flat, disbelieving voice.

'Yes, you see, she booked to go away with my grandad, but he died before... you know... and my mother persuaded me to come with her to keep an eye on her, but I don't think Gran realised she'd booked a hotel for singles.'

'Are you single?'

'Yes, but—'

'You'll fit in nicely.'

'I don't want to fit in. I want a hotel suitable for my eighty-four, I mean three, year old grandmother.'

'Admittedly, she is outside our normal demographic, but you're not. Is she with you?' The rep scoured the courtyard as if she expected to see an old lady hiding behind a fountain.

'But that's the point, *I'm* not inside the "demographic" either. I'm most definitely outside it.'

'Wow, you look good for your age, you must tell me your secret.'

'I'm not too *old* to be here, I'm too *young!*'

'Oh. Sorry, for a second there I thought... oops. I did say you looked good for your age though, didn't I?'

'I'm twenty-eight.'

'Yes. Right. Back to your... er... problem. We can't move you to another hotel.'

'Why not? Clearly you can see we don't fit in here. They had Gran prancing around holding a cardboard penis yesterday, and last night she sneaked out at god knows what time to go dancing on top of a bar.'

'*Talk of the Town?* I love it there.' The rep clapped her hands together. 'Such a good atmosphere.'

'Not for someone in their eighties.'

The rep gave Nina a shrewd look. 'How does your grandmother feel about moving hotels?'

'She'll be fine,' Nina muttered. 'Just put us somewhere a bit more suitable.'

'But that's what I'm trying to tell you. *Athena Holidays* only caters for the thirty-to-forty-five age bracket.'

'And that's what I'm trying to tell *you*, both of us are outside that "age bracket".' Nina used her fingers to make quotation marks. 'One of us is double your upper age limit. She should never have been allowed to make the booking in the first place.'

'You'll have to take that up with your travel agent when you go back home. In the meantime, I'm telling you we can't put you anywhere else.'

'Why ever not?'

'*Athena Holidays* has only got one hotel in this area – we don't want to saturate the market. Our nearest hotel is in Antalya, and you'll have the same problem there. Of course, there's nothing stopping you checking out of this hotel and checking into another.'

Nina seized on the suggestion. 'We'll do that then. Can you arrange it?'

'Sorry, but you'll have to do that yourself, and cover the cost of accommodation.'

Wonderful. Nina didn't have the funds available for that, and she suspected Flossie didn't either. Even if her grandmother did, Nina suspected Flossie would refuse anyway; for some reason, the old lady seemed to like it here.

Nina slunk back to the beach (keeping a look-out for potential sky hazards at the same time) and sat on the edge of her sunbed, cross and hot.

One good thing – Flossie was where Nina had left her, with an untouched crossword in her hand and a smile on her face. At least her grandmother was having a good time.

Chapter 12

'You were the one who wanted to go on this bloody jeep thing in the first place, so move it, grumpy.' Nina gave her grandmother a nudge. They were being picked up from the hotel in just under an hour, and Flossie would need her breakfast first, or else her insides would suffer.

Flossie rolled over and opened one eye. 'Shut up. There's a ruin or two for you to moon over, so the day won't be all about me.'

Later, sitting in the jeep, Nina was not so apprehensive about the excursion. It promised to be a long and possibly wet day, but at least they'd get to see something of Turkey other than the hotel and the resort. After the not-as-bad-as-she-remembered climb up the steep road from the coast into the hills, Nina didn't want to admit it, but the journey to their first stop at the ruins at Tlos was quite a pleasant one – if you ignored driving under waterfalls and being shot at by rival jeeps. Okay, maybe that was an exaggeration; the waterfalls were in fact sprays from strategically placed overhead pipes with holes in them which the driver of each jeep deliberately drove under. With the temperatures already hitting thirty-seven degrees Celsius at ten thirty in the morning (just short of ninety-nine degrees in old money as her gran would say because she still worked off Fahrenheit – but only when it was hot; when it was freezing Flossie liked to think it was zero degrees along with everyone else in Europe), a gentle spray was quite refreshing, and Nina found herself looking forward to the next drive-under.

She wasn't as keen on being bombarded by water guns wielded by a truckload of delinquent children and their equally mad parents, though – until Flossie produced two massive water pistols, unwrapping them from their carrier bag with a flourish and presented one to Nina the next time the jeep pulled alongside a large barrel filled with water to "reload".

'I thought you'd only bought one,' Nina said.

'And have you miss out on all the fun? Here, fill 'er up.'

Nina didn't need telling twice. 'I'm going to get those little shits back, if it's the last thing I do,' she vowed.

'That's my girl!'

Their driver, sensing the mood of his passengers, hared off up the road with his foot to the metal, and with a complete disregard for health and safety or the speed limit, racing to catch up with the truck. Nina had assumed their little convoy of three jeeps were the only ones doing this excursion, but she'd not made allowances for the numerous other tour companies who all had an assortment of jeeps and trucks on the road, and a kind of war had broken out with rival "gangs".

The truck, heavier and slower, ground up a hill, it's speed dropping off in direct proportion to the steepness of the incline. The occupants of their own jeep whooped and hollered, Nina joining in without realising. As the jeep gained ground and drew level, Nina primed the pump on her gigantic gun and let fly with a jet of water aimed at the mother's head. It slapped the woman in the chest instead, and she squealed, her thin top soaked in seconds, prompting the husband and all the little trucklets to lay down return fire.

Within a couple of minutes everyone, including both drivers, were drenched, the cannons were out of ammo, and each side were hollering that they'd won.

'I'm laughing so hard I think I might have peed myself,' Flossie announced. 'Can't really tell.' She pulled her dripping shift dress away from her lap and grimaced.

'Surely you know if you've wet yourself?' Nina asked, crossing her own legs in case of a similar unfortunate accident.

'Not when you get to my age, you don't,' was Flossie's reply.

When they arrived at Tlos, Flossie opted to stay in one of the little make-shift bars at the base of the steep hill.

'My old legs won't make it all the way up there, especially not in this heat,' she said, so Nina set off alone, trying to ignore the numerous other tourists who'd been brought to the ancient site in a variety of different vehicles, coaches seeming to be the most favoured mode of transport. Those tourists were easily recognisable – they were the dry ones, but Nina found she didn't resent their air-conditioned comfort. She'd actually had fun, she realised as she tackled the start of the path.

The lower slopes of the citadel weren't too steep, but as Nina followed the zig-zag track to the crumbling fortress on the top she wondered whether she would have been better off staying with Flossie and a cold drink. It was an awful lot steeper than it appeared from the bottom and the heat was fierce.

Made it! The view of the Xanthos valley was breathtaking but not as impressive as the ruins themselves. Nina ran a hand across the warm stones, awed by the knowledge that the site had been settled over four thousand years ago, and had been inhabited in turn by the Romans, the Byzantines, and the Ottomans. She sat on one of the walls and let the atmosphere soak in. With the valley below and the mountains as a backdrop, it was impressive. She tried to imagine it as it had once been – a living, thriving community, where people lived and loved and died.

This was why she loved the past so much, it was the basis of everyone's present, and so much could be learned, if only people took the time to listen and to see, and not just tick the site off their must-visit list.

She stayed as long as she dared, ignoring the other sweaty, puffing tourists, even though she was one herself, she acknowledged reluctantly. Conscious of the time (it had taken her longer than she'd anticipated to reach the summit) and not wanting their jeep to leave without her, she hastened back down, but couldn't resist stopping now and again to admire the rock tombs carved into the face of the hill. She wished she had more time to explore and that she'd had the foresight to have purchased a guide book. As she trundled back down, sweat coating her back and dribbling disgustingly between her boobs, she would have loved to know which tomb belonged to the fabled Belleraphon and to have been able to see the lion carved on the rock inside the tomb for herself.

After a quick and very welcome cold drink, it was then on to Saklikent Gorge and lunch. Nina was hoping for another water-fight along the way – anything to cool her down!

Wow! Just wow! Suddenly Nina was very glad indeed that Flossie had talked her into coming on this trip. She'd never seen anything as magnificent as that gorge. Cut into the side of a huge cliff face, it appeared out of nowhere – an intimidating cleft in the rocks, narrow and deep, towering above them for hundreds of feet, a boiling churning river at its base. Where the river calmed as it flowed out of the gorge, pontoons floated on the water, decked with low tables and cushions. It all looked so very Turkish, and very inviting.

'I wanna see the inside of the gorge,' Flossie announced as soon as they left the jeep, with strict instructions to meet at a nearby restaurant in an hour and a half, where lunch would be provided.

Nina halted outside the entrance to the gorge and read the warning signs with trepidation.

'We can go so far, Gran, but then it looks like you have to wade through waist-deep water.' It would be more like neck-deep on her diminutive grandmother.

A wooden walkway hung off the rocks on one side of the gorge and Nina stayed close behind her grandmother, ready to catch her if the old lady slipped on the slick, wet wood. Nina shuffled along the balustrade, clinging on with white-knuckled fingers and eyeing the churning water below with trepidation, while her grandmother strode ahead, as sure-footed as if she was in her own living room.

Without warning there was a scream, and Nina saw a splash out of the corner of her eye. Someone had fallen in! Another plummeting body followed the first, and another. But why were the voices around her sounding so happy and unconcerned, and why wasn't anyone sounding the alarm?

A brown head bobbed to the surface, followed by the rest of his body, and Nina let out the breath she'd been holding. At least one of them was still alive.

Then she realised – the fallers were actually jumpers, and they seemed to be enjoying the experience immensely. Young boys, not one of them older than about fourteen, their bodies nut-brown from the sun, water cascading off their skin and hair as they climbed nimbly out of the river and up the rocks, laughed and chattered – and did it all over again.

Nina admired their bravery. They seemed fearless, invincible. With the arrogance of youth, they believed nothing could touch them, because from where she stood all Nina saw was a sickening drop, the roaring river, and sharp rocks.

An unexpected pang shot through her – had she ever been as carefree and as courageous as these otter-like, monkey children, who were equally at ease climbing up wet rocks or plunging into raging cold rivers. Hell, she couldn't even remember climbing a tree.

'If I was ten years younger…,' Flossie said.

Thank goodness, she wasn't, Nina thought, with visions of Grannie plunging off the side never to be seen again as the thundering, swift-flowing river swept the old woman downstream and out to sea, playing through her mind.

Her relief was short-lived. When they got to the end of the walkway, Nina was dismayed to be confronted by a mass of water-drenched, slime-covered rocks. There was no way her grandmother would be able to negotiate that. People were gingerly walking over them, ankle deep in water in places, and every so often someone would slip and fall.

'That's it, Gran. This is as far as we go.'

'Nonsense.'

'You're not walking over that.'

'There's a café over there.' Flossie pointed.

'There are cafés on this side too, outside the gorge. We could sit on one of those floating pontoons. I'll even buy you a vodka.' Nina didn't want to encourage her grandmother to drink, but she would buy her one if it meant Gran behaved herself and didn't insist on trying to break her neck. Nina felt a bit like a parent trying to distract an unruly toddler.

'I can buy my own vodka, thank you very much, and stop treating me like a child.'

Nina rolled her eyes. 'If you fall don't blame me.'

'Oh, give it a rest. If it happens, it happens.'

'Not if I can help it, not on my watch,' Nina muttered then spoke a little louder. 'Yes, but I'll be the one picking up the pieces.'

Aside from physically manhandling her grandmother and wrestling her to the floor, Nina had no way of stopping her, and Flossie was determined. Nina vowed her mother would have to accompany Gran on any and all future trips; she washed her hands of the daft old bat.

'I help,' a firm voice declared, and a boy of about eight-years-old took her grandmother by the arm. Another appeared on Gran's other side, and between them they grappled her over the rocks, their bare feet gripping the slippery surface with confidence. Nina prayed their self-assurance wasn't misplaced. One wrong foot and all three of them would be on their backs like upended turtles. Gran would have to be stretchered out!

Safely on the other side (though the ground was still wet and you had to be careful), Flossie instructed Nina imperiously, 'Pay them. They don't do this sort of thing for nothing.'

Nina gave the boys a five lira note each, trying to calculate the exchange rate in her head – was it enough? Too much? What *was* the going rate for escorting old women over small waterfalls these days?

Flossie, meanwhile, had trotted off to the kiosk and was on her way back with two cans of cola and a cross expression.

'No vodka. No alcohol of any kind. Only beer. Beer makes me fart,' she said loudly and Nina cringed.

Lovely! Nina took the can with a feeling of relief. She hadn't been looking forward to dealing with a half-cut Flossie, because as sure as god made little green apples, her grandmother would not have stopped at just the one drink.

They sat on a wooden bench to sip their drinks and watched the incredible and rather amusing sight of people wading through deep water and only keeping their feet by hanging on to a rope which stretched from one side to the other. The main body of water gushed out of a cavern on the right of the gorge, whilst the river flowing through the gorge above the cavern was little more than a shin-deep trickle. She could see people paddling through it with confidence once they'd braved the torrent and reached the other side. From the looks of it, the river bed was actually dry in places, and Nina wondered how much rain fell in the winter months; quite a lot if the tide mark on the rock walls were anything to go by. Head tipped back, she gazed up at the top of the canyon. The walls narrowed as they got higher and the sky was a cerulean strip high above them. The sun wasn't visible from where they sat, and mist from the water cooled the air to a more comfortable level.

Voices chattered in so many different languages that Nina lost count and there was constant traffic back and forth. So many people that she wondered how much more of the gorge was traversable.

Little did she know it but she was about to find out.

When she lowered her gaze from the top of the gorge, feeling like an ant with all that towering rock above, Flossie had disappeared.

Chapter 13

Nina's first thought was that Flossie must have wandered off in search of the loo. Her next, and more accurate, thought was that Gran had taken it upon herself to go exploring. Nina narrowed her eyes, pushed her sunglasses further onto her head, and studied the people both at the river's edge and those wading across.

There she was!

Bloody hell! The woman was only being carried across like Lady Muck, in the arms of a strapping young man and was smiling up at him brightly.

Nina threw her drink can in the nearest bin and ran as if a swarm of angry bees were after her. 'Gran! What do you think you're doing?' she yelled, wading in up to her knees, the tug of the fast-flowing water bubbling around her legs.

She took another step, feeling for the bobbing rope, slipped, and lost a flip flop, watching helplessly as it floated off at a rate of knots. 'Bugger.'

'Wait, lady,' one of the seal-children said, with a huge smile. He threw himself headlong into the water and Nina cringed; if he was to drown because of her stupid shoe she'd never forgive herself.

Reaching down carefully so as not to overbalance, she slipped off the other shoe and held it tightly. Her grand-mother had already reached the other side and had been placed back on her feet. Pulling at his shoulder, Flossie urged her rescuer (or should Nina call him "the idiot who her gran had managed to coerce") to come down to her level. Nina watched as she said something in his ear, then both of them turned to look at Nina, and the bloke waved at her.

'Wait there,' he mouthed, miming wading back through the water.

No way! She was not going to be carried over the river like a helpless female. Besides, she wanted her grandmother on this side with her, not both of them on that side. Nina shook her head and pointed at him, then at her grandmother, then back at him again, making walking movements with her fingers.

Flossie, one step ahead of her, smiled sweetly, turned around, and picked her way up the shallow stream, leaving Nina no choice but to wade through the rushing water if she wanted to keep an eye on her stubborn grandmother.

'You'll be the death of me,' she muttered at Flossie's back, throwing her a venomous look, and stepped into the flow. The temperature took her breath away. Within seconds she couldn't feel her feet. Where was this water coming from, the Arctic?

Gasping, she waited, thinking her body would become acclimatised, but when the only thing to happen was for her feet and legs to start to go numb, she took the plunge. Not literally of course, for there was no way she was going to immerse herself in freezing water, but as the river crept higher up her legs, she wondered just how deep it was going to get.

She wasn't quite half way, with her attention on the frothing water and the slippery too-thin rope, when she bumped into a naked chest.

'Sorry,' she said, not looking up. One rope with lots of people all trying to hang on to it, made for awkward fumbling and close body contact as everyone skirted around one another, whilst trying not to be swept downstream. Really, it shouldn't be allowed. It was far too dangerous. There should be a proper bridge, or not let anyone go across at all. Somebody was going to drown, and Nina was worried it was going to be her!

'Eek!' she squealed, as two very hard arms lifted her off her feet without warning. Nina found herself with her nose squashed into a broad chest. She was so startled she nearly dropped her remaining flip flop.

'Put me down!' she yelled.

'I will, as soon as we're on the other side.'

Scared he was going to fall, she wrapped her arms around his neck and clung on with the desperation of a small child, and didn't release her death-grip until the water level dropped to her saviour's knees. Not that she'd needed saving – she was quite capable on her own – but it was rather nice to be held by a strong man, and he smelt nice, too, all coconutty with an undertone of deodorant. When her grip lessened, she was free to lean back a little and look at him properly.

Oh my. Bronzed, muscled, chisel-jawed, smiley mouth, chocolate eyes, and far too young for her. He was at least five years her junior, maybe more. Still a boy really.

But a treacherous little voice said in her head, boys aren't usually built like this, and his voice, when he spoke, was deep and rumbling, and not boy-like at all.

'Are you okay?' he asked. 'Can I put you down now?'

'Oh… er… yes. Thanks.' Damn it! She'd been enjoying that.

Then she remembered the reason it had been necessary to be carried in the first place – Gran. When she caught up with Flossie, she was going to give the old woman a piece of her mind; not that it would do much good, but it would make Nina feel better.

Smiling her thanks, she shot off barefooted, stones and pebbles cutting into her feet. Flossie was nowhere in sight – she must have gone around the bend in the gorge. Nina followed, cursing under her breath, to find the other woman calmly sitting on a rock, sandals off, dangling talon-like toes in a slow-moving, shallow eddy.

'You do realise we've got to cross that thing again?' Nina cried, as she drew closer. 'What were you thinking of?'

'I wanted to experience it for myself,' Flossie said. 'Not watch from the side-lines. Anyway,' she waited until Nina dropped onto the rock, 'it was worth it to be manhandled by such a fine young man. Didn't you think he was handsome?'

'Yes, Gran.' Nina massaged the soles of her feet.

'It would be better if you put your shoes on,' Flossie said. 'Those stones look sharp.'

'They are,' Nina growled. 'I lost one of them.' She waved the remaining flip flop under Flossie's nose.

'How did you manage that?'

'Crossing the damned river.'

Hunk and Co – yes there were more of them, and all made out of the same mould, but painted in slightly different colours – passed Flossie's rock and smiled. Nina thought Hunk may have winked, though it was difficult to tell with the sun in her eyes. It was now directly over-head and blasted down into the floor of the gorge. The temperature rose alarmingly; it was what Nina imagined it would be like if she was an ant and some sadistic little boy tried to burn her with a strategically-angled mirror. In this instance, the trickling water was the mirror, as it bounced the light around the rock walls and directly into her face. Nina reapplied her factor fifty with haste.

'Have you seen what you wanted to see?' Nina demanded.

'Yes, thank you,' Flossie replied, primly, as if she'd been asked whether she'd enjoyed a meal rather than being asked about a death-defying plunge into an ice-cold, raging torrent.

The journey out of the gorge was less exciting, though just as cold and frightening. A stringy Turkish youth, who was clearly much stronger than he looked, carried Gran. Nina had to wade. Sopping wet, probably looking like a drenched scruffy bag-lady, minus the bags and hopefully without the smell, though she did have a hint of l'eau de river about her, Nina scrambled towards the exit, and they made their way back along the scary walkway, out of the gorge, and crossed over the river via the road bridge.

On the far end, stuck through holes in a fence, were hundreds of assorted footwear. A young lad guarded them jealously. Nina spotted her poor flip flop and stretched out a hand to remove it.

'Ten lira,' he said with a big smile.

'Excuse me?'

'Shoe, ten lira.'

Nina gave him the money, guessing she was being fleeced (she'd got them on sale from Primark for ninety-nine pence), and she put it on, the soles of her feet very grateful even if her purse wasn't. Her mood didn't improve when, on the way to the restaurant, they passed several stalls, all selling flip flops and sandals for five lira.

But it did improve when Nina and Flossie had been shown to a communal table and Nina saw Hunk walk in.

Another wink. She wasn't imagining it this time. Using her hands to fan her hot face, she flushed even harder when he walked up to her.

'I thought you were walking further up the gorge,' she said.

'So did I, but we saw the time and realised it was lunchtime. We'll come back again and walk it then. I'm Martin, by the way.' He held out a hand.

She took it and they shook.

'Nina, and this is Flossie, my grandmother,' she said. 'Nice to meet you, and thanks for, you know...' She jerked her head towards her grandmother who was attacking the wine with enthusiasm. Nina hoped the carafe would be refilled, or everyone else seated at their table would have to make do with water.

She realised she was still holding his hand and that he had an amused smile on his lips. She let go and looked away. What was wrong with her? He was at least five years too young, and it wasn't as if this was the first good-looking bloke she'd ever met. On the other hand, most good-looking blokes didn't look at her the way he had been – with a kind of appreciative light in his eyes.

'You'll do another excursion to Saklikent?' she asked.

'I doubt it. We'll probably get a dolmus next time and do it ourselves. This was just an orienteering mission.'

'Dolmus?'

'Public bus. This excursion is so we can get our bearings.' He spotted his friends. 'Over here, bro,' he called, and five more exuberant, tanned, confident males sauntered over to Nina's table and sat down. Flossie simpered as the introductions were made. She looked like she was in seventh heaven, with hunk number two on her right, and hunk number three sitting opposite.

A waiter came around asking for meal choices; chicken, fish, or meatballs. Nina opted for fish. A basket of bread was already on the table, along with a jug of water and the carafe of wine. Half a carafe since Flossie had started on it. The men ordered Efes beer and Nina did the same, feeling reckless.

The restaurant wasn't what she had expected when the rep who had sold them the excursion told her lunch was included. Nina had anticipated a quiet little place, with table cloths and more than three choices on the menu. This set-up was worryingly similar to a school dining room, with people who didn't know each other crammed onto long tables. But the food was nice enough and the company was lively, and not to mention very good-looking. No wonder people enthused about the view at Saklikent!

During the meal Nina discovered Martin and friends were on a lads' holiday. They were all into outdoorsy stuff – diving, paragliding, white water rafting, going down the river in an inflated tyre.

Wait, what? 'This river?' Nina pointed towards the gorge and its turbulent contents.

'Yeah, the Xanthos river. You can hire an inflatable here and let the river take you downstream into the middle of nowhere. Our jeep will meet us there. You could have a go?' Martin suggested.

'No thanks,' Nina said, at the same time as Flossie cried, 'Yes, please,' and clapped her hands together.

'No, Gran, it's not safe.'

'Life ain't safe, girl; haven't you learned that yet? Oh, I forgot, you live in a Nina bubble of too-scared-to-do-anything-outside-your-comfort-zone.'

'Comfort zone?'

'I watch Loose Women. They know all about comfort zones and G-spots.'

Did her grandmother just say G-spot at the lunch table? Oh dear, she did.

'I'm fed up of you telling me "no",' Flossie was saying, as Nina tried to process her grandmother and G-spot in the same sentence.

Nina turned to Martin in exasperation. 'See what I have to put up with?'

Martin was on Flossie's side. 'I think it's great if she wants to do it.' He put a hand on Flossie's arm. 'You're only as young as you feel, eh, Flossie?'

Her grandmother giggled. Nina growled.

'I'll go with her, if she wants to try it,' Martin offered. 'You should have a go too.'

'I'm not in the market for a man,' Flossie announced. 'I've lost mine. He died, you know,' she added in a theatrical whisper. 'But *she* is.'

'Gran!' Nina was mortified.

'I'll be okay on my own. You stick with Nina,' Flossie said.

The rest of lunch was spent listening to the guys' tales of daring and adventure. It was enough to make Nina's hair curl. Why would anyone want to throw themselves off the side of a mountain, or be spun around in a dingy while hoping a raging river wouldn't slam you into sharp rocks and drown you? Where was the fun in that?

Flossie clearly thought there was plenty of fun in it. 'I wish I'd done those kinds of things,' she said, wistfully.

'It's not too late,' Martin said. 'You can do whatever you set your mind to. It's all about attitude, man.'

'It's all about not ending up in a nursing home,' Nina said. 'Because that's where she'll be if she isn't careful. Either that or six-foot under.'

'I don't want to get to eighty and look back on my life with regret,' Flossie stated.

'Eighty?' Nina assumed she had misheard.

'I'm seventy, you know,' Flossie said to the rest of the table, giving Nina a sneaky kick on the ankle.

'You don't look a day over sixty,' one of Hunk and Co said, the one with the bleached blond hair and the spider-web of tattoos over his chest and arms. They suited him.

Her gran looked every inch her eighty years, but Nina held her tongue as Flossie lapped up the compliment. Age to Flossie, Nina was beginning to understand, was moveable, much like Easter. Any time after the end of February seemed to work for Easter, and anything north of seventy seemed to work for her grandmother – it merely depended on who she was talking to.

'How old are you?' Flossie asked him, polishing off the rest of the second carafe of wine. No one else had managed as much as a sip of the stuff, and Nina suspected the restaurant owners weren't prepared to bring out any more for free.

'Twenty-three.'

'Do you like older women?'

'Er…' The poor bloke was bewildered, and Nina didn't blame him. Welcome to my world.

'Not for me,' Flossie said. 'For her. I like my men with a bit more experience, but I doubt my granddaughter is too fussy.'

Nina flushed scarlet. How could Flossie do this to her? What was wrong with the woman; didn't she have a filter on that mouth of hers? Dear lord, take me now before I do something we'll both regret, Nina prayed.

'Will. You. Stop. Trying. To. Set. Me. Up.'

As a collective, Hunk and Co were pissing themselves with laughter. No wonder, and Nina would be too, if she were in their shoes. One of them had his hands over his face, shoulders shaking, and odd snorting noises coming out of his nose.

'Sorry guys,' she said. 'My Gran seems to think I need a man. I don't.'

'Oh, Nina love, you're not a lesbian, are you? Not that I've got anything against them, you understand, but I want to see you get married and have babies.'

More snorting and lots of falling off their seats from the men around them.

Martin took a shuddering breath, his face bright red, and said, 'You don't need a man to have babies.'

Flossie sat up straighter in her chair. 'I know very well where babies come from, young man, and the immaculate conception only happened once. My Nina is no virgin.'

'Arrggg! Stop, you've gotta stop. I can't take any more,' Martin cried. The rest of his mates were unable to speak.

Nina wished Flossie couldn't speak either, and if the old woman didn't shut up, Nina was gonna make her.

'Anyone got any gaffer tape?' Nina asked, and it wasn't a joke. She turned to Flossie. 'One, a woman can get sperm from a donor, she doesn't need to have a husband or a partner to have a baby. Two, women can marry other women, men can marry men. Three, I am not a lesbian, and if I was, it would be none of your business.'

Flossie thought for a moment. Hunk and Co waited with barely supressed excitement for the old woman's next words.

They weren't disappointed.

'I have got this bit right though,' her gran said. 'You're definitely not a virgin, are you?'

Chapter 14

Flossie couldn't understand why Nina was in such desperate haste to leave the restaurant and return to their jeep, and Nina was too incensed and humiliated to enlighten her.

'Lovely boys, didn't you think?' Flossie asked. 'Such good manners. Not many young people are willing to spend time with the elderly, and listen to what they've got to say. You could learn summat from them.'

'I'm here, aren't I? Be grateful.' If Mum didn't have Flossie committed when she got home, Nina would never speak to her mother again. Her and her bloody ears. There was nothing wrong with her mother's ears; it had been an excuse not to go with Flossie. Her mother had set her up. Nina had been plucked, stuffed and trussed like a chicken for the oven. Mum had known exactly what she'd been doing and she'd happily sacrificed her daughter's sanity for her own.

'I didn't ask you to come,' Flossie said, looking hurt.

'No, you didn't,' Nina snarled, but her mother did, that woman who was supposed to love her and keep her safe, had gaily thrown her to the lions. Flossie was like a pack of them, all lying innocently in the sun one minute and savaging you to death the next. Who needed claws and teeth when Flossie had her mouth and a brain without a filter. And Nina wished her gran would stop saying she hadn't asked Nina to come. It made her feel guilty, and that was one emotion Nina could do without right now, since she had so many others vying for attention: shame, embarrassment, humiliation, anger, despair. The despair bit was knowing that they were only three days into their holiday, and the remaining days would be spent on the edge of her seat, waiting for Flossie to say or do something else outrageous.

For a second, Nina seriously contemplated Googling any and all available flights. There must be a plane leaving tomorrow; she didn't care where it was going, though the further away the better, as far as she was concerned. Let Flossie fall off a bar-top and break her hip, let her drink herself to death, or drown, Nina didn't care. Flossie was right, Nina wasn't her keeper or her carer – she was her granddaughter, and Flossie was a grown-up who hadn't been sectioned (yet), and Nina ought to just let her get on with it.

Which was exactly why, when they arrived at Patara Beach, a twelve kilometre stretch of golden sand, bordered by sand dunes, and famed for where turtles nested, Nina made sure she picked a decent spot to lay out their towels. It was also why she bought a couple of cold bottles of water from the jeep driver, and ensured Flossie was comfortable before she went off to explore the beach (not that she intended to go too far, she wanted to try to keep Flossie in view, even though she felt like staking her grandmother out in the sun, smearing her with jam, and letting the ants do their work).

The beach was beautiful, mile after mile of golden sand, with a backdrop of trees, with the glittering sea with long rolling waves and the Xanthos River flowing into it.

Nina hoped she wouldn't see Martin and friends shoot by because they'd missed being picked up.

At this stage in its life, the Xanthos didn't appear to be the same river. If she looked upstream (and not down, where the water became a cauldron of choppy waves and swirling eddies at the point where the river poured into the sea), the water was smooth and placid, flowing serenely with barely a ripple.

She dipped a toe in – it was icy, but refreshing, and she sat on the grassy bank for a while, letting the peace soothe her. Birds chirped in the trees, the river gurgled drowsily, and she almost fell asleep until her conscience prodded her. She'd left her grandmother alone for long enough. Reluctantly, she stood, taking one last lingering look, soaking up the calm before returning to the storm that was her grandmother.

Nina cut across the beach towards the sea and paddled through the wavelets, careful not to enter the water too close to where the river flowed into it. She'd heard about rip tides and stuff.

The sea was warm, and she ventured a bit further in, up to her knees. Soft golden sand swirled around her feet, tickling her skin. She dug her toes in, and smiled. Hot sun (maybe a bit too hot, but she had a hat and T-shirt on), the never-ending sea with waves rolling in for what seemed like miles away, a beautiful beach, and the absence of other people and their noise. Others were in sight, but they were far enough away not to bother her, and she certainly couldn't hear them. The only sound came from those wonderful waves, and Nina had the urge to jump through them, to kick and splash, and dance in the water.

She wished she had someone to share it with.

Sighing, she turned her back to the sea and put her flip flops back on. The sand might look gorgeous, but Nina knew how hot it would be, so she made her way cautiously back up the beach to where she had left Flossie.

Shielding her eyes with her hand, Nina spotted their towels.

No Flossie. A trail of grandma sized footprints angled down the beach towards the water's edge. Nina frowned; she hadn't spotted her grandmother, but the beach was huge and the people she'd seen dotted across it and in the sea had been exactly that – dots.

With her hand still over her eyes, Nina scanned the beach, trying to remember what Flossie was wearing, but there was only one solo figure in sight, and though he was at least half a mile away, Nina could tell he was male.

With dread creeping up her spine, Nina turned her attention to the sea. Maybe Flossie had gone for a paddle, like Nina had just done, but there was no one matching her grandmother's description in the shallows.

Wait a sec, could that be her, the distant speck bobbing in the water several hundred feet out? Nina had no idea how good a swimmer Flossie was, and even if she was Olympic standard, there might be off-shore currents and undertows, and *sharks*…!

'Help!' Nina cried as she shot off down the beach, kicking her flip flops off as she ran, and discarding her clothing along the way. Thank god she had her bikini on underneath.

And why wasn't anyone rushing to her aid. Admittedly her travelling companions were scattered along the sand, as far away from each other as it was possible to get, but surely someone must have heard her cries of alarm.

She splashed into the water, and began to wade.

And carried on wading.

Further out she went, expecting the sand beneath her feet to drop away.

It didn't. She was half way to her grannie and the sea, despite the waves, still only came up no further than the tops of her thighs. In fact, the water seemed to be getting shallower.

It wasn't until she reached the old lady, that Nina realised Flossie was sitting on her backside on the crest of a sandbank, letting the waves wash over her stomach.

Nina flopped down beside her, panting, put an arm around her grandmother and squeezed her tight. Flossie gave her a bright, unconcerned smile.

As her heartrate gradually returned to normal, Nina sincerily thought this keeping-Grannie-company business was going to be the death of her.

Chapter 15

Flossie didn't like being reminded she was old, but this time it was her body doing the reminding and not Nina. The excursion had taken it out of her, and Nina was left to her own devices after the jeep dropped them off at their hotel.

Flossie had needed help to get out of the vehicle and had climbed the steps to their apartment slowly and stiffly. She'd gamely dressed for dinner and had managed a healthy portion (and drank some wine, of course), but when the meal was finished she'd asked to go back to their room.

Nina saw she was exhausted, and no wonder after a night flight, followed by dancing on the top of a bar in the wee small hours and showing the world her knickers, then a long day out. They'd only been here three days, but it felt like a week already. Nina wasn't sure if that was a good thing or a bad one.

She accompanied her grandmother to their room, saw her into bed, then left the other woman to sleep. Nina was physically tired, in a nice way, but her brain was still very much awake, so she snatched her book off the table along with the room key, and headed for the courtyard. She'd go back and check on Flossie every so often, more to make sure the exhaustion wasn't a ruse and her gran wasn't planning on escaping again. Nina knew she had trust issues, but who could blame her – the old woman was sneakier than a weasel. Nina felt sorry for the bad press weasels suffered, because her gran could beat the poor animals hands down when it came to cunning.

All three hotel bars sounded lively, but she wasn't in the mood (was she ever?) and instead she wandered into the courtyard with its tinkling fountain and secluded, covered seating area, and ordered a coffee.

She'd enjoyed today, despite Gran's indiscretions. Nina had even found the river crossing to be fun. In hindsight, now Nina wasn't up to her backside in fast-flowing, ice-cold water, Gran was good company. Once Nina had gotten over that final humiliation in the restaurant and her fright at her grandmother's escapades, Flossie had been unknowingly funny, and if she was anyone else's gran Nina would have found the whole thing absolutely hilarious. Flossie was stubborn and annoying, but funny with it.

Nina never realised her grannie could be so adventurous and outgoing, and in a way it was a good thing that Flossie seemed to be coping with Grandad's death as well as she was, because Nina had imagined a much more sombre holiday, with her Gran sobbing into her beach towel and hours spent talking about him. Not that she'd mind, if that's what Gran wanted to do, if it made the old lady's life easier to cope with, but Flossie had surprised her. In a good way. Mostly. Even if the pensioner did seem to be experiencing a second teenage-hood. Nina understood regression into childhood could happen to the elderly, so maybe old people degenerated gradually, and behaving like a teenager was the start of the slippery slide towards a second babyhood.

The book sat unopened on her lap as Nina drank her coffee and stared unseeingly into the distance. Maybe both her grandparents had been losing their marbles (why else would they book a holiday where the clientele were all under forty, were all single, and were all looking to hook up with the opposite sex). Maybe Grandad dying was a kind of blessing in disguise, because Nina didn't want to think of her grandfather slowly and inevitably travelling towards the hell of dementia. Susan, a work colleague, had a mother with Alzheimer's and her descriptions and stories didn't make for pleasant staff-room conversations.

Nina smiled to herself; she wanted to remember her grandmother like she was now, dancing on top of a bar or begging to be allowed to float down a raging river on a fragile inflatable tyre. Suddenly she was very thankful she'd been given the chance to spend this time with her, even if the old lady drove her to distraction.

'May I join you?'

With a mental sigh and an urge to reply "No, you may not", Nina looked up at the man standing next to her chair and gestured for him to take a seat. After all, it wasn't his fault if he didn't know she wasn't on this holiday for casual sex, or to find The One, or any permutation in between. Besides, on reflection, she was a little tired of her own company and he looked pleasant enough, not in Hunk's league, but at least he didn't appear to be young enough to sit in on one of her GCSE classes. GCSE's – the results of those dreaded exams would be out soon, and she prayed her kids would do well. They deserved to, all of them; most of them, she amended, thinking of Connor Wilson who spent most of every lesson mucking about, annoying the kids who did want to work. Pity, because he was a bright pupil. He just hated school.

'You look like you're in a world of your own,' the stranger said. 'Another?' He gestured to her empty cup as a waiter appeared.

'Please.' Glad to have her mind taken off work, this time Nina's smile was genuine.

'I'll have the same. Been here long?' he asked.

'Day three.'

'I'm seven days in,' he said with a sigh.

Nina laughed; they sounded like a pair of convicts comparing prison sentences. 'It's not that bad, is it?'

'Depends what you're looking for,' he replied.

'I'm not looking for anything – I'm here as a sort of plus one.' She didn't really want to confess she was on a singles holiday with her gran; it sounded a bit sad, even if it wasn't strictly true.

'Two girls together, eh? Must be fun.'

'Yeah, it's so much fun that I'm sitting here on my own, reading a book and drinking coffee,' she said, with a grimace.

'You don't have to be on your own,' the man said.

Woah, now, Nina thought, hoping he wasn't suggesting what she thought he was suggesting.

'I like it,' she replied huffily, wishing he'd take the hint and go away. She had no objection to a civilised conversation but she didn't fancy being propositioned. Especially since the whole purpose of anyone else coming on a holiday like this was to get your leg over with as many people as possible, in as short a time as possible. Except her. Getting her leg over was the last thing she wanted, thank you very much!

'There are three bars to choose from,' he continued, 'and all of them are chock full of singletons wanting a bit of company, myself included, though I think I'm getting a bit old for this chatting women up in bars malarkey – I can hardly hear myself think because the music's too loud and to be honest, most of the women I've met only seem to be after one thing.'

Maybe she'd misjudged him.

Leaning back in the squashy seat, she examined him a little more closely. Hmm, not too bad. He seemed nice enough in a lawyer-ish, or accountant-ish way.

'What do you do when you're not on holiday?' Nina asked.

'I'm a stripper.'

Oh. Nina was at a loss; especially as he looked a bit… well… paunchy. Round the middle. Not much, just a bit. Maybe he sucked his stomach in when he took his clothes off. It would take a bit of sucking though.

'You should see your face,' he chortled. 'I wish I was a stripper, but I don't have the guts for it.' He grabbed a handful of stomach and squeezed. 'Guts! Get it?'

She got it alright.

'No seriously, I do voice-overs for TV adverts.' He took a breath and said in a dramatic tone, 'Panty Pops, so you never get caught unawares". Yeah, that was one of mine; do you recognise it?'

'I think so. Feminine hygiene, or something similar, aren't they?'

He pulled a face. 'Disposable knickers. Just pop them on and away you go. Aimed at the laugh-and-leak brigade. Not one of my finest moments, admittedly, but it seems to be the most memorable.' He let out a big sigh. 'Personally, I prefer to be remembered for the one where I did a voice-over for a well-known brand of shampoo. Pity I wasn't allowed in the bathroom with her.'

He saw Nina's aghast face. Nina knew it was aghast because she was wearing the same expression as she did whenever Romy from the Science Department told a dirty joke, and everyone laughed harder at Nina's expression than they did at the joke itself. Nina was sure Romy went out of her way to find the filthiest joke possible, just to see Nina's shocked and rather disgusted face.

'Sorry, I'm trying too hard, aren't I?' he said.

'Um… just a bit. Maybe tone it down a little?'

'I blame TV,' he said. 'All that innuendo tends to rub off.'

Now that he wasn't being such a dick, he seemed a bit nicer. 'Do you enjoy your job?' she asked.

'Hell, no. Take, after take, after take. More inflection on the word "cake", Wayne; can you say that again with a little more feeling, Wayne. Though just how much feeling can you put into double glazing, I don't know. And none of the millions of takes matter, because after the fiftieth version they usually go back to the very first one you did.'

'Like women and shoes.'

'Huh?'

'The myth is that women go into every shoe shop in town, before coming back to the first pair they saw.'

'My first wife used to do that.' he said glumly. 'I hated going shopping with her.'

Right. First wife, eh. 'How many times have you been married?'

'Just the once.'

'You said, "first wife".'

'That's because she is. I'd dearly like to have a second, but meeting the right woman isn't easy, is it? And I intend to hang on to the next one.'

'Is that why you came on this holiday? To find a wife?'

'Not exactly, but I did hope to meet some ladies who'd consider going on a date with me after the holiday ends. It's a bit like speed dating here – you get to talk to lots of different people who are all in the same boat (well, most of them are), and you can decide if you'd like to sit and chat for the rest of the evening, or if it's time to move on to the next table.'

Nina was curious. 'Have you been on many speed dates?'

'A few. Hideous things, they are.'

'Is this any better?' Nina gestured around the court-yard, with its mosaic tiled wall, lush planting, and soft lights.

'Yes and no. It's a false situation, being on holiday, don't you think? If you're not careful you can get seduced by the sea, and the sun, and the exoticness of it. I've got a feeling everyone will look a bit different when their tans have faded and they've got a mug of cocoa in their hand instead of a glass of raki and ice.'

Exactly! Holiday romances should remain on holiday. Even Cara in the school kitchen said so, and she'd brought home a Moroccan waiter several years ago and they had three kids together. Actually, three lively, demanding kids may well make you wish you'd left your holiday romance sobbing on the tarmac before you got on the plane. The poor woman looked worn to a frazzle!

There was no way Nina would ever have her head turned by a bloke on holiday. It was far too risky.

Chapter 16

Day five dawned in exactly the same way as days one to four – warm, (sticky if the air con had been turned off in the middle of the night), sunny, blue sky, blue sea, with the prospect of spending the next eight hours or so in a bikini. Nina could get used to this. For the first time ever, she wasn't wishing the summer away in order to return to school to fill her days with teaching, marking, organising, and planning.

Today they were going diving, and though Nina was hesitant (because of her grandmother, not because of the actual diving), she was looking forward to it too. If she bottled out, there was always the option of being a bubble-watcher, someone who sat on the side and watched everyone else try their hand at organised drowning. She'd also made a purchase of a mask and snorkel, to join in a bit if she didn't fancy going all the way, as a sort of half-way house.

It was Gran she was worried about. It had taken Flossie all day yesterday to recover from the jeep safari, and it wasn't until she'd got on the outside of several vodka cocktails (called, rather inappropriately, Nina thought, Sex on the Beach) that Flossie started to move less like an old woman and more like her old self. She'd also lost the pinched, drained look she'd been wearing all day. Nina had been quite worried, and was fully prepared to call the diving off if her grandmother didn't perk up.

By last night, Flossie had perked up all right, enough to drink the bar dry of peach schnapps – an essential ingredient of the cocktail, it seemed. Nina hoped it was because the bottle of schnapps had been almost empty and not because Gran had been grabbing secret top-ups every time one or the other of them went to the loo.

'I hope I won't be sea sick,' Nina said as they settled into a seat in the room where the pre-dive talk was being held. 'I'm not usually too good on boats.'

'When was the last time you were on a boat?'

'I was about twelve, I think.'

'I remember. It was a rowboat on Wetherton Lake when we went for a camping holiday. Your mother insisted we come along, but your grandad and I booked a guest house, because I didn't fancy peeing in a bucket.' Flossie paused. 'You'd eaten half a ton of candy floss and a three-scoop ice cream. No wonder you were sick.'

'Oh yes, so I did.'

'You'll probably keep your fruit and rabbit food down,' her grandmother stated. 'And if you don't, it'll be food for the fish.'

'Ug. Ew. Not nice.'

'Then try not to chunder,' Flossie suggested bluntly.

The boat itself was lovely, with a carved dolphin on the front. It was run by a lively British bloke by the name of Alan, who was in his late fifties, still fit, funny and enthusiastic. He had everyone on board laughing with tales of the antics of scores of previous novice divers. Nina hoped she wouldn't add a tale to his extensive repertoire.

He stressed that this was a ten-foot, three-metre-maximum taster dive, and he was shit-hot on health and safety. He went through all the hand signals, making them laugh when he did the signal for shark.

'No seriously, this means shark,' he said, placing his hand on the top of his head, thumb pointing backwards while resting on his hair, fingers aimed at the sky. 'It means the last one out is lunch – the shark's lunch,' he joked, while Nina peered over the side of the boat nervously, expecting to see a torpedo shape shadowing the hull.

The sea today was choppy but not enough to make her feel sick, though Nina did suspect Alan's jokes and constant stream of chatter was a method he used often to put his new divers at ease and to keep their nerves in check.

By the time the boat chugged into a sheltered cove, Nina was ready to get in the water. Alan made it sound so easy, and as everyone was helped into their wet-suits and the equipment was secured, he appointed one instructor to every two divers.

'Your instructor will not leave you. If one of you has to ascend, the both of you will. You will never, ever be left alone under any circumstances. Follow your instructor's directions,' Alan said, serious for the first time since they'd left the busy harbour. 'They know what they're doing and they'll keep you safe.'

Nina was suited up well before Flossie, and she had to bite back laughter as she watched an instructor trying to stuff the old lady into a wet suit. Gran fussed and flirted, and made him laugh, which Nina hoped wasn't at her expense as the pair of them stared in her direction. The instructor nodded. Nina had a feeling something was going on, but forgot about it when Alan, seeing that the instructors were ready, sent them into the water ahead of the newbies.

He selected Nina to descend with another woman.

'Can I go down with my grandmother?' she asked.

'Because of her age, she's going to have an instructor all to herself, aren't you, my darling?' he called to Flossie, and gave her a wink.

Flossie waggled her fingers at him, unable to do anything else because she'd put the goggles on and shoved the regulator in her mouth (Nina had recently learned the name of the breathing thing) and her grandmother looked like a cross between an elderly Biggles and a space man.

Starting off in the shallows, getting used to putting their heads underwater and breathing through their mouths, Nina quickly got the hang of it. She had one dodgy moment, when they started the dive proper, and she looked up to see the underside of the sea, the *wrong* side (humans were meant to be above the divide, not below it), and she felt a bit panicky, but she breathed slowly and regularly, as per Alan's instructions, and the moment passed. It helped that Nina was a strong swimmer, and the surface was only a few feet above.

When she settled down, she finally looked about her. What she saw stole her breath. Never, in all her twenty-eight years, had Nina experienced anything like the sensation of floating in the middle of the ocean. She forgot her diving companion; she forgot the instructor; she forgot the rest of the world existed. All that mattered was here. Now. A deep serenity swept over her. She felt like Alice in her looking-glass and Lucy slipping through the wardrobe, rolled into one, awed, mystified, and slightly disbelieving at the same time. She never imagined it could be so magical.

A tap on her arm. She made the "okay" sign with her thumb and forefinger. She was more than okay, she was bloomin' marvellous.

The three of them swam slowly and majestically toward the sea bed, only a few feet below, and their instructor halted. He pointed to a pile of rocks, then to his eyes and back to the rocks again.

Oh, yes, they were going to feed the fish; Nina had forgotten, in her excitement. But it wasn't fish they were going to feed, she discovered, it was something much more thrilling.

Octopus. A little one, admittedly, but a real live octopus all the same.

It crept and flowed out of its miniscule hole, while Nina marvelled at how it could possibly have fitted into so tiny a crack in the rocks. It reminded her of the expanding foam her dad had once used; a tiny squirt had turned into a massive dollop which grew and grew with an alien determination.

She squealed into her regulator when the creature gently touched her hand with a tentacle, gliding over her skin until it came to the little silver ring she wore, with its turquoise stone. The octopus stoked it, appearing fascinated.

Nina held her breath until the instructor, who was positioned directly behind her, gave her a nudge to remind her to breathe. She resented the intrusion, however necessary it might be. For a blissful minute nothing else and no one else had existed – just her and the cute, enchanting, incredible creature from another world, and she sent a silent thank you to it for allowing her this brief contact.

If Nina lived to be as old as her grandmother, she would never forget this. And she vowed she'd never eat octopus again, either.

'Oh my god, it was fantastic,' she enthused as she was helped (or rather, hauled) aboard, turning to her instructor who was still bobbing in the water, awaiting his next assignment of newbie divers. Nina wanted to go again. And again. Maybe she'd see if there were any diving lessons she could sign up for when she got home and—

Flossie sat there in her normal clothes, wet suit off, with a huge grin on her face.

'Did you see it?' Nina said. 'The octopus?' Oh, she couldn't have. It had only been Nina, the other woman, and the instructor around *her* octopus. Maybe there were more of them, secreted all over the seafloor, waiting for their complimentary meal of fish scraps from successive boatloads of tourists.

Flossie shook her head. 'I didn't go down.'

'I'm sorry, Gran.' She sat by her grandmother and dug a bottle of water out of her bag to wash away the salt-taste. 'Did you lose your nerve?'

'I never had any to start with.'

Nina blinked, confused. 'What do you mean? I don't understand.'

Flossie accepted the water, taking a slug. 'I didn't have any intention of diving,' she said.

'But you were all suited up – I saw you.'

'Would you have gone, if you thought I wasn't going to?'

Nina had nothing to say.

'Thought not,' Flossie smirked.

'You mean to tell me, you had no intention of diving, even when you booked this trip?'

'Give the girl a medal.' The words were a tad on the sarcastic side, but Flossie's expression was all smiles and love.

'Why?' Nina was glad she'd dived, she would not have missed the experience for the world, but *why*?

'Because you needed a push. Because you never would have entertained the idea of going diving. Because I thought you might like it, and even if you didn't, at least you tried it.'

'I did love it! It was the best thing I've done in a long time, maybe ever.' Nina finished the water, thinking furiously. 'Is that why you booked the jeep safari? Is that why you crossed that stupidly dangerous river?'

'No, not totally – I wanted to go. I didn't want to spend the whole holiday flat on my back on a sunbed, with a vodka in my hand. Life's too short for that, and whatever time I've got left is getting shorter by the day. And to answer your second question about the river – yes. But it wasn't as dangerous as you make out.' Her eyes took on a wicked twinkle. 'Not if you can get a lovely young man to carry you across.'

'Gran,' Nina hesitated. 'I hope you haven't planned anything else for the sole purpose of getting me to try new things – like paragliding?'

'Would you go, if I did?'

'No and don't you dare, you batty old bird! I'm really, really not going to do that!' She twisted in her seat and gave her grandmother a hug. 'Thank you,' she said. 'For everything.'

Chapter 17

Dear lord, Nina had never felt so hot in all her life! An oven came to mind as she helped Flossie out of the taxi and they stepped into the heat of a Fethiye morning. The city, with its lovely big harbour, was a half-hour drive from their resort, and on Tuesdays it held a market.

Funnily enough, Flossie hadn't particularly wanted to come. Nina would have thought she'd have jumped at the chance of mooching around stalls selling everything from pins to pianos (okay, the piano may be an exaggeration, but in a market this size one never knew) despite her protestations during the welcome meeting where they'd booked their various excursion.

Instead of pleasure, Flossie had pulled a face when Nina suggested it.

'Markets are for old people,' she'd grumbled yet again, and she was still grizzling under her breath when she took Nina's arm as they prepared to dive into the fray of people. Only Nina's promise not to sulk (Nina never sulked, so she didn't know where her grandmother had got that idea from!) when they went on the Sunset Cruise later that evening, had persuaded the other woman to go.

'You drive a hard bargain,' Nina had stated at the time, not fancying a night of staged games and cheesy entertainment. Right now, she was almost wishing Flossie had driven an even harder one – so hard it would have put

Nina off coming to the market. The noise, the smells, the sheer volume of people, and not to mention the heat (had she already mentioned how hot it was?), were all overwhelming.

Covering the market was a billowing mass of white tarpaulin, shading people below from the sun. Unfortunately, they also reduced any breeze (not that there was much of a breeze to start with) and Nina's first purchase was a fan – the plastic and paper variety, painted with pictures of Turkish scenes, costing an arm and a leg, the seller obviously aware he had a captive audience.

Nina was fascinated as they walked into the first aisle, the air awash with the scents of the herbs and spices piled into colourful, fragrant heaps in tightly woven baskets and open-topped jars. Huge melons, fat juicy grapes, olives, and oranges were amongst the variety of fruit on sale. Vegetables, nuts, cheeses, honey, Turkish delight – the list was endless, and everywhere she looked stall holders shouted their wares, offering portions to taste.

The market was as much for locals as it was for tourists, Nina was pleased to see, watching the bescarved women wearing a kaleidoscope of colours and patterns, head, arms and legs covered, as they bartered for their weekly shop, filling bag after bag with glorious fresh-looking produce.

Flossie kept a tight grip on Nina's arm. 'If I wanted to look at a sack of spuds I could have gone to Waitrose,' the old woman muttered.

'Look, Gran, bags. You like bags.' Nina pointed to the next section of stalls, decked from floor to tarpaulin roof with bags of all sizes, shapes, and colours; handbags, shoulder bags, clutches, shoppers, evening bags, fancy rucksacks, briefcases, manbags… if you could imagine it, this stall sold it.

'Lookie, lookie, cheaper than chips. Yes, lady, you want I show you a nice bag? For you?' the man said to Nina, then grinned at Flossie. 'You are sisters, yes?'

He chucked the old woman under the chin. Flossie slapped his hand away and Nina supressed a laugh. There was no getting around her grandmother when she was in this mood. Good luck, mate, you're gonna need it if you think you'll get my grannie to part with money she doesn't want to spend.

'Bloody hell,' Nina muttered ten minutes later, as the man wrapped an enormous leather shopper (they knew it was leather because the stall holder had insisted on trying to set light to it to prove it didn't melt like a plastic one would) and handed it to Flossie.

'How much did I pay for that?' her grandmother asked as they strolled off. She gave Nina the bag to carry.

Nina did a quick calculation in her head. 'He was asking ninety pounds and you got him down to thirty-five.'

'I only saved fifty-five pounds?' Flossie cried, dismayed. 'It sounded like more than that.'

'That's because of the exchange rate. You did have a good deal,' Nina added. 'A leather bag that size would cost you at least three times as much back home.'

Flossie huffed a bit, but Nina knew she was secretly pleased, especially when they stopped for refreshments and her gran insisted on transferring everything from her old bag into her new one.

She was so pleased with it, she took it with her on the cruise.

"Food, wine and dancing, and a romantic swim in the warm Mediterranean Sea under the silver moonlight" the leaflet had advertised.

Nina guessed there wouldn't be a moon tonight, though the boat did head out towards the setting sun, which more than made up for it. When she looked back towards the land, the mountains were lit up in gold and orange. There wasn't going to be any swimming either, not for her, not in the dark. Things came out at night, and she wasn't talking about the mozzies. There were much scarier things living in the deep than the cute little octopus. He might have a cousin for a start, a really big one with tentacles thicker than her waist. And sharks. They came out at night too, didn't they?

She wasn't all that convinced about the dancing either, not on a rocking boat. She had enough trouble keeping her balance sitting down, let alone bopping around. She'd sick her dinner back up. There'd not be much alcohol either, for the same reasons: balance and the nausea factor.

'See that mountain there?' Flossie, hanging onto her new bag and wearing her finery even though they were going to some distant beach to have a barbeque and a dip, pointed to the peak rising above the resort. The tip of it shone white as if it was covered in snow.

Nina nodded. It certainly was impressive. The whole area was very beautiful.

'Nearly seven thousand feet high, it is,' Flossie said. 'The paragliders take off from there.'

'Yeah, good luck to them. It's nice to look at, but you won't get me up there in a month of Sundays.'

'It's Sunday tomorrow,' Flossie said slowly.

'So?'

'Nothing. Just saying.'

As the sun dipped below the skyline, the boat reversed into a secluded cove. Or it would have been if it wasn't for the three other boats already lined up as they drew alongside.

'I like walking the gangplank,' Flossie stated as they staggered off, the so-called gangplank bobbing with the waves. 'It makes me feel like a pirate's moll. I love a nice pirate. That one with the dreadlocks, he was lovely. What was his name?'

'Jack Sparrow?'

Three people within hearing distance joined her gran in a chorus of '*Captain* Jack Sparrow.'

Music played, and the bonfire was in its full roaring glory. The smell of wood-smoke infused with barbecuing meat, hung on the night air, mingling with the cleansing scent of the sea. Someone had gone to a lot of trouble to drag huge logs into position to sit on. Nina was handed a glass, which she took without thinking. She'd promised her gran there would be no sulking and she intended to live up to her word.

Wine, nice and chilled, and tart on the tongue, was a perfect accompaniment to the evening. Despite there being quite a few people, Nina felt as though they had been marooned on a deserted island, and the atmosphere steadily soaked into her reluctance, rinsing it away until she felt relaxed and happy.

She nudged her grandmother. 'Thank you for talking me into this. It's really pretty here, isn't it?'

Flossie stared at her for a while before answering. 'Are you really glad you came?'

'I am, and I don't just mean tonight. The holiday has been fun.'

'There's plenty more where that came from – we're only half way through.'

'We've crammed a lot into a week, and there was me, thinking I'd spend lazy days by the pool and the evenings playing bingo.'

'I bloody hate bingo,' Flossie declared solemnly.

'I'd have taken you for a bingo lady.'

'You don't know me at all, do you?'

'I didn't,' Nina replied thoughtfully. 'But I think I'm beginning to. It's funny isn't it, how us young 'uns,' she bumped Flossie with her arm, 'forget the elderly weren't always old. That you were children, teenagers, once young like me. Pensions, and winter fuel allowances, and wrinkles and dentures hadn't crossed your mind.'

'It's not until you get old you understand what it's like, but you never really forget what it's like to be young either, not really, not deep down. I think most old people just don't like comparing what they were to what they are now, so they brush their memories with a layer of "it-wasn't-like-that-in-my-day" and varnish them with nostalgia.'

'That's so insightful.' Her grandmother's words almost brought tears to her eyes.

Flossie threw back the last of her wine. 'Yeah, I read it in a magazine, and been waiting for a chance to use it.'

Nina held out her hand. Flossie shoved her glass in it. 'Get me another, there's a good girl.'

'Gran, you don't fool me. You really meant it.'

'Of course, I did! My glass is empty.'

Nina smiled ruefully. Her gran clearly wasn't much of a one for sentiment. 'I don't care if you don't want to talk about it anymore,' she said to her. 'But I just want to say one thing before I have any more to drink and you think it's the booze talking – I love you.'

Chapter 18

'I hate you, Gran!' Nina squealed as she was forced to run awkwardly down the slope, Mehmet at her back, his legs doing all the work, his hands operating the ropes.

Ropes? Ha, more like thin nylon strings of death.

Without warning, there was no more ground, no more earth; she felt as though a giant hand had taken hold of the chute and pulled them skyward.

She let out a shriek, screaming, 'Put me down, put me down, put me down.'

'You okay?' Mehmet asked.

'Do I sound it?' she cried.

'You are safe. The thermals are good.'

The only thermals Nina ever wanted to come into contact with were the clothing variety in the depths of winter. She'd give anything to be stuck in a freezing field right now, shivering her tits off, with a load of equally miserable pupils doing their Duke of Edinburgh Award.

'Take me back,' she shouted. 'I don't like it.'

Her pilot (they really were called pilots – yeah, a pilot without a plane didn't inspire her with confidence) chuckled. 'Sorry, one-way ticket. Down. Relax and enjoy.'

'Noooo…' She knew she was hyperventilating, her own breathing sounded harsh and frantic and panicked in her ears. I'm going to die, I'm going to die, was the only thought in her head.

'Arggg!' The world tipped to the side as they came about, describing a huge circle in the sky at least a hundred feet above the top of the already stupidly high mountain.

'Open your eyes and enjoy the view,' Mehmet suggested.

'I've got my back to you,' Nina said, through a jaw so clenched her whole head ached – or was that the altitude? 'How do you know my eyes are closed?'

Another chuckle. 'I guessed.'

She gripped the ropes with knuckle-cramping hands, terrified that if she let go of them she would tumble, screaming, to her death. The sensation of turning ceased and Nina opened her eyes for a brief peep, hoping they'd descended a significant amount.

There was land beneath her alright, and not too far away either; but it wasn't the land she was hoping for. This particular land was the top of the mountain she'd unwillingly thrown herself off.

They hadn't gone down – they'd gone up!

And there was her treacherous deceitful grandmother grinning up at her and waving.

'I hate you,' she mouthed.

Flossie nodded and smiled.

'You'd think I'd learn wouldn't you,' Nina muttered under her breath. 'But no, the sneaky old bat out-manoeuvred me again. First the diving, then this.'

Eeek. Another turn, gradual and graceful, with little sense of movement, yet the ground rushed by underneath, then abruptly dropped away. The only sound was the flutter of the canopy and a creak or two as the nylon ropes slid against one another.

'I don't feel as though we're moving,' she said over her shoulder, not needing to raise her voice. Any second now a pterodactyl would come swooping majestically out of the cloud and Nina wouldn't be in the least bit surprised.

'It is because we travel at the same speed as the air,' Mehmet said. 'No noise, no speed.'

Now and again a voice reached them, reminding Nina they weren't alone up here.

Then without warning they were below the scant cloud and the whole world was spread out before her. She could see for miles, like being in an aircraft coming into land. Nina never knew the world could be so beautiful. She let out a sigh of sheer joy. Gone were thoughts of dropping like a stone; gone were thoughts of what she'd do to her grandmother when she caught up with her; gone was the crippling fear she had felt the second before the wind had taken the chute, blowing her into the abyss.

A remarkable peace stole over her as she watched the ground grow slowly larger, coming closer with each breath she took, with each beat of her heart. She was curiously and abruptly delighted that Flossie had pulled her either-you-go-or-I-will stunt.

She could cheerfully have brained the old woman when Flossie dragged her out of bed at stupid-o'clock, informing her that she was paragliding this morning. Nina could either come with her to the top of the mountain, or remain at sea level, to watch her grandmother float in.

Float? Ha! Drop with the speed of a brick, more like. The conversation, as Nina recalled quite clearly, went something like this:

Nina. 'You're not going.'

Flossie. 'I am, too.'

Nina. 'You're not, I forbid it.'

Flossie. 'Who died and made you my mother?'

Nina. 'Please, Gran, you can't. People have died paragliding.'

Flossie. 'People have died in their beds. Want me to stop sleeping?'

Nina. 'You're being silly.'

Flossie. 'I'm enjoying life.'

Nina. 'You might not have any more of it to enjoy if you carry on.'

Flossie. 'Are you threatening me?'

Nina. 'No, what I meant was you might get killed.'

Flossie. 'You really don't want me to go, do you?'

Nina. 'No, Grannie, I don't.'

Flossie. 'Right, you can go instead of me.'

Nina. 'I don't think so!'

Flossie. 'It's either you or me, chick, so make your mind up.'

Nina. 'Okay, I'll do it.'

Flossie. 'And don't think about leaving me here, and you chickening out at the last minute. I'm coming to the top with you.'

Which was why her grandmother was waving gaily at her as if Nina was on the other side of the street and not nearly seven thousand feet in the air, her life in the hands of a total stranger and a bit of flappy fabric.

And to her unbridled surprise, Nina realised she felt alive for the first time in a very long time (before the cynical part of her chirped up with the idea that you probably only feel this alive when you're just about to die). But she wasn't going to die, was she? This man, this stranger, sitting so close behind her that she could feel his breath on the back of her neck, seemed to know what he was doing. He'd done it hundreds of times before. He

143

wouldn't knowingly jump into the arms of death, and take her with him – not unless he was a psychopath, and he didn't strike Nina as the type. He probably wanted to stay alive just as much as she did.

So she let go of her fear (mostly) and enjoyed the ride.

Leaning forward, just a smidge, Nina spied their hotel directly beneath her feet. If Flossie had been sitting by the pool and not sitting in a minibus rattling her way down the dusty road off the stupidly high mountain, Nina would have been able to have a conversation with the old lady, it was so quiet.

Despite enjoying the experience immensely (though she tried desperately to keep the last few feet of the flight out of her mind – the bit where she and the ground met), Nina fully intended to have a conversation with her grand-mother, and she didn't anticipate it being a particularly pleasant one.

'Oh god, oh god.' The ground was rushing up at her.

'Remember what I said, as soon as we touch down, you need to run,' Mehmet said.

'Don't you mean "fall"?'

Tense and frightened, Nina braced for impact.

'Go!' Mehmet shouted in her ear, and Nina's legs scrabbled in the air, finally finding purchase as they touched the ground. She only needed to run a few steps, leaning backwards in an instinctive move to slow her speed. As they came to a halt, the chute whispered to the earth behind them in a sigh of silken nylon.

She'd made it. She was alive, and in one piece, and totally and utterly elated.

'Whoop, whoop.' She fist-pumped the air, as she was helped out of the harness, and had the urge to drive straight back up that mountain to do it all again.

'Did you enjoy it?' Mehmet asked, and Nina saw the twinkle in his almost-black eyes.

'Oh yes!' she cried, and she kissed him.

He happily kissed her back, his lips cool on hers, his arms around her waist. She'd never kissed a man with a beard before, and the hairs on his face were soft and tickly.

He tasted of coffee, cigarettes, and freedom.

Nina pulled away. 'Sorry, I... er...'

'No worries. It was good, yes?'

Nina had no idea whether he referred to the flight or the kiss, and she realised it didn't matter.

'Yes, very, very good,' she agreed.

Chapter 19

Ephesus. Nina couldn't wait! Her grandmother might have gotten her out of her "comfort zone" (Nina made quotation mark fingers in her head) on this holiday, but the visit to Ephesus would place Nina firmly back in it. It boasted the Temple of Artemis, for goodness' sake! – one of the Seven Wonders of the Ancient World. Who couldn't fail to be impressed?

Flossie, for one…

'It's an awful long way to go to see a lump of stones,' she grizzled.

'You can always stay here?' Nina suggested, crossing her fingers Grannie wouldn't call her bluff and take her up on the offer. There was no way Nina could disappear for a few days, leaving her grandmother free to get up to all sorts, though since the bar-dancing, knicker-showing episode, Flossie had actually behaved herself; it had been Nina doing all the silly dare-devil stuff. Flossie had cheerfully thrown Nina in at the deep end instead, and had laughed when she was drowning, but the pensioner hadn't actually done anything outrageous herself. However, Nina was well aware of the old saying regarding a cat being away and the mice having a rare old time. There was no telling what her gran would do if she was left to her own devices for forty-eight hours.

'You don't think I'd let you loose in a foreign country all by yourself?' Flossie asked. 'No chance, my girl.'

'What do you think is going to happen? I'll be fine,' Nina said, before giving herself a mental slap – at this rate she'd talk Flossie out of going and then Nina would feel obliged to stay with her. Shut up, Nina.

'You could be abducted by slavers. They'd like a nice blond English girl like you.'

'I think I'm a bit old, Gran,' was Nina's reply. Slavers, indeed! Where did Flossie get her ideas?

'This is nice,' Nina said, as she got on the coach half an hour later, expecting Flossie to be right behind her as she traversed the aisle to pick a seat.

'No, it's not,' Flossie called. 'I can't get on, I'll be sick. I might even have one of my turns.'

What turns? This was the first Nina had heard of any turns.

Their tour guide, who had been supervising the loading of their case (one between them, was enough for a couple of changes of clothes and their toiletries, though Nina still felt a little uncomfortable at the thought of her white cotton, short-style knickers snuggled up to Flossie's simply enormous pants – it didn't seem right, somehow) came up behind Flossie.

'I am Yasin. I am here to facilitate you.'

'Oh good,' Flossie said.

Nina returned to the front of the coach, hovering at the top of the steps, wondering whether she should get out to see what her grandmother was playing at now. If the old biddy really didn't want to go, she should have said so earlier, not when they were boarding the coach, keeping everyone else waiting. Nina shot apologetic smiles to the man sitting in the front seat and the assorted couples scattered towards the back. She heard a loud sigh from a middle-aged man with a Kiss-Me-Quick hat (did they actually make those – Nina had assumed they were an urban myth) and she did a "what-can-I-do" shrug. Come on, Gran, make your mind up; go, stay, stay, go, just make a bloody decision.

'I need to be facilitated into a front seat, otherwise I can't travel,' Flossie stated. 'Or maybe I'll get on anyway and we'll see if we can manage to get to Elephant without having to stop too many times. Or call an ambulance, if I have one of my really bad ones.'

Nina was flummoxed. She didn't know whether to applaud the other woman's bare-faced cheek or give her a good telling off. Those kinds of lies could come back and bite you in the bum – karma, fate, or whatever.

'You need to be sitting in a front seat?' Yasin clarified.

'Yes, and my granddaughter needs to be sitting with me, just in case.'

'Maybe you should not be going?' the guide suggested, looking concerned.

'Yes, I should definitely be going,' Flossie insisted. 'I will only be unwell if I can't travel in the front seat.'

'But I am having to sit in the front seat. It is so I can speak to everyones and give informations.'

'There is another pair of front seats,' Flossie pointed out.

'Peoples are sitting in them.'

'Just the one people,' Flossie said. 'Can you ask the people if he would mind moving?' Flossie raised her voice so the man in question heard. 'Would you be kind enough to let a ninety-four-year-old woman sit in the front?' she called to him, her voice quavering.

Nina knew her gran didn't quaver. Flossie had never quavered in her life.

'Of course.' The man in the front seat stood, picked up a rucksack from the floor and moved back one.

Flossie got on.

'What on earth are you playing at?' Nina hissed in the old woman's ear once they were both seated and Flossie had fished a bag of boiled sweets out of her handbag. The driver started the coach and they began to move.

Flossie hissed back out of the side of her mouth, 'Shut up – I got you a front seat, didn't I?' Then in a more normal voice and with a hand cupped to the side of her head, she said, 'Sorry lovey, I can't hear you, you'll have to speak up.' She shuffled so she could see the poor bloke behind. 'I'm a bit deaf, you know,' she said, throwing him a butter-wouldn't-melt-in-my-mouth smile.

Nina gritted her teeth. Flossie needn't think she'd got away with it. There was always later, even if she had to wait until they were alone in their shared hotel room.

'Would you like a sweet?' Flossie asked nicely, and the man took one. Nina noticed he didn't attempt to unwrap the half-melted sticky mess, and she thought he'd only taken it out of politeness. That was nice of him, humouring an old lady. Nina hadn't done much more than glance at him until now, too embarrassed to notice anything other than he appeared to be on his own.

'Thank you for moving seats to allow my ninety-four-year-old grannie to sit here,' she said, through stiff lips. When she got to the ninety-four part, she kicked her grandmother on the shin.

'Ow!'

'It didn't hurt. It was a gentle tap,' Nina said.

'Skin this old is like tissue-paper, you know.' Flossie lifted her chin. 'I bruise easily.'

'Like the bloody princess and the pea,' Nina muttered darkly.

Thankfully, the bloke behind seemed oblivious to the exchange. 'My pleasure,' he said.

He appeared nice enough, ordinary, was clearly quite considerate and had good manners, Nina thought.

'Are you travelling alone?' This was from nosey Flossie, who seemed intent on shoving Nina at any, and all, remotely eligible men within a ten-mile radius. Thankfully, she hadn't seen Nina launch herself at Mehmet, else in Flossie's mind Nina would be married to him and have had his babies by now. Exciting though the kiss had been, Nina had no intention of repeating such an out-of-character action.

Nina's soft feelings and previous closeness to her grandmother, which had lingered through the couple of days since the dive and had grown during the Sunset Cruise, had evaporated quicker than the steam from a boiling kettle after the paragliding escapade. Flossie, with this kind of talk, was doing nothing to make Nina feel all fuzzy-wuzzy about her again. The way her grandmother was behaving this morning, had Nina seriously contemplating asking the driver to pull over and leave the pensioner on the side of the road. It would serve her right if the old bat was abducted by slavers. Though Nina had a feeling anyone kidnapping her gran would bring her back within half an hour of snatching her, offering Nina their profound commiserations.

'For this excursion, yes,' the bloke said, 'but I'm actually on holiday with a friend.'

'Male or female?'

Nina gasped; her grandmother had no shame.

'Male.' His smile was bemused and rather indulgent. And rather nice, in a gentle sort of way. He had nice lips.

'Do you bat for the other side,' Flossie asked.

His smile widened, and he took off his sunglasses to reveal quite blue and very amused eyes.

'No, I don't,' he said. His voice was nice too, not too deep, but manly all the same, and he sounded quite well-spoken, with a faint accent she couldn't quite place.

'Married?' Flossie asked.

Bloody hell, the woman was relentless.

'No.' He bit his lip.

Nina turned around to face the front, shrank down in her seat, and cringed in embarrassment.

'Fiancée? Girlfriend?'

'No, and no.'

'What's wrong with you? Got a nasty habit?' Flossie demanded with all the force of the Gestapo questioning a prisoner.

'Not that I'm aware of. I'm single by choice.'

'More of a wham-bam-thank-you-ma'am type, then?'

Nina sneaked a peep at him through the space between the headrests, wondering what his reaction would be. If Nina was in his shoes, she'd tell the nosey old biddy to mind her own business.

He guffawed, a deep belly laugh which shook his whole frame. 'Certainly not. I respect women. I just haven't found one I want to have a long-term relationship with.'

'Have you met my granddaughter?' Flossie asked, with an excruciatingly bright smile.

Oh. My. God. Her gran didn't just say that, did she?

Nina sat up sharply and whipped her head around fast enough to cause a serious crick. 'Ignore her,' Nina said to the poor bloke. 'She's going gaga.'

He smiled (he had nice lips, Nina noticed again, irrelevantly). 'She seems lucid enough to me.'

'No, believe me, she doesn't. She's missing some marbles. The deck is half empty, or whatever the collective noun for a pack of marbles is.'

'A round of marbles, a play, a bag?' he offered.

'Her name is Nina,' Flossie said.

The man's eyes crinkled and his lips narrowed. Nina simply knew he was trying not to laugh. 'Leo,' he said.

'The lion? As in the star sign?' Flossie asked with a frown.

'Er… no, Capricorn, I think.'

'Goodie,' she said, clapping her hands. 'She's a Virgo, all precise, fussy and a bit narrow-minded. You're a perfect match for her.'

'I'm not any of those things!' Nina protested. 'Anyway, it's all a load of bull.'

'We'll see,' Flossie said with a pleased grin, and did Nina imagine it, or was there a cunning glint in the other woman's eye?

Nina leaned in close to her gran and whispered, 'Don't say you can't hear me, because I know you can. If this is another one of your plans to get me to let my hair down, then stop it right now. I'm not looking for romance, and especially not a quick holiday fling.'

Flossie produced another one of her mega-watt smiles and Nina knew she was up to something.

'My dearest wish is to see my granddaughter married before I die,' the old lady announced solemnly. 'Which won't be long. Did I tell you I am ninety-four?'

Leo barked out a laugh. 'You did. Oh, I am *so* going to enjoy this trip.'

'Glad one of us is,' Nina growled.

He shuffled forward. 'Don't worry, I'm taking it all with a large pinch of salt,' he said in a low voice to Nina. 'But you've got to admit it, she is funny. I love old people.'

She's not and I don't, Nina wanted to say. 'She's lovely in small doses,' she actually said instead. 'You try living with this twenty-four seven.'

'Yet, you are on holiday with her,' he pointed out.

'I was conned into it. I didn't realise she was this bad. She hid it well.'

Leo laughed again. He had a nice laugh. Everything about him seemed nice; in a nice way, not a boring way. Mr Slightly-Above-Average. Not too good-looking for his own good, and not too nerdy (though who would go on a trip like this if they weren't a bit of a nerd – oh, yes, she would…).

'Do you like history?' she asked.

'I do. It's one of the reasons I booked this excursion.'

'What are the other reasons?'

'There's only one other reason, and that's to get away from my friend, David.'

That sounded a bit mean. Maybe Leo wasn't quite as nice as he first seemed. 'Oh?' Nina questioned.

'He came out of a bad relationship a couple of months ago, and hasn't been coping well. He caught his fiancée in bed with another guy, yet he still thinks the sun shines out of her arse – sorry for swearing,' he added to Flossie who was following the exchange avidly.

'Nothing wrong with "arse",' Flossie said. 'I've got one myself.'

Leo chuckled. 'Anyway, I persuaded him to come on holiday to try to cheer him up and take his mind off her, thinking a change of scenery would do him good.' He frowned. 'Unfortunately, it worked a bit better than I thought.'

'How so?'

'He's only gone and fallen in love with some German bird, and they've spent every day and night together for the past week. I've resorted to sleeping on the balcony with the door firmly shut.'

'Why would you...? Oh! I see.'

'They can't use her room because she's sharing with three others,' he explained, wearily. 'I wonder if you can buy ear defenders in Turkey because the pair of them are at it every night like a couple of rabbits. Once or twice I've stayed on the beach, watching the stars, and gone back to the room to sleep after the love-birds had gone to the pool.' He sighed. 'Not only is the lack of proper sleep killing me, but I'm worried about the fallout when Frieda leaves. Dave will be in bits again.'

'Nah, he'll be fine,' Flossie interjected. 'He's just shagging that other one out of his system. He'll feel better when he goes home, mark my words.'

Did Flossie just say "shagging"? Nina blew out her cheeks and prayed Leo hadn't noticed.

'I just hope he's not getting in too deep. I'd hate to see him hurt all over again.' He sat back in his seat and pulled some headphones out of his pocket. 'That's the problem with holiday romances – they burn too fast and too hot, and when you add several hundred miles into the mix once each party is back home...' he trailed off.

Amen to that, Nina thought, and reached for her trusty guidebook.

Chapter 20

It might have been the bang that woke her or the coach's abrupt deceleration, but when Nina opened her eyes to see the driver on his mobile yet again (weren't there any laws in this country against using a mobile phone whilst driving?) and heard his rapid-fire Turkish, she experienced a flash of irritation. Their guide, Yasin, was reaching for the microphone. He hadn't said much after the coach had picked up the rest of the passengers from an assortment of hotels and apartments along the way, except for introducing himself and giving them a brief rundown of what to expect during the day, then left them to it for the past hour. Nina spent some of that time watching Turkey speed past at sixty miles an hour, before the rhythm of tyres on tarmac and the heat sent her to sleep.

She was wide awake now and watching the drama unfold. Flat tyre apparently, she gathered, as they pulled over onto the side of the dusty road.

No one got out, apart from the driver and Yasin, everyone else was content to wait in the comfort of the air-conditioned coach until the tyre fairy solved the problem.

Only, the tyre fairy wasn't able to come to them any time soon, and after half an hour everyone piled off. Yasin led them across the road and into what looked like someone's back garden. A few large tables were set out under some trees, and a boy gestured for them to sit. His father (Nina assumed it was his father) brought out several huge green melons and cut them open with a massive knife.

She understood the coach had broken down, but couldn't they have gone somewhere else, like a proper service station, or a café?

Nina realised she was being grumpy and put it down to having been woken from a lovely nap. Her mood lifted when Leo approached, asking if he might sit with them. Flossie gave him a watermelon grin, juice dripping down her chin, and he sat down, accepting his own slice with a smile.

'Have you seen the size of that man's knife?' Nina hissed, taking a piece gratefully. 'He could be an axe murderer.'

'An axe murderer who used a knife instead, and feeds you water melon before he kills you?' Leo bit into the melon, and pink juice dribbled down his own chin. He and Flossie grinned at each other.

'You know what I mean,' Nina said, smiling at a woman (the mother?) who held aloft a large silver teapot whilst one of the other children grasped a tray of small Turkish tea glasses sitting on individual silver saucers.

'Cay?' the woman asked, and the child shoved the tray in their direction.

'Got any Tetley?' Flossie asked hopefully.

The question was met with blank stares.

'Cay?' the woman repeated.

'I suppose.' Flossie gave in and the child handed her a glass. A bowl of sugar was placed on the table.

Flossie's dentures rattled against the glass as she took a sip. 'Not bad, for foreign muck,' she said.

'Gran.' Nina growled at her and waggled her eyebrows in warning.

'What? You know I only drink Tetley tea at home. That's why I have coffee abroad. No Tetley tea bags. Maybe they've got coffee.' She twisted around in her chair but the tea lady and her helper had moved on.

'I believe they've offered us what they have,' Leo said. 'I had a quick chat with Yasin and he knows the family; I think they're second cousins of the driver's mother. Or was it his father? Anyway, the driver managed to get the coach as far as here because he knew we'd be welcomed.'

After several cups of tea and some very sweet and tasty baklava, they were ready to go again, the tyre fairy having put in an appearance after all. Nina was pleased, for as nice as it had been sitting under the trees, chatting and getting to know their fellow passengers, the day would be long enough without the delay.

'Have you used the facilities?' Yasin asked, as they filed onto the bus one at a time. 'For there is no stopping between now and the restaurant where we will have lunch. We have used all the stoppings.'

The "facilities" were a hole in the floor, albeit a tiled floor with quite a clean hole.

'Traditional Turkish toilet,' Leo said, when he returned from his visit. 'At least we're getting to see more of the real Turkey. They ought to put this on the itinerary for every trip to Ephesus.'

Nina opted to pass on the experience, hoping her bladder didn't give out before they arrived at the restaurant, while Flossie thankfully, had seemed to manage on her own, although a brace of middle-aged ladies who had been sitting the back of the coach kept giving her grandmother very odd looks indeed since their visit to the bathroom after Flossie. Nina had no intention of asking what had gone on; she guessed she was better off not knowing.

'Are we nearly there?' Flossie piped up as they took their seats once more and the coach pulled off.

'Not yet, Gran. We stop for lunch in an hour or so, and I think it's at least another hour after that,' Nina said, thinking great, we'll get there just at the hottest part of the day.

Lunch gave Nina the opportunity to find out what the hell Flossie was playing at, as the table her and her grandmother were directed to sit at had only two seats left, forcing Leo to sit elsewhere. Or maybe he was relieved to get away from the grumpy woman and her weird grandmother – she thought she would be, if she were in his shoes.

Flossie waggled her fingers at Leo, who lifted a hand in response. Nina watched him charm the ladies at his table, while also engaging their menfolk in conversation. He had an easy, relaxed way about him, she noticed, liking his modest confidence.

'May I ask you what all the questions were about? *Are you gay?*' she huffed at her grandmother. 'What sort of thing is that to ask a total stranger?'

'Leo didn't seem to mind,' Flossie retorted tucking into her plate of kofte and rice.

'What is that?' Nina asked, making a face.

'Spice minced lamby things. Bit like a burger. Try one.' Her grandmother speared one of the pieces, which looked far too much like something a cat might leave in a litter tray, and pointed it at Nina.

Nina shook her head. No thanks; she'd stick with her salad. You knew what you were getting with a bit of lettuce. 'Well?' she persisted.

'Just making conversation,' Flossie said.

'What you were asking him was rather personal, don't you think?'

'No point in wasting time when you get to my age. Gotta cut to the chase.'

Nina lowered her voice. 'Oh yes, that reminds me – your *age*.'

'Got you a front seat view, didn't it?'

'Have you no shame?'

'I've had two kids and more internals than you can shake a stick at. Shame packed his bags a long time ago.'

Nina paused, trying to push the image of her grand-mother naked from the waist down, with her legs in stirrups, and a doctor poking around at the grim end. Ew!

'What do you mean "at your age"? He's young enough to be your grandson.'

'Not for me, you prat – for you.'

'I can find my own man, thank you very much.'

'You've not done a very good job so far. You couldn't find one if he sent you a written invitation and a SatNav.'

'I object to that,' Nina hissed.

'No sex Nina,' Flossie hissed back, rather too loudly.

The chatter on their table ceased abruptly. Nina managed a sickly smile, dropping her head so low she practically had her face in her salad bowl. Perhaps the green of the leaves and the cucumber thingy would coun-teract the tomato red of her face.

Things didn't improve when they all trouped back onto the bus.

'You sit next to Nina,' Flossie said to Leo. 'She could do with talking to someone her own age. How old are you anyway?'

'Thirty-one.'

'Got all your own teeth?'

'Yep. See.' Leo opened his mouth to show her as he reached his seat.

Flossie manoeuvred around him so he was nearer her own seat than his.

'I thought you had to sit in the front,' he said, and Nina winced.

'Oh that,' Flossie waved a hand in the air. 'My turns, they come and they go. I'll not be having one today.'

'How do you know?'

'Because I do. Now sit down, there's a good boy, and keep my granddaughter company. Oh, before I let you loose on her, what do you do for a living?'

'I do research.'

'Wonderful! You can tell my granddaughter all about it.' Flossie plonked herself down in Leo's seat, giving him the choice of either sitting next to the old woman, or sitting next to Nina. Nina thought it was touch and go for him for a second – lesser of two evils?

He chose her.

Why did she feel so pleased?

'You're a researcher?' she asked, as an opening gambit after several minutes when he'd said nothing while she wished he would. She was acutely aware of his tanned arm close to hers and when she shifted position, the soft golden hairs on his forearm tickled her skin. He moved to the right, giving her a little more space.

'Yes.'

'What is it you research?'

'Quantum mechanics.'

'Oh.' That certainly wasn't an area she was terribly familiar with. 'Where?'

'I'm based at the University of Bristol.'

'I'm a teacher in a school near Worcester,' Nina offered, wondering if all his answers were going to be as short. If so, it was shaping up to be a long ride indeed.

Leo showed a bit of interest with a cock of his head. Nina took it as an invitation to carry on.

'History. GCSE and A-level,' she said.

'Is that why you're on this excursion?'

'Partly, though neither syllabi cover Greek or Roman history, more's the pity. I did try to offer classics as a subject but got no takers. Apart from needing to get away from your friend, are you here for the history too?'

'I wasn't going to pass up a chance to see one of the Seven Wonders of the World. I went to Egypt last year and saw the pyramids. Fantastic!'

Oh, so he was a box-ticker, was he. A been-there, seen-that person.

'There are only three of the Seven Wonders left. Such a shame, all that knowledge and history gone to waste. Thank goodness we are better at preserving our past than we were. To think the Lighthouse at Alexandria was systematically torn down, stone by stone, to use for other buildings.'

'It was more or less destroyed by a succession of earthquakes before that,' Nina pointed out. 'It was in ruins already.'

'So are most of the Norman-built castles in Britain, but you wouldn't advocate pulling *them* down, would you?'

Nina smiled. He *was* passionate about history. Ephesus wasn't a touristy thing for him, like it wasn't for her.

For Nina, it was almost a pilgrimage; the chance to see something so old, so steeped in the past... For a while she wished she'd taken archaeology at university and not a teaching degree in history. But as usual, she'd chosen the safe option, the one with more job prospects at the end, the one with a straightforward career progression. The one which was stilted and prescribed, giving her no chance to follow her heart.

Oh well, too late now. She'd made her bed and she had to lie in it.

'Tell me about Quantum Mechanics,' she said, hoping Leo hadn't stifled his own passion for the dryness of physics, and he appeared to need no further invitation. Nina prepared to be bored to death, but to her surprise, she discovered he hadn't sacrificed his passion at all.

Leo, she found, was a passionate man. Very passionate indeed.

Chapter 21

He was still enthusing about the ins and outs of wave particle duality (whatever that was – Leo did sort of explain, but it went over her head a bit. Okay, a lot. But he made it sound so interesting, even if she didn't have much of an idea what he was talking about. He had a nice voice though, rumbly and quite soft, with the gentlest hint of an accent she still couldn't place) when Yasin picked the mic up once more, sending a surge of squeaks and squeals down the length of the coach.

'Sorry, sorry,' he said, tapping it, and making the noise worse. 'Can you hear me? Good. We are almost at our destination. It is,' he checked his watch, 'three o'clock. You have until five-thirty in Ephesus Ancient City.'

Nina's heart sank. She'd known they didn't have long, but two and a half hours to explore a site of such size was nowhere near enough.

'At the exit, there is a place to purchase cold drinks and souvenirs. This will be our meeting place. After Ephesus Ancient City, we drive for an hour and forty minutes to our hotel for the night, which is near to Pamukkale, and the terraces. Once we are at the hotel, we will enjoy dinner.'

I'll be the judge of that, Nina thought, remembering the less-than-wonderful lunch.

After selling them bottles of cold water and reminding his passengers to wear hats and put on sun cream, Yasin finally freed them from the coach.

Nina gasped. Dear lord, the heat was tremendous. She turned to her grandmother – the old lady couldn't be expected to traipse around in this, no matter how sprightly she was.

'Perhaps I'll stay on the bus,' Flossie said, flapping a hand in front of her face. She looked exhausted and Nina sympathised. Travelling for hours on end was tiring. There was no way her grandmother would make it around the ruins. Not today.

'You cannot stay on the coach,' Yasin said. 'It will be locked, however you can sit in the lokanta.' He saw their bewildered expressions. 'A lokanta is a place which serves drinks and food, more than a bar perhaps, but not a restaurant. It is at the exit where we will be meeting, over there.' He pointed to a building a couple of hundred feet down the road.

'Do we have to go through Elephant… I mean Ephesus, first?' Nina asked, wanting to get her grandmother out of the sun as quickly as possible.

'No. It is where the drivers sit. You can walk along the road.'

'Come on, Gran, we'll go and have a nice cold drink, and wait for the others. I might even treat you to an ice cream.'

'There's no need to speak to me like I'm three,' Flossie retorted, huffily. 'I'm not senile yet, and I don't want a cold drink; I want a strong cup of coffee.'

'Sorry.' Her grandmother was right. Nina had slipped into "I'm-talking-to-an-old-person" speak. How patronising of her and how irritating for the elderly person being spoken to.

'I can make my own way there,' Flossie continued. 'You go and enjoy Elephant. I'll be here when you finish.'

'I'm not leaving you on your own.'

'I've been on my own before, you know,' was the tart reply. 'I'll be fine.'

Nina was torn. She'd come all this way to see Ephesus but it wasn't fair or right to leave an old lady all alone in a foreign country when she couldn't speak the language. Anything might happen.

It did. The driver and a pack of cards happened.

Yasin said, 'Mustafa will accompany her and will stay with her until you return. She will be as safe as if she were in your own care.'

'But he doesn't speak English and she doesn't speak Turkish,' Nina objected, feeling horribly guilty at the possibility of being able to explore the ruins after all.

'We don't need to say anything,' Flossie said, her eyes lighting up when the driver waved the pack of cards and gave her a gap-toothed grin. 'But how do you say, "you're cheating" in Turkish? That might come in handy,' she asked Yasin as she took Mustafa's arm.

Nina hovered uncertainly, watching the old lady trot down the dusty road, hanging onto a man neither of them had met until this morning.

Poor bloke. He had no idea what he was letting himself in for.

'Go. Enjoy. I have my phone. If there is a problem I will call you,' Yasin said to Nina, and they swapped telephone numbers.

With a much lighter (though still guilt-ridden heart), Nina strode off in the direction of the entrance. So much to see, so little time.

To her surprise, Leo lounged against a wall waiting for her, one leg cocked, arms folded. He was tall and lean, and she noticed the way his shirt pulled across the tops of his arms at his shoulders as the muscles bunched underneath. He really was quite fit under all that niceness.

She hoped he was going to continue being nice and not think she'd abandoned her grandmother. Unfortunately, she couldn't see his expression because of his sunglasses.

'I didn't really want to leave Flossie,' Nina began, but Leo interrupted her.

'It's okay,' he said. 'I understand. She'll be fine, believe me. Shall we go in?' He gestured for her to lead the way and she gave him a grateful smile.

Ephesus (or Elephant as it would be forever known), was right in front of her. She was here, really here, on this site which had been occupied since before the rise of Christianity. She opened her guide book, wanting to make sure she didn't miss anything.

'There was a settlement in this area in Neolithic times,' she read aloud, 'and Elephant itself was constructed around three thousand years ago – bits of it – the later stuff is Roman.' She guessed Leo probably knew this already, but she was so excited she simply had to share.

He was more interested in something else. 'Elephant? You do know it's called Ephesus, right?'

'Elephant is what Gran calls it. When I said I wanted to visit here, she pretended to be deaf, and she calls Pamukkale, Pinky Moon.'

Leo mouthed Pamukkale a couple of times, trying to transform it into Pinky Moon. 'I sort of get it.'

'I think she'd switched off at that point,' Nina said, pulling a crumpled straw hat out of her bag, tugging it into shape, then popping it on her head. She knew she didn't look particularly glamorous, but the sun was fierce enough to give her heatstroke if she wasn't careful. She hoped her gran was sitting in the shade, preferably somewhere inside. 'I only persuaded her to come on this trip by having to agree to go on a jeep safari and diving with her.'

'Diving? Wow! She's really good for ninety-four, isn't she?' Leo said.

Nina coughed, and suddenly became very interested in the communal Roman toilets. Ninety-four indeed!

Although there was no roof (had there ever been?) on the ancient toilet block, the outline of the building was still very clear; large and square with waist high walls, all four sides had a kind of seat running around it with holes at regular intervals.

'Imagine the men, and women too, coming here for a social poop,' she said to change the subject about Flossie's age. 'It goes against our sense of propriety a bit. I'm not sure I could pee alongside someone else, let alone do anything more substantial.'

Leo barked out a laugh and the two of them stood side by side, peering down into the round holes chiselled into the long slab of marble. The stone was smooth and Nina wondered if it had been worn away by the friction of countless bottoms.

'Water constantly flowed through these channels, taking the waste away,' Leo pointed out. 'Quite sanitary really, though I do wonder where it ended up.'

She wrinkled her nose. 'Better than the medieval method of throwing it into a ditch running down the middle of the street.'

They looked at each other and grinned.

'What have the Romans ever done for us?' Leo misquoted.

Nina, delighted they were on the same wavelength (she adored *Monty Python*, and *The Life of Brian* was possibly her favourite film ever), joined in with enthusiasm. 'The aqueduct?'

Leo carried on in character, using a funny voice, 'Yeah, yeah, that's true, they did give us that. But what else have they given us?'

'The sanitation,' Nina quoted.

'All right, I'll give you the sanitation and the aqueducts.' He wasn't quite word perfect, but he was close enough.

'And the roads,' she giggled.

'Obviously the roads. But apart from sanitation, the aqueducts and the roads, what else have they given us?'

'Irrigation, education, medicine.' Did she have that in the right order? Oh, who cared. 'And wine.'

Returning to his normal voice he said, 'I love that film.'

'So do I.'

Their eyes met, Leo gestured to the toilets, and they started laughing again, unable to help themselves. He bent over, clutching his sides, and spluttered. 'Then there's that scene where the centurion catches Brian writing graffiti on a wall, and tells him to conjugate the verb to go...' he mimed painting the words and snorted.

'And then orders him to write out the correct sentence a hundred times!' Nina had tears in her eyes from laughing so hard.

'I hope you don't threaten your kids with that if they get their spellings wrong.'

'God forbid. You're not even allowed to tell them off these days,' Nina replied, gasping for breath.

'They should have lived in Roman times, then they'd know what it's like to be hard-done-by.'

'At least they'd have toilets, and roads, and aqueducts,' she chortled.

'Please don't, you'll start me off again.' Leo put a hand out as Nina staggered, howling with laughter, and caught her arm.

She sobered at his touch, a warm frisson travelling across her skin where his hand gripped her, and she paused, enjoying the feel of his hand on her arm. When she looked up at his face, she found him staring back at her, his sunglasses pushed on the top of his brown hair. The blueness of his eyes held her captive.

She felt a connection, a faint stirring of desire, and she wished he'd lower his head to hers and kiss her. A noise brought her out of her daydream. Leo let go of her arm and the strange mood faded away. Had she imagined it? She recalled the impulsive kiss she'd bestowed on Mehmet, and wondered if she was having a bit of an early mid-life crisis. Yes, Leo was nice, sexy even in a laid back, unassuming way, but it was a long time since she'd had such a reaction to a bloke, and she wasn't even sure she believed in this instant attraction nonsense.

'Oh dear, I think we've drawn a bit of a crowd,' she said, noticing the world around her for the first time in several minutes. 'Sorry,' she mouthed at a Japanese man wielding a camera almost as large as his head.

She moved away, to give him a better shot of the public toilets, bemused when the eye of the camera followed her, as he took a photo of her instead. Was she really more interesting than two-thousand-year-old toilets?

'Shall we move on?' Leo suggested. 'I don't want to come all the way here and have to admit the only thing I saw were the toilets, fascinating though they are; people might get the wrong idea, thinking I've eaten a dodgy meatball.'

'They were a bit dodgy, weren't they?' Nina added, as they carried on walking down what had once been a main street thriving with stalls, shops, houses, and *people*. It was easy to forget about the actual people themselves, all those individual lives summed up in generalisations about culture, beliefs, and society.

She buried her head in her guide book, her mood suddenly sombre.

'That way,' she said, pointing, 'is the Temple itself.' She held up the guide, showing Leo the map, and traced her finger along the route. 'We haven't got long, so I suggest we see the biggies, and fit the smaller things in if we can.'

'Good idea.'

The rest of the tour was conducted with considerably less hilarity, as they marvelled over the sights and basked in the feel of the place. Nina, to her intense annoyance, found herself distracted, unable to concentrate on the wonderful building in front of her. Instead, she was far too conscious of the man at her side. She kept getting whiffs of his aftershave, citrussy, woody, manly, the scent oddly disconcerting. On a couple of occasions she actually caught herself moving closer to him for a better sniff, before scuttling away at a rate of knots. He must have thought she was deranged.

When he accidentally brushed against her, she jumped, as if a bolt of *something* travelled through her body, coming to rest in the pit of her stomach. Once again, she had a fantasy of those lips on her mouth, those large hands on her body.

What the hell was wrong with her!

Whenever their eyes accidently met, Nina looked hastily away, fearful he would notice the attraction she felt for him, though when he concentrated on a statue, or a column, or a marvel of architecture, Nina would steal surreptitious glances at him out of the corner of her eye. Once or twice, she caught him staring at her, and she turned away in confusion.

Again, what the hell was wrong with her?

With less than half an hour left and Nina a distracted mess (not that she let on, of course – how humiliating would that be?), they made their way to the amphitheatre, Nina feeling as though she had hardly touched the surface of Ephesus.

'Would you look at that...' Leo breathed.

The amphitheatre was magnificent. 'It can hold twenty-five-thousand people,' Nina said, her eyes wide, the man at her side forgotten for a moment as she took in what lay in front of her.

Row upon row of terraces climbed up the steep hillside, the lower seating constructed of marble, and the higher ones, where commoners sat were made of stone. The whole thing had been built in a massive semi-circle around a gigantic stage at the front.

'Makes Wembley Stadium look like somewhere to host kids' parties,' Leo said.

Nina had never been to Wembley, but she knew what he meant. Despite the still-vicious heat, she wanted to climb the terraces to the top. Leo plodded manfully behind her, as she puffed and panted her way up the series of steps. If she didn't go back weighing several pounds lighter from the impromptu workout, she'd be most disappointed.

The last step. She turned, keeping her attention on the stone seats and sat, tipping her head back, closing her eyes, and catching her breath. When she was ready, she opened them.

It was magnificent.

'Words fail me,' Leo said.

Spread out below them was the whole amphitheatre. The view was perfect, and so were the acoustics. She wondered if the family who were exploring the remains of the massive stage below, realised she could hear every word they uttered. What must it have been like in its hay day, with throngs of people lining the seats, dressed in their finery, waiting for the show to begin.

'They used to hold religious and political discussions here, as well as plays and concerts,' she said.

'And don't forget the gladiator fights.'

It took a little more imagination to picture gladiators here. Nina associated gladiators with a circular structure like the Colosseum in Rome, where it was impossible for the fighters to escape. This was more like a modern theatre.

'Look.' Leo pointed beyond the amphitheatre.

A vast valley spread out below and beyond the ancient city, with a river running through it, trees lining its course. Nina, lost in her own world, envisaged the workers in the fields, farming the land, providing food for the citizens.

'I have to come back,' she said regretfully, conscious of the lack of time. 'Someday, I'll come back.'

'Me, too. Let me know when you do and I'll meet you here, at this very spot.'

Nina brought her attention back to the present. That sounded rather... romantic? Or did it?

'I don't have your phone number,' she said with a ghost of a smile, turning to look at him sitting beside her, up in the gods, with the world spread out in front of them. It was a beautiful, magical, wonderful place. And it had clearly got to him.

'Remind me to give it to you,' he said.

Then he leaned towards her and kissed her.

Chapter 22

Er… she hadn't been expecting that. She wasn't sure she wanted it now it was happening, scared of her attraction to him, but as his mouth met hers and she tasted him, breathing in his scent once more she sighed, and opened her lips.

He pulled away with such speed she nearly fell off her seat.

'Oh god!' he cried. 'Sorry, I didn't mean to do that. I don't know what I was thinking. Well, I do know – I was thinking how pretty you looked and how nice it would be to come back here with you, and your hair is so shiny and you look so happy, and… Bugger, I've gone and spoilt it. Sorry.'

'Nothing to be sorry about,' Nina replied primly. Great, not only had a man suddenly kissed her, out of the blue, but as soon as she'd started to enjoy it (when was the last time she'd been kissed like this anyway – throwing herself into Mehmet's arms didn't count) the man in question immediately regretted it.

It was all the fault of her shiny hair, apparently!

'We'd better make a move,' she said, standing up and brushing dust off her skirt.

Leo hesitated, before getting to his feet, and she wondered if maybe he didn't want to walk back to the bus with her after all, but he fell in beside her as she trotted down the steps, making her way out of the monument and towards the exit. He followed in silence.

'There she is,' Nina said, eventually spotting Flossie sitting underneath a large umbrella. The table was laden with empty glasses, miniscule coffee cups, and hands of cards. Her grandmother was surrounded by five burly coach drivers.

Yasin was flitting around, rounding up his charges, urging them to buy a drink and do other necessary things before the journey to the hotel. Thinking of toilets reminded Nina of the communal Roman ones – life had been much less complicated a couple of short hours ago.

Leo had been just behind her when they'd scooted through the exit, and though she fully expected him to have loped away on his long, lean legs, she glanced around anyway. He was still there, and when he caught her eye, he winked.

Perhaps they could be friends after all, despite the kiss.

'Ooh, look at the pair of you,' Flossie called as Nina and Leo approached the gambling den. 'You make a lovely couple.'

'Did you enjoy your coffee?' Nina asked sarcastically, eyeing the almost-empty glass in Flossie's hand. She relieved her of it, sniffed, and took a sip. Yuk – aniseed. The woman had been drinking raki with the locals, men who had probably been weaned on the stuff.

Her grandmother burped loudly. The drivers cheered, raising their own glasses. Nina hoped those hadn't contained raki too, else everyone would be spending the night here, because she had no intention of being driven anywhere by a bloke who'd been boozing all afternoon.

'Have you ever driven a bus?' she asked Leo out of the side of her mouth.

'Pardon?'

'Never mind.' There had to be a hotel or two nearby. They could get a taxi to it, or walk.

'Give me my drink back,' Flossie demanded. 'I haven't finished it.'

'Have you been drinking all afternoon?'

Flossie lifted her chin in defiance. 'What if I have? It's nice, with ice. Nice, with ice, nice with ice,' she chanted. 'I've developed a bit of a taste for it.'

'You don't say.' Nina sighed. Leave her grandmother alone for five minutes and look what happens – she gets blotto. Wonderful. *I just hope she isn't sick on the bus*, Nina thought with a grimace. She knew she should have stayed with her.

Yasin appeared, in a vain attempt to herd them towards the coach. 'It is nearly six pm and we will have to leave Ephesus Ancient City now to arrive at our hotel,' he said.

'I'm not getting in any bus with someone who's been drinking,' Nina said.

Yasin looked horrified. 'You cannot leave her here. The hotel, it is booked.'

'I'm not going to leave her. I'm staying too, and I suggest everyone else does the same.'

'I do not understand. You wish to remain here, at Ephesus Ancient City?'

Nina wished he would stop calling it that. It's Ephesus, just Ephesus. And it wasn't sodding Elephant, either.

– 'I wish for you to arrange a hotel,' Nina said snootily, and promptly wished she hadn't sounded like a stand-up comedian doing a bad imitation of the queen.

'We have a hotel. It is near Pamukkale, Cotton Castle. It is part of the tour,' Yasin protested.

'I don't care about Pamukkale. I just don't want to die in a coach driven by a drunk driver.'

Yasin gave her a sharp look and spoke to the gaggle of drivers in rapid Turkish. They were in the middle of stubbing out cigarettes and draining coffee cups, but they all paused when Yasin spoke.

'No lady, we not…' One of the drivers lifted a glass to his lips and pretended to drink. 'We have kahve.'

'He is speaking truth,' Yasin added. 'They do not drink alcohol. None of them. They are all good Muslim men, and even if they were not, they would not dare to drink. They would lose their jobs. They drink coffee – kahve – and water.'

Great, not only had she accused them of drinking on the job, she had also managed to offend their religious beliefs.

'It is your buyu, your grandmother, who has enjoyed the raki,' Yasin added.

'I'll get us all some cold drinks for the bus, shall I?' Leo offered, and strode off towards the lokanta.

Nina watched him go, not blaming him in the slightest for running away. If he hadn't thought she was barking mad before, he certainly did now. Gathering her courage to apologise to the departing drivers and with Yasin translating, Nina said sorry, and wondered how far down the bus Leo would sit. Maybe there was an empty seat at the back, or on the roof…

'They say she cheats,' Yasin said, and Nina apologised again, wondering how much Flossie had fleeced the poor drivers for.

Yasin smiled and waved her apology away. 'Do not be sorry, they love her anyway. She bought them coffee, much coffee, and she shared her cigarettes. She is a lady.'

Implying that I am not – Nina did her own translating, reading more into Yasin's comment than he was perhaps aware.

'In return, they bought her raki,' Yasin added. 'They wanted to see how much she could drink.'

'Don't they know how old she is?'

Yasin nodded enthusiastically. 'Yes, and they are very impressed. She is a grand lady. They say she is cok guzel, it means very beautiful.'

Flossie smirked and patted her hair. Beautiful, indeed, Nina thought. He wouldn't be saying that if her grandmother threw up all over the bus.

'I'll sit behind, you sit in the front,' Flossie said as they climbed the steps onto the coach. 'I want to have a nap, and I can't do that if I'm worrying about flying through the windscreen every time the coach breaks.'

Nina made a move to sit next to her grandmother.

'Sit with your young man,' Flossie said. 'I can't spread out with you squashing me.'

Nina looked at Leo. He sat in the front as instructed and patted the seat next to him. Nina sat. Neither of them said a word.

After a while, her mind full of sunlit stones and heavenly kisses, Nina's head began to loll. She scooted down, leaned against the headrest, and closed her eyes. If Leo thought she was asleep, the lack of conversation might not be so awkward.

She awoke to find her head on his shoulder, his arm holding her close to him, and drool on her chin.

Lovely.

'Nearly there,' he said, seeing she was awake and removing his arm, forcing her to sit up.

She glanced around at Flossie. Her grandmother smiled at her, looking quite smug. Nina frowned.

Yasin ran through the check-in procedure (all that fuss for one night) and told them where to meet for dinner. 'After dinner, there will be entertainment. Belly dancing. You can try it.'

Nina glanced behind again. Flossie gave her an innocent stare.

For the final time of that long, long day, the passengers descended the coach's steps, stepping into a balmy evening, stretching cramped limbs and dodgy hips. Nina realised she was the youngest person there. Even Leo was older than her. Clearly this type of excursion didn't appeal to the average twenty-something.

The hotel was large and reminded Nina of a block of London flats, but the room was nice enough. Thankfully they had been allocated a twin room and not a double, and Nina left Flossie to choose a bed and lay out a cotton nightie, whilst she went for a cold shower.

Feeling cooler, she pulled on the flowy dress she'd brought with her for the evening, and brushed her hair. A flick of blusher across her cheeks, a swipe of gloss, and she was ready to go.

'You look pretty,' Flossie said when she emerged from the bathroom. 'You've caught the sun; a bit of colour suits you.'

Treacherously and stupidly, Nina hoped Leo would think she looked pretty, too.

Dinner was an odd affair. The buffet was okay, if a bit nondescript (they'd been spoilt because the food in their hotel back at the resort was so good), and the company was subdued at first. Their whole party seemed drained, the early start combined with all the travelling was catching up with many of them. Conversation was desultory and sporadic, as most people concentrated on their meal, but as the trips to the bar increased, the evening gradually livened up.

For everyone except Nina. To her immense annoyance she kept looking for Leo, who had yet to show.

Dinner came and went, and still no Leo. By the time the belly dancer began shaking her assets, Nina had come to the conclusion he was either too embarrassed to face her, or he was making sure she understood The Kiss had been a mistake. She tended towards the latter explanation.

'Come, come...'

A jingle of bells and a flash of olive stomach topped and tailed by a scarlet belly-dancing outfit a foot away from her face, diverted Nina's attention. She eyed the outstretched hand with caution, and shook her head. No way was she prancing about in front of all those strangers (it wasn't just their coach party staying at the hotel), and shaking what she didn't have much of to shake, not in the boob department anyway, though her butt might not stop wobbling once it got going.

Flossie had no such inhibitions.

Grabbing the dancer's hand, Flossie almost leapt out of her chair in her haste to join in the fun. She was met with cheers and wolf whistles. The belly dancer persuaded a few more women to join her in the cleared area between the tables, and proceeded to show them some moves, first shaking her shoulders, then her hips, and finally undulating her belly.

When her victims had got the hang of the sequence, she speeded up, rolling and shaking faster and faster, her victims giggling as they tried to keep up.

Flossie, feet planted wide apart, her hips gyrating, and her shoulders shaking, was laughing at the top of her voice, and Nina smiled. It was nice to see the old woman having fun.

Nina kept smiling, until Flossie's false teeth shot out of her mouth, sailed into the air, and landed with an audible clink into a half-full pint of Turkish beer. Flossie clamped a hand to her toothless mouth, her eyes wide, trying not to laugh. Nina wanted to be anywhere other than here. How embarrassing. She got up and hurried over to the shocked man who found himself staring at a pair of gnashers through the sides of his glass.

'I'll buy you another,' Nina offered, horrified.

'Sharon, did you get that on camera?' he demanded to his wife.

A woman nodded, waving her phone. 'It's all there, I checked. And I got that woman's face too.' She pointed at Nina. 'It was a picture.'

'Let me get you a new drink,' Nina said picking up the glass and trying not to look at its toothy contents. 'Efes, was it?'

'Don't bother, love, it was an accident. Anyway, the missus will send it off to *You've Been Framed* and we'll get two hundred and fifty quid for it,' he guffawed. 'Watch out for your face on the telly.'

Great. It would be out there for the whole world to see. She could hear them now – the ribbing, the hushed sniggers, the notes left on the whiteboard, and that was just from her colleagues. Goodness knows what the kids would say; she'd never hear the last of it.

Thanks, Gran, for yet another unforgettable memory.

Chapter 23

Leo showed up, just when Nina was about to retire for the night. She intended on leaving Grannie with a gaggle of oldies, who were reminiscing about the good-old days, and playing a virtual game of holiday Top Trumps. They were focusing on mishaps, and so far, no one could top being stung by a jelly-fish off the coast of Mexico and being peed on by a passer-by, though they were all having a good go. Nina suspected that most of the stories were made up, and as the night wore on the tales would become increasingly outrageous.

She sat in a secluded corner, curled up in a chair, nursing her third glass of white wine. The alcohol was going to her head a bit because she rarely, if ever, drank, but she didn't care. She intended to finish this one then go to bed, and try not to think about lips, and stubble, and hairy chests.

Okay, she was making the hairy-chest bit up. She had no idea whether Leo's chest was as smooth as a baby's bottom or if he had more hair than a gorilla, or was somewhere in between. She liked a bit of hair, not too much, just a smattering.

'Penny for them?'

'Eh? Oh, hi. I was... er... um... just thinking about you,' Nina blurted, caught off guard.

'Nothing bad, I hope,' Leo said, lightly.

'No.' She was glad the night hid her blushes. The lights around the bar and the candles on the table were soft enough to hide her pink cheeks. 'I thought you were avoiding me,' she said, then wished she hadn't. She'd had no intention of referring to what happened at Elephant in the slightest, and here she was, coming right out with it.

'Not at all. I fell asleep. It seems like ages since I've had a proper sleep in a decent bed.' He yawned, and Nina remembered his friend Dave and the German girl.

'I take it I've missed dinner?' he asked.

'You didn't miss much. It was okay, I suppose.'

'Do you fancy a walk? I noticed some shops and things near the hotel.'

Yes, she did fancy a walk. She hadn't fancied one at all before he'd mentioned it, but now he that had, the idea appealed very much indeed.

Leo, it turned out, wasn't after a gentle, romantic stroll. Oh no, Leo was hunting supper.

'Can I get you anything?' he asked, after pausing outside a kiosk-cum-stall affair with tables dotted randomly on the pavement.

A part of Nina, the sensible have-you-washed-your-hands-before-handling-any-food part, shuddered at the thought of eating from anywhere which looked as if it might have printed its own hygiene certificate off the internet. The other part, the I-only-picked-at-my-dinner part, had other ideas as her stomach rumbled loudly.

The smells wafting through the air were delicious and nearly every table was full of what appeared to be regulars. That was always a good sign.

'I'm having a chicken kebab,' Leo said. 'Don't worry, they're nothing like the ones you get at home after a skin-full of beer when your taste buds are shot to hell.'

'I've never had a kebab.'

'You don't know what you're missing!' Leo exclaimed. He turned to the bloke behind the counter. 'Two chicken doners, please, in pitta with salad.'

'Drink?'

'Two colas.' Leo glanced at Nina, who nodded her agreement.

'One moment. Sit, please. I will bring.'

They sat, and in a short while two kebabs were placed in front of them. They looked scrummy. Nina picked up a succulent piece of chicken and popped it in her mouth. Spices and herbs exploded on her tongue as she chewed. Mmmm.

'You like?' Leo asked around a mouthful of food.

Nina smiled. 'I like. Now shut up and let me eat.'

She was licking the last of the taste off her fingers before she knew it. All gone, every last morsel. Taking a swig of her drink, she asked, 'Was it by chance you found this place, or did you know about it?'

'Yasin told me. None of the tour guides or the drivers eat in the hotel. Not because the food is bad,' he added hastily, 'but because they get charged for it. And the rooms. Yasin and Mustafa sleep in the coach, as do all the others.'

'That's awful!'

'It's the way it is. Fancy a drink at the bar?'

'An orange juice would be nice. I've had enough wine.'

'Juice, it is.'

They strolled back in companionable silence, and Nina felt relaxed in Leo's company, just happy to be wandering down a foreign street in the height of summer with a gorgeous man, until Leo said abruptly, 'Sorry about earlier... you know, The Kiss.'

Was it her imagination, or had he capitalised the words too? She was perturbed. It was the last thing she expected him to say. Okay, him saying "I prefer men" was the very last thing, but she hadn't anticipated him apologising for kissing her either. She'd been hoping it could be ignored, brushed under the carpet, never referred to again – in the great British tradition of not talking about anything which made you feel uncomfortable.

'Don't be sorry,' she said. 'There's nothing to apologise for. I've forgotten it already.'

'You have?' Nina thought Leo sounded a little put out.

'I've not really forgotten, you're a good kisser so how could I forget, I meant I'd just put it to the back of my mind, the heat of the moment and all that…' She knew she was babbling so she trailed off, wondering what on earth she was supposed to say.

'Oh. Okay. Friends?'

'Friends,' Nina replied firmly.

When they returned to the hotel, Nina insisted on paying for their drinks, saying, 'You bought the last lot, before we got on the coach, and wouldn't take no for an answer.' She hadn't paid for the kebab either, though that was sitting a little heavily in her tummy.

Leo waved her away. 'It was nothing. I was thirsty and I thought you might be too.'

They picked a spot away from those guests who were still up, enjoying a night cap – or several by the sound of it.

Nina sipped her juice and cast around for something to say. She would have liked to have talked about the day, about the marvellous things they'd seen, but she didn't want to mention Elephant in case the subject of The Kiss came up again, just when they'd put the subject to bed.

Leo kept looking at her.

'What? Is my mascara running?' She wouldn't be surprised in this heat. Perhaps she should have bought some waterproof stuff back in England.

'Sorry, it's just… you look beautiful,' he finished in a rush and looked away. Was he blushing, Nina wondered? It was difficult to tell in this light.

'Thank you,' she said softly. Maybe he wasn't regretting The Kiss as much as she thought he was.

Oh hell. She had nothing to lose – except her dignity and her self-respect if he turned her down, but she was on holiday and apart from earlier she hadn't been kissed by a man for nearly a year (a peck on the cheek from her dad didn't count, and she didn't think her quick snog with Mehmet really counted either). She'd enjoyed the feel of Leo's mouth on hers, the taste of him on her lips, so this time she leaned over and kissed him.

It must have caught him by surprise because he hesitated for a second and she wondered for one awful moment if he was going to pull away, or worse, push her off him.

He did neither.

To her relief, he slid one arm across the back of the sofa and another around her waist, drawing her closer as she melted into him, her arms snaking around his neck. She pressed herself against his chest.

Their tongues met and the kiss deepened.

Oh my. He really was a very good kisser. She felt it from the top of her heat-frizzed hair to the ends of her curled-up toes. It was a long time indeed since a man had made her toes curl – in a good way.

When Nina came up for air, panting, she was delighted to discover Leo was panting too, but he gave her less than a second to catch her breath before he kissed her once more.

She lost all sense of time, location, and self. All her awareness was concentrated on what he was doing with his lips. And his hands. They stroked her shoulders, sending shivers up and down her spine, his fingers working their way down the small of her back until they rested on her bottom.

She had one moment when she could have stopped it there, left it as a passionate and very thorough kiss, which would never be repeated but was divine while it lasted; but she didn't want to. She was going to live a little, do something her heart and soul were crying out for her to do. For once she would ignore the little voice telling her to be careful, to think about it first, and what would everyone think if they knew. And if she hated herself in the morning, then so be it.

Tonight, she intended to throw caution to the wind, so when he pulled away, got to his feet, and held out his hand, she took it.

She intended to enjoy every second.

Chapter 24

Who knew there could be so many "seconds" in one long, lovely, delicious night. Nina was pleased to find she regretted none of them. In fact, another second would be more than welcome, but she saw the time and groaned.

'I'd better get back. I don't want Gran waking up and wondering where I am,' she said.

'She'll know exactly where you are and what you're doing,' Leo replied, catching her about the waist as she tried to climb out of bed, nibbling the side of her neck. Her insides melted. If he kept doing that, she might liquidise and he'd have to scrape her up off the floor.

She slapped him away, laughing. 'Stop that, I've got to go,' she insisted, wriggling out of his embrace.

He let her go with obvious reluctance, trailing his fingers down her back as she slithered away from him. She looked over her shoulder, drinking in the sight of him; his deceptively broad chest, a sprinkling of hair on it (yum), the satisfied gleam in his eyes, the lazy smile of his face, his tousled hair, and wearing slightly more stubble than the day before. He looked good enough to eat. Oh wait – face flaming, she giggled to herself.

It flamed even more when she remembered what he'd done to her, and her insides did a slow roll of lust and desire. She'd dearly like him to do it to her again, but there was Flossie to think of. Nina suspected she already looked like she'd had a good night, without making it obvious she'd had a good morning too. She felt as though she wore a glowing, neon sign illuminating her from within, advertising what she'd spent last night so happily and joyously doing.

Leo watched her get dressed, never taking his gaze off her. 'See you at breakfast?' He didn't sound confident; he sounded unsure, hesitant even, as if he expected to be turned down.

'Eight o'clock on the dot,' she replied, returning to the bed to kiss him and show him just how sure of her he should be. She wasn't going anywhere, not unless he wanted her to…

She slipped from Leo's room smiling broadly. She'd have to wipe her happiness off her face a bit sharpish if she didn't want her gran to suspect anything. Not that Nina wanted to hide what had happened last night (and this morning!) or that she was ashamed of it, but she wanted to keep it to herself for a while. She needed to work out in her own head how she felt, before she gave the rest of the world a peep at it, though she was under no illusion the whole thing was nothing more than a lovely evening spent with a gorgeous man. If she saw him again during the rest of her holiday it would be wonderful, but if she didn't…

It would be lovely to spend more time with him after today, but she wasn't counting on it. As she crept back to the room she shared with Flossie, she mused on her new outlook. Even as little as a week ago, if someone had suggested she would spend the night with a man she'd only just met, she'd have laughed in their face. But that's exactly what she'd done and she felt no shame, just a warm glow deep inside.

The glow was abruptly extinguished when she realised she didn't have a key to her room. Flossie had it in her handbag last night, and would have used it when she went to bed.

Nina pressed an ear to the door and listened hard.

It was no good – she couldn't hear anything. Her grandmother could be fast asleep, or sitting in a chair, very much awake and tapping her feet, waiting for her wayward granddaughter to show her shameful face.

Nina had three choices and none of them held much appeal. She could either wait in the hotel's lounge and pretend she was an extremely early riser (an early riser who was wearing last night's clothes), or knock on the door and wake Flossie – assuming she wasn't doing the tappy-feet thing. Nina decided on the third option – go to reception and ask them to let her into her room.

The day staff hadn't begun their shift yet, and the night porter understood little English. At least that's what Nina told herself, but she had a sneaking suspicion he understood more than he was letting on and was enjoying her discomfort.

'I need key to room,' she enunciated slowly, pretending to turn a key in a lock. 'I have no key. My…,' would he understand the English for grandmother? '…friend is sleeping.' She put the palms of her hands together, laid them on her cheek and bent her head so it almost touched her shoulder. Then she broke in to a loud snore just to make sure he got the message.

The porter looked at her blankly.

'I.' She pointed to her chest. 'Need key.' She pointed to the pigeon holes behind him some with keys in, some without.

'Ah, roomkey,' he said running the two words into one. 'Number?' The "r" came out as a sort of trilling growl.

Thank goodness. 'Two thirty-one.'

The porter looked at the pigeon holes. 'Two three one?'

'Yes.'

He pointed to room two thirty-one's empty pigeon hole. 'No key.'

'Yes, I know. That's what I'm trying to tell you. I haven't got the key. The key is in the room. Room Two Three One.'

'No key.' He shook his head whilst patting the inside of the pigeon hole theatrically.

Nina sighed. If this farce carried on much longer it would be too late for an effective sneak – Flossie would be up and dressed, and thinking of her breakfast.

'Madam, may I help?'

A man in a suit who spoke English. Yay!

'Thank you, that would be great. I'm locked out of my room,' she explained.

The man held a quick conversation with the porter, who pointed to her room's empty pigeon hole. Both men paused, looked at Nina for a second then the conversation resumed.

'He wants to know if you've lost your key,' the man said.

'No. I am sharing a room with my… friend. She went to bed before me and now I can't get in.'

'It was a good night, yes?'

'Er, yes. Lovely thanks.'

He spoke to the porter again, who grabbed a large bunch of keys from somewhere under the desk and beckoned her to follow.

'Thank you,' she called over her shoulder. The stranger gave her a nod.

Flossie was asleep when the porter, with shushing noises from Nina, unlocked the door and let her in. As quietly as possible, she grabbed the extra-large T-shirt she'd been using as a nightie and removed her dress.

Getting into bed and lying down, she closed her eyes willing sleep to come, but her head was full of a muscly chest, strong arms, and other assorted bits of Leo's anatomy.

'What are you grinning at?' Flossie demanded.

Nina jumped. 'Oh, I thought you were asleep,' she said.

'I was, but I'm not now.'

What was that supposed to mean, Nina wondered.

'Did you have a good time?' her beady-eyed grand-mother enquired.

Should she come clean? Or would Gran be horrified? She tried to stall for time. 'When?' she asked.

'Last night, of course.' The lower part of Flossie's face was all pursed and crumpled. Her teeth were probably sitting in a glass in the bathroom glaring at anyone who ventured in there. Nina hoped the gnashers had recovered from their impromptu dunking of the night before.

'It was okay,' she said. Maybe her grannie was talking about the belly dancing. Or even if Flossie had seen Nina leave the hotel with Leo, it didn't mean that anything else had taken place.

Flossie spoke. 'Just okay? That's a shame. He looked like he knew his way around a woman.'

'Gran!'

'Well, he did! Nice manners too, and he's got all his own hair and teeth.'

'Having one's own hair and teeth might be a bit of a novelty at your age,' Nina said. 'but it's quite normal for a man in his early thirties.'

'Well, I don't suppose you can have everything,' Flossie sighed. 'Nice manners count for a lot. You can teach him the other stuff.'

The other stuff… was her grandmother talking about what Nina thought she was talking about?

'They're not born knowing how to please a woman,' Gran carried on. 'They've gotta learn it.'

Yes, Flossie *was* talking about being good in bed, and Nina *so* didn't want to discuss sex with her grandmother.

'I'm going for a shower,' she said, changing the subject.

It didn't work. Flossie shouted through the bathroom door, taking up the conversation where Nina had tried to end it. 'They've got to be shown where the J-spot is.'

'I think you mean G-spot, and how do you know…? Tell you what, I don't think I want to know.'

'It was on *This Morning*. They have all kinds of interesting things on there. Make sure you tell that nice young man of yours to check his privates on a regular basis.'

'He's not my young man,' Nina muttered under her breath, knowing it was futile but needing to say it anyway. And there was no way she was going to get onto the subject of Leo checking his bits and pieces.

She had a few minutes of respite when Flossie made her own visit to the bathroom, during which Nina scoured the meagre contents of their shared case, wondering what to wear. She wanted to look nice; sexy even.

Flossie, teeth in and curlers out, emerged looking presentable. She had her one-piece costume on ready for her dip in Pamukkale's thermal pools and she pulled a loose-fitting dress out of their communal case to pop on over the top of it.

'Put some slap on,' the old lady instructed, seeing Nina standing by the door ready to go. 'You want to make him think you made an effort.'

'No, I don't. He can take me as I am or take a hike.' But she made the excuse of needing a quick wee before they left, to check her face in the bathroom mirror. Maybe a bit of gloss…?

Leo was sitting at a table when they entered the dining room, looking relaxed and gorgeous. Nina's heart skipped a beat when he smiled at her, the rest of her innards jumping up and down with lust, though she tried to tell herself it was because she was happy to see him. Yeah, she was really happy; jaw-droppingly, slobbering over him, sort of happy; happy to whisk him off to bed this very instant, type of happy.

'Coo-ee,' Flossie called, waggling her fingers in greeting.

Leo waved back and stood up. 'Let me get you a coffee,' he offered.

Flossie nudged Nina in the ribs.

'Oof!' What had Gran done that for?

'See what I mean,' Flossie said in a loud whisper. 'Nice manners.'

'Gran,' Nina warned, praying the old woman wouldn't say any more.

'You can work on the other stuff. Bet he's a quick learner too,' her gran said with a leer.

Nina raised her eyes skywards. 'Dear lord, please make it stop. I'll have Turkish tea, please,' she called as Leo halted at the self-service drinks machine and held up a coffee cup, raising his eyebrows.

She watched him, admiring his easy grace, the way he seemed comfortable in his own skin. He placed the cups in the dispenser and pressed the buttons. She recalled how those hands caressed her body. When he half-turned, giving her a smile, she thought of his mouth on hers and it sent a delicious shiver down her back.

'He couldn't have been all that bad,' her grandmother noted. 'Not if your expression is anything to go by.'

Nina plastered a frown on her face and it wasn't a pretend one either. Leo, returning to their table with two steaming cups, shot her a concerned look and mouthed, 'What's wrong?'

She shook her head a fraction and jerked her gaze in Flossie's direction, following it up with a penetrating stare. He smiled, and she knew he'd realised the source of her irritation as he turned his attention to his own drink.

When Flossie left the table to attack the breakfast buffet, Leo asked, 'I take it she knows about us. Did you get into trouble?'

'Far from it. She thoroughly approves and is pestering me for the gory details.'

'I hope they weren't that gory,' he said, with a smile.

'You know what I mean.'

'Seriously, do you have any regrets?' he asked.

'Why? Do you?'

'No, I don't,' was his firm reply, and Nina let out a breath she didn't know she'd been holding.

For a minute there she'd thought… Aw hell. Regrets or not, it had happened and there was no turning back the clock. She'd enjoyed herself (immensely) and would treasure the memory of her Elephant lover. Oh, no! She hadn't meant to think that at all, though nothing had been lacking in the trouser department, but she hadn't meant to imply he was hung like an elephant either, even if the conversation had taken place in her own head.

'Do you?' he repeated and she realised she'd been too busy thinking about his you-know-what to answer.

She put her hand over his. 'No, not at all. It was lovely.' A big smile spread across her face as she remembered how truly lovely it had been.

He answered her with a grin of his own.

Nina caught the eye of the gentleman who'd helped her with the porter. He was directing some hotel staff and she realised he must be a manager of some kind. He nodded and she nodded back, her head held high. She refused to feel embarrassed. Anyway, he'd probably seen it all before, and had far more interesting tales to tell than hers.

'Righto, love birds. Get some breakfast down you. Nookie is all well and good but it won't keep your bowels regular,' Flossie announced.

Ug. Trust her gran to bring everything down to earth.

Chapter 25

'It's not what I was expecting. I thought it would be pink.'

'That's because you insist on calling it by the wrong name, Gran. It's Pamukkale.'

'Yes, Pinky Moon, that's what I said. But it's not pink, it's white.'

'Pamukkale means cotton castle in Turkish and it's called that because it looks like a white cotton-wool castle on the side of the mountain,' Leo said.

'Why is it white?' Flossie asked.

'Mineral deposits in the water. Over centuries the thermal springs have left a limestone deposit on the stones, and the way the water flows over the rocks has formed a number of terraces.'

Flossie was unimpressed. 'I still think it would look better in pink.'

'Do you fancy a paddle?' Nina asked hoping her gran would say no; there were signs everywhere warning how slippery the wet rocks were. She watched as people traversed the terraces with almost comical caution, but when one lady fell hard, Nina wasn't happy about the idea of Flossie walking on them. Anyway, the supposed benefits of bathing in the mineral rich waters were bound to be exaggerated.

'Nah, I think I'll give it a miss,' Flossie declared. 'I dare say even if I drowned myself in one of those pools, I'd not come out looking any younger. I'll find a spot in the shade to sit and wait for you. You two go and have fun.'

Kudos for being tactful, Nina thought, though tact hadn't appeared to be one of her grandmother's strong points up to now. She found the old lady a seat and left her with their shoes and strict instructions not to move from the spot until they returned.

Flossie promised she would stay put. 'Cross my heart and hope to die,' she said, an innocent expression on her wrinkled face, but why did Nina have the uneasy feeling her grandmother was up to something.

Goodness me, the signs certainly hadn't been exaggerating, Nina thought, as she gingerly made her way across the rocks towards the first water-filled terrace. None of the pools appeared to be more than knee deep, and the sliminess underfoot didn't add to her desire to get any more of herself wet. In fact, the warmth of the water was a little off-putting, a bit like swimming into a suspiciously warm patch in the local swimming baths.

They didn't stay long, Leo as keen to leave as she was, and to her astonishment Flossie had remained exactly where they'd left her. She was happily chatting away to a couple of ladies around the same age (her real age, not her ninety-four age), and said goodbye when Nina and Leo picked up their shoes.

'They seemed nice,' Flossie said. 'Couldn't understand a word they said, mind you. Foreign, they were,' she added sagely.

Leo took Flossie's arm, gallantly guiding her towards the restaurant. Next to it was a large grassed area with seats and sun loungers, and a deep pool which looked far more inviting than the murky terraces.

'Do you want to stay here, or would you like to see Hierapolis with us?' Leo asked.

'Hairy what? Penis?' Flossie asked, cupping a hand to her ear, and Nina swore she was doing it on purpose. Flossie's deafness tended to be selective. 'I don't want to see a hairy anything, thank you very much, especially not a penis. Don't like beards either, or hairy backs. Has this one here got a hairy back?' she asked Nina, jerking her head at Leo.

'No.' Nina's answer was short. She did not want to discuss Leo's back, or any other part of his body with Flossie. Her grandmother might not stop at backs. She might start on fronts. At least she hadn't asked whether he had a hairy...

'Hang on a sec – Did you say Hierapolis?' Nina asked Leo.

'Yes, the other part of Pamukkale – the Roman spa city.'

'There's a Roman spa city?' she squealed. 'Why didn't anyone tell me!'

'I'm sure they did,' Leo said. 'Maybe you didn't hear. Yasin definitely mentioned it, and it's on all the excursion details.'

'Maybe she had other things on her mind,' Flossie said, with a wink and a nod.

'Maybe she was so caught up with going to Elephant, she didn't realise there was more to Pinky Moon than some thermal springs,' Nina replied loftily.

'Go, go.' Flossie shooed them away. 'I see enough ruins on a Monday morning in the doctor's surgery. I'll get a drink, have a smoke, and find someone to talk to.' She looked at the other tourists hopefully. 'There's bound to be someone here who speaks English, even if they do have a funny accent.'

'Not very PC is she?' Leo laughed, taking Nina's hand as they braved the midday heat to go explore old stones for the second time in as many days. Tingles shot through her fingers and up her arm at his touch.

'Tell me about Hierapolis,' she demanded, to take her mind off how nice it felt to be holding hands. She caught a whiff of his aftershave and supressed a groan. He smelled so *good*.

Leo stopped and turned her to face him. 'Okay, but you've got to do something for me first.'

'What?'

'Kiss me.'

'I think I can manage that.' She stood on tiptoe to reach his mouth, and wrapped her arms around his neck. Mmm, she liked tall men. She also liked strong ones, and she giggled as he lifted her off the ground.

'I may never put you down,' he said, his lips on hers.

Wait a minute – what? Did he mean it, or was she reading too much into a simple bit of flirting? And if he did, wasn't everything moving a bit fast? They'd only met yesterday and her ovaries might be in raptures, but her head was telling her to think logically.

Oh, goodness, she'd only met him yesterday, and she'd already spent the night with him. Did that make her a loose woman, a tart, a tramp? It did, didn't it? But it made him one too – loose man, that is, not woman, because he had a…

His difference pressed against her, and she sighed. You know what? she asked herself – it didn't matter. No one back home knew, she knew no one here, and no one would care if they did. This was between her and Leo, and her and her conscience. If she could live with what she'd done then everyone else could just get lost and mind their own business.

And if Flossie blabbed, Nina would deny everything.

She melted into the kiss, thoroughly enjoying it. She'd have been up for another one, but a gaggle of tourists led by a man with a rainbow umbrella came around the corner and shot them filthy looks.

'Come on Romeo, show me some piles of stones,' she said, laughing at herself, knowing if the shoe had been on the other foot and she'd been the one to stumble across a couple in a passionate embrace, she'd have been the first person to tut and roll her eyes.

Talking of rolling her eyes, she hadn't done quite so much of that since she'd met Leo. Or perhaps she simply wasn't as bothered by things as much (and by "things" she meant her grandmother!), though the old lady was still supremely annoying. But in a nice way, a funny way.

Hairy Penis wasn't as impressive as Elephant, though if she'd visited Hierapolis first she'd have been perfectly happy with what she found.

'I'll be comparing every other Roman ruin with Elephant,' she cried forlornly as she gazed around more ruins, disappointed to find Hierapolis wasn't in such good nick as Ephesus. 'All future sites will be spoilt for me,' she declared.

'Aw, let me kiss it better,' Leo offered, and Nina was more than happy to let him.

'It'll take a lot of kissing,' she warned. 'Are you sure you're up for it?'

Leo bit his lip, a smirk playing about his mouth. 'What do you think?'

'Then what are you waiting for?' She closed her eyes, lifted her chin, and was rewarded by a thoroughly good kissing. If anyone disapproved, let them look somewhere else, she was enjoying herself far too much to care.

'There's something else you need to see,' Leo said when they finally came up for air. 'Another amphitheatre. Maybe I can kiss you in this one, too?'

'Yes, please.'

'Oh, it's fabulous!' Nina clapped her hands when she saw it.

Though smaller than the one at Elephant, it had something the other amphitheatre didn't have − a series of niches at the back of the platform or stage, and a couple of them still had statues in them, flanked by huge marble columns.

Nina and Leo stood on the floor of the amphitheatre, and Nina shaded her eyes as she stared up at the steep rows of seating. 'What does that say?' She pointed at an inscription written on a block of stone, and they sauntered over to it.

'Can you read any of it?' Leo asked her.

'Not a chance.'

Leo consulted his guide book. 'It says, "Hierapolis, foremost land of broad Asia, mistress of the Nymphs, adorned with streams of water and all beauty." It certainly has streams of water, though you can't tell what they might have looked like then.'

'Let's climb to the top,' Nina suggested.

'You've got a real thing about amphitheatres, haven't you? Race you!'

Nina let him win. Really, she did. She could have taken him if she wanted to, but she had no intention of getting any hotter and any sweatier than she already was, thank you very much!

When she finally reached him, he pulled her onto his lap and with his lips on hers, he murmured, 'This is getting to be a habit. Do I have to kiss you at the top of every amphitheatre in the world?'

Was he offering to, or was this more flirting? And how was she supposed to answer? She didn't, lifting her face to his, and their lips met once more. Crisis averted.

When the afternoon heat drove them to seek shade and cool drinks, they headed back to where they'd left Flossie (Nina had her fingers crossed her grannie would still be there). Leo halted for a moment, looking back at Hierapolis, thoughtfully.

'I know of somewhere even more astounding,' he said.

'Where?' Nina asked, hoping it was within travelling distance – Turkey was a far larger country than she'd realised.

'Pompeii.'

Oh, not doable from here then. 'Have you been there?' Nina would love to go, and not just for the romance of Italy either, because there was nothing romantic about those unfortunate people at Pompeii.

'Not yet, but I will,' Leo said, his focus on somewhere deep inside, and not the scene before him.

As they made their way to the present day, leaving the ancient past to sleep on in the sun, Nina had only one thought on her mind – she wished he would take her with him.

Chapter 26

Two days ago, Nina had gotten off the bus outside *Aphrodite Hotel* and watched the coach drive slowly away. During the time it took to reach the bend and turn the corner, they'd never taken their eyes off each other, Nina craning her neck, Leo half-standing in the aisle.

It wasn't until the coach was out of sight, that Nina realised they hadn't exchanged phone numbers and she had no idea which hotel he was staying in. Not that she intended to go looking for him if she did. It was over, whatever *it* was. It had been nice while it lasted, but it couldn't have lasted any longer. It had been an enjoyable way to spend a couple of days (she refused to think too deeply about that night right now, no sir, not yet, maybe not ever). No strings. No expectations. No pre-conceived ideas. No commitment.

No heartache.

So why did she feel so empty? They'd returned from Elephant two days ago, and Nina hadn't felt right since. Maybe it was something she'd eaten. That service station they'd taken a pit-stop at on the return journey to their resort hadn't been the best.

Their holiday was over half way through now, though it actually felt as though they'd been here a lot longer. Four days and she'd be home, back to normal, with the exam results looming and a new term to prepare for. For the first time Nina didn't have that faint stirring of excitement at the thought of returning to school, no sense of satisfaction at the resumption of the steady stamp of the days, the weeks, the terms. Just a disturbing flatness. Something was definitely lacking; she felt no joy, no pleasurable anticipation, only faint stirrings of discontent with her lot in life where there had been previously been nothing but contentment.

That was it, Nina realised, she no longer felt satisfied with her lot.

Lying on a sun lounger next to the turquoise Mediterranean Sea, her skin glowing from a light golden tan, with a good book in her hand, Nina was aware she felt positively disgruntled. What kind of a word was disgruntled anyway? And was there an opposite – gruntled? If so, her gruntle had well and truly upped and left her.

She blamed Leo.

He'd been so darned enthusiastic about his job, so lit from within when he spoke about it, that it highlighted the shortcomings in her own. She couldn't imagine waxing lyrical about Free School Meal statistics or school league tables; she couldn't see herself getting all worked up about yet another meaningless meeting just to tick a box to say it had been done.

She did however love the kids. Most of them. And sometimes there was the occasional pupil who showed real promise, real enthusiasm, but when she looked back over her teaching career (okay, it wasn't that long a career), she didn't think she'd lit a fire under any of her pupils.

It might be her fault, the way she taught. Or it might be the tight, restrictive nature of having to teach pupils nothing other than what was necessary to get them through their exams.

What a shame, what a waste.

Nina enjoyed her job (until very recently) and it did consume most of her waking days, but she abruptly realised the reason her job meant everything to her was only because she had little else in her life. How sad.

Her grandmother, at eighty-four had more fun than Nina did, and even with her husband of nearly sixty years no longer with her, Flossie still found joy in life.

Joy – that was exactly what Nina was missing and she wished she knew what to do about it.

Was a man the answer? A lover, a soul-mate, The One?

On the rare occasions she went out with her friends, the diminishing number of unmarried ones spoke reverently of The One, and the married ones basked in the smug satisfaction that they'd found their happily-ever-afters.

What did Nina have? An almost non-existent social life, a totally non-existent love-life, and a job she suddenly found herself not as enamoured with as she'd previously believed.

Time for a stiff one. Or several.

'Want a drink?' she offered.

'Vodka?' Flossie replied and Nina could tell by the look on her face that her grandmother didn't expect her to come back with anything stronger than an expresso.

Nina returned with doubles, and it sure as hell wasn't coffee in those glasses.

Flossie took a sip and the shocked expression on her gran's face was a picture.

'It's not lunchtime yet,' the old woman said. 'You don't like me drinking alcohol before lunch.'

Am I really that disapproving, Nina wondered. She held up her identical drink. 'I'm joining you.'

'Why? What's wrong?'

'Does there have to be anything wrong?'

'Frankly, yes. You're not exactly the life and soul of the party, are you?'

'No,' Nina sighed, 'I'm not, am I? I think I've become stuck in a bit of a rut,' she confessed.

'And you think a large vodka and orange before lunch will snap you out of it?' Flossie raised her glass. 'Game on. Bottoms up,' she said and downed hers in one.

Nina took a couple of tentative sips. Wonderful, Nina was the one who wanted to get drunk (or have a few to take the edge off) and now it looked like her gran was going to be the one getting plastered instead. Nina had no choice but to stay sober, in order to keep an eye on the old lady. They couldn't both be drunk at the same time; what if something happened?

'For the love of all that's holy, will you just enjoy yourself for once!' Flossie exclaimed when she saw the amount remaining in Nina's glass. 'You're boring, do you know that? You're my granddaughter and I love you dearly, but a wet weekend in Hull is more fun than you are. Live a little, before it's too late.'

'Are you saying, that because I don't get rat-arsed every five minutes, I'm boring?' Nina demanded slugging her drink back. 'I don't need alcohol to enjoy myself,' she called primly over her shoulder as she headed back to the pool bar.

'No, but sometimes it bloody well helps,' Flossie yelled after her.

In less than half an hour Nina was sozzled; pickled, plastered, three-sheets-to-the-wind, off-her-face, pissed – she hadn't had so much fun in ages, though she couldn't feel her lips, or her feet. In fact, most of her lacked feeling, though she thought she could feel her hair. She knew hair had feelings, and she wondered if trees did.

'Do you think trees feel happy?' she asked, delighted her mouth worked. 'Or sad. Or lonely?'

'Do *you* think they do?' Flossie replied. Her grandmother sounded as sober as a sober thing. How did she do that? 'Why would a tree be lonely?' Flossie added.

'Because the other trees don't love it. Poor tree.'

'You're drunk,' exclaimed a delighted Flossie.

'Not.'

'Are.'

'Not.' Nina poked herself in the nose. She didn't feel a thing. Fancy that, her nose was numb. 'Okay, maybe a bit squiffy,' she admitted, prodding her nose again. She turned to Flossie. 'I'm lonely,' she said. 'Like a tree.'

'I know, dear.'

'How can you tell?' Maybe it was some kind of mark on her forehead which was invisible to her, but everyone else could see it – like those UV stamps they used to put on the back of your hand in a nightclub to show you'd paid. Not that she'd been to a night club recently. Maybe they could go to one now?

'I can see it in your eyes,' Flossie said.

'Eh? See what?'

'Your loneliness.'

'I'm not lonely. Who said I was lonely?'

'You did.'

'Didn't.' Nina stuck her tongue out and wobbled off in search of more alcohol.

She came back with a jam jar full of lime green liquid, bristling with umbrellas and plastic stirry things, and paper shapes which were flat until you opened them, then folded around themselves to make 3D shapes.

Nina, with an intense look of concentration, took them out one at a time, closing them and unfurling them again. 'Magic,' she proclaimed sombrely.

Wasn't there something she wanted to do? Ah, I know, she remembered, getting unsteadily to her feet and listing slightly to the left.

'I wanna dance,' she declared, waving her hands in the air while keeping her feet firmly planted on the grass in case she fell over, because the ground was very, very unven... unenven... bumpy.

Bet they had moles. Moles made grass bumpy and lumpy. The golf course her dad was a member of had moles. So did MI5. 'Cept they were bigger. 007 used to catch them.

Nina got down on her knees and felt the ground. Maybe the hotel should give James Bond a ring. He'd catch the little beasties.

'Have you lost something?'

The voice sounded familiar but when she looked up the sun was directly in her eyes, blinding her. She hoped it wasn't budgie-smuggler man. He had a habit of standing in the sun, forcing her to squint. Maybe he thought he looked better back-lit. Nina giggled. He'd look better *unlit*, in the dark. Not that she wanted to be anywhere in the dark with him and his budgie. She giggled again.

'I think she's looking for her dignity,' Flossie said.

Oh, Nina hadn't realised she'd lost anything. 'Is it under here?' she asked trying to peer beneath her sunbed.

'How much has she had?' the familiar voice asked.

'Too much,' came Flossie's wry reply.

'Does she often get drunk before lunch?'

'No, and she doesn't get drunk after lunch either, or at any other time. I don't know what's got into her.'

'Are you gonna help me look or wha?' Nina slurred, her backside in the air and her head jammed under the lounger. What did a "dignity" look like anyway? She couldn't remember ever seeing one.

'What exactly is it you've lost?' the man repeated.

It didn't sound like the bloke with the white budgie smugglers, or that other one from the courtyard. It might be one of the bar staff or the entertainment team. But it actually sounded like...

'Oohhh oohhh!' she squealed. 'It's you, isn't it?'

'It is. I most certainly am me.'

Nina scrabbled backwards until she was free of the sunbed and scrambled to her feet, with only a small stagger and a wobble. 'My lovely, lovely Leo the lion,' she sang. 'I love Leos, they're all liony.'

'How much has she had?'

'Either too much or not quite enough,' came Flossie's cryptic reply.

'Dance with me,' Nina crooned, grabbing hold of Leo's hands and trying to twirl him around.

'We thought we'd seen the last of you,' Flossie said. 'Well, *she* did. I expected you might show up sooner or later. You've got that look about you.'

'What look is that?' Leo was attempting to keep Nina upright. She wasn't too keen on the idea. She wanted him down here with her, on this nice sunbed where they could cuddle and kiss, and stuff.

'Come down here and cuddle with me. It's in the shade and everything.' Nina dropped her voice to a loud whisper which was no quieter than her normal speaking voice. 'We could kiss.'

'As inviting as that sounds, I think I'll pass,' Leo said. 'Shall I take her back to the room and put her to bed?' he asked Flossie. 'And what do you mean "that look" about me.'

'The in-love look,' Flossie replied.

'I'd like to go to bed with you, but shhh,' Nina put a finger to her lips. 'Don't tell my grannie.'

'Grannie already knows, dear,' Flossie said to her. 'And Grannie wholeheartedly approves.' She tapped Leo on the arm. 'If you wouldn't mind helping her to bed before she passes out. But before you go, tell me what took you so long?'

Yeah, Nina wanted to know the answer too. She stared up at her grandmother and Leo, blinking. Her eyes wanted to close without her permission. Why would they do that? They needed to behave, else she'd give them lines to write.

'I needed to work out what this was – is,' Leo said.

'Have you come to a conclusion?' Flossie had her arms crossed as if she were about to give him a telling off. Oooh, Nina thought, Leo's been naughty.

'I have,' he said, stroking Nina's hair as if she was a fluffy dog.

Both her grandmother and Leo ignored her when she barked like one.

'What is it?' Flossie demanded.

'I want to see her again, when we get back to the UK. Do you think she'll want to see me?'

'Look at her.'

They looked.

'I've never seen Nina drunk before, not even a little tipsy, and I blame you,' Flossie declared.

'She got drunk because of me?'

'I did,' Nina piped up. 'It's Leo the Lion's fault.' Her eyes filled with stinging tears. 'You didn't call me. You don't care.'

'I didn't call you because I didn't have your phone number, and you're wrong, I do care.'

Nina thought he said, 'More than I want to', but she wasn't sure. It could have been wishful thinking. Not that she herself cared – she didn't – but it would be nice if he did. She couldn't remember the last time she felt wanted.

'Do you want me?' she said in a little girl voice. She was aiming for take-me-or-leave-me-I-don't-care-either-way but the words came out the wrong way.

'Yes.'

'Good,' she said, before falling face down on the sunbed. 'G'night.'

Chapter 27

'Do you feel okay?' Leo asked as they got on yet another coach.

Nina nodded, albeit slowly. Her head was still a little fragile, despite having slept through lunch and most of yesterday afternoon. She wasn't sure whether she'd been disappointed to find Leo had returned to his hotel, or relieved he hadn't stayed around to witness the state she was in when she finally woke up. She'd been delighted though, when Flossie had told her what she'd arranged with Leo.

'He's smitten,' her grandmother had said. 'And I think you are too. Make the most of the time you've got left because he's going home on Friday and just enjoy yourself.'

Flossie's blessing hadn't stopped Nina from feeling guilty at leaving the other woman on her own all day, but the offer was hard to resist. A whole day (more or less) sailing down a boat on a river, with a lovely, sexy, glorious man. How romantic.

The romance was made more poignant because this was nearly their last day together. Leo went home on Friday, Nina on Saturday. After that, they might never see each other again and Nina wasn't sure how she felt about it, but she put the depressing thought of going home to the back of her mind and settled down to enjoy the day.

Leo's dark brown hair had lightened slightly in the sun, giving him auburn highlights and, combined with his tanned skin, he looked yummy enough to eat. And that led to thoughts of the night they'd spent together and the impossibility of a repeat performance, not with Dave occupying the one room, and Flossie the other.

You should be ashamed, she told herself, but she wasn't. 'How's Dave?' she asked instead.

'Distraught. Inconsolable. A right misery. Take your pick.'

'I assume the German girlfriend has gone home?'

'Yep, and Dave's heart has been broken all over again. He's going to be impossible when we get back. He's already talking about going to Germany to visit Frieda.'

'Aww, that's so sweet.'

'It would be if she'd answer any of his phone calls. Either she's ignoring him and hoping he'll take the hint, or she's given him a duff phone number.'

'That reminds me,' Nina said. 'I still haven't given you mine.'

'Flossie did, yesterday. I didn't bring my mobile with me today, but when I get back to my hotel, I'll text you so you've got my number too.'

Just that simple thing of knowing he cared enough to get her phone number gave her a warm feeling. Maybe they would keep in touch after all.

Today was going to be a good day, she thought, hugging herself in barely contained happiness, but she almost changed her mind when the coach made the first stop at a gold centre, whose sole purpose was to persuade tourists to part with as much of their money as they could.

Nina had the bright idea of staying on the coach, (she had no intention of being talked into buying a piece of jewellery she'd never wear and couldn't afford, and she'd heard stories of their hard-sell tactics) but yet again the bus was locked. When it came to a choice between roasting like a couple of chicken wings on a grill, or hiding from the sun inside a (very) cool shop with the possibility of a glass of tea, the shop won.

Soon after making that decision, Nina regretted not taking the roasting option, after being followed mercilessly around the huge room. Every time she and Leo tried to stand still, a formally-clad sales assistant pounced. Oh no, here comes another one!

'Excuse me, lady?'

Nina tried to avoid eye contact with the sales girl, but it wasn't easy when said sales girl planted her diminutive frame right in front of Nina, and stared into her face with all the cunning of a mongoose trying to pin a snake down. Nina didn't stand a chance of escaping.

'The engagement rings are this way,' the mongoose said.

'Er… ah… we aren't… I mean, you've got the wrong end of the stick.' Nina tried to put her off.

'Sorry?'

'We aren't engaged,' she said.

'Yes, I see.' The mongoose woman looked pointedly at Nina's bare left hand. 'Which is why I show you engagement rings. Follow, please.'

Beside her, Leo shook with surprised laughter. Nina trod on his foot.

It shut him up – for a second anyway.

'Show me what you've got in the region of four carats,' he said, shooting Nina an evil smile as he followed the delighted sales woman to a nearby counter. Nina was pleased to see he limped slightly. Served him right.

She hung back, not wanting to show any interest but Leo didn't let her off the hook that easily.

'What do you think of this one, darling?' He pointed to a ring with a rock Kim Kardashian would be proud of. 'How much is it?' he asked the sales girl.

Nina smiled sweetly and before the mongoose had a chance to answer, said, 'If you need to ask, *dahling*, then you can't afford it.'

'I just want you make sure you have what you deserve, *my love*,' he retorted, his smile as saccharine as hers. 'Do you prefer a round one, a square one, one on its own or one surrounded by lots of other little ones?'

'You're wowing me with your technical knowledge,' she said. Actually, thanks to her friends, both the marrieds and the nots, she knew what she liked and didn't like when it came to engagement rings; after all, she'd seen enough of the sodding things. Having been forced to coo over and admire so many, she knew she liked square cut solitaires the best. If she was ever going to get engaged, that's what she'd plump for. Not that she was planning on getting engaged any time soon, if ever, and the reason was simple really – no man.

'I prefer ones like that,' she said, pointing to the perfect ring.

Leo said, 'Would madam prefer yellow gold, white gold or platinum?'

'Platinum. White gold looks a bit dull don't you think?'

'As a man, the only consideration is, will the lady in question say yes, and then pray she doesn't lose it,' Leo retorted.

'In order for the lady to say yes, she first needs to be asked,' Nina replied archly.

'That's the problem,' Leo said to the bewildered sales assistant. 'I haven't asked her, so for the moment, I think we'll leave it, thanks.' He offered Nina his arm. 'Shall we retire to the coach?'

She took it. 'Yes, let's.' And they swept out of the room as if they owned the place.

'That was a bit mean of us,' Leo said when they were safely outside and they'd finally stopped laughing.

'It was, but if those sales assistants hadn't been so pushy...'

The excursion stayed on roughly the same level when, at the well-publicised and rather-too-hyped-up thermal mud baths in Dalyan (apparently the mud had rejuven-ating properties but all Nina could think about was the thousands of other people who'd wallowed in it, and the disgusting feel of the slimy mud between her toes) Nina saw a photo of herself, her bikini-clad body covered from head to toe in slightly stinky mud, with only her eyes showing. She looked delightful. To be fair, Leo didn't look much better, but he carried the muddy body mask off with far more aplomb.

Sprawled out in the sun to let the mud dry, Nina said, 'That wasn't particularly pleasant, was it?'

'Oh, I don't know, you look quite cute slathered in mud.'

She scraped a globule of the stuff from her stomach and flung it at him. It landed on his nose, and she collapsed into giggles. 'I can't stand this any longer,' she said. 'I'm going to have a shower.'

The "showers" were lengths of pipes with holes in them, suspended about seven feet in the air, the water running continuously. Nina squealed as the icy spray hit her hot skin.

'They're trying to kill me!' she cried, desperately trying to wash the half-dried mud off whilst not getting wet.

Leo took matters into his own hands, picking her up and carrying her to stand underneath the freezing spray.

'You git! I hate you,' she spluttered as he gamely attempted to rinse the mud off whilst holding a struggling, squirming Nina.

When he put her back on her feet, she looked down and saw she was clean-ish. Pity. She quite liked being held by him, in those strong arms, against that solid chest. Oh stop it, she thought – you sound like a virgin in one of those romances her gran liked so much, going all swoony over a man.

Lunch was the usual communal affair of chicken, meatballs, or fish, with rice, bread and salad, which she'd come to expect on these excursions – not haute cuisine, but it filled a hole, and she wasn't particularly hungry anyway, though Leo ate like a horse.

'It's the fresh air,' he said when she asked him where he put it, annoyed he seemed able to eat what he liked and as much as he liked and still be lean and lovely, whilst she only had to look at a calorie for it to attach itself to her bum like a heat seeking missile. She'd have to do some serious gym-work when she got back.

There was that phrase again "when she got back" – it lurked behind other thoughts waiting to ambush her. For someone who didn't want to come on this holiday, and was only here out of duty, she sure didn't want to go home. Get over it, she warned herself. The way you're going your mood will be lower than a snake's ass in a waggon rut, and you'll spoil the rest of the day if you're not careful.

There was actually little chance of spoiling anything, because the rest of the day was simply magical.

They boarded a boat and chugged off down the Dalyan river. Apart from the noise of the engine, it was remarkably peaceful. Leo sat behind her, his arms around her and she leaned back into him, resting her head on his chest, watching the world go by.

'Look.' She pointed to caves carved into the rocks on a bluff high above the river. 'Rock tombs. I've read about them, and there was some at Tlos too.'

They weren't caves, so much as elaborately carved entrances, reminding Nina of temples, with their pillars and engravings, and to think they were nearly three thousand years old. She could imagine people carrying the dead to their final resting place so they could look out over the river and the delta beyond for all eternity. What a stunning place to be laid to rest.

Thoughts of ancient Lycians were replaced by scenes from *The African Queen* as they puttered into one of the open channels between banks of towering reed beds.

'Do you think the film was shot here?' she asked, delighted when Leo knew what she was talking about. She'd watched *The African Queen* as a child, and again more recently, and admired Katharine Hepburn's sass, and her unwavering love and loyalty to the rough-diamond she'd fallen in love with.

'Maybe. Google it,' Leo suggested.

Nina took her phone out. 'Battery's dead,' she said. 'Damn it, I wanted to take some photos too.'

'I keep all mine up here.' Leo tapped his temple. 'The secret is to visit them often so you don't forget. I'll play this whole day over and over in my head, reliving every moment, when it's cold and wet outside and I've had a stressful day at work.'

'How much stress can you get from sub-atomic particles? See, I *was* listening,' she teased, pretending to yawn. He stopped her from saying any more with his mouth.

Mile after mile the boat wove its way through the reeds, until eventually the delta opened out into one deep long channel, the river waters coming together in a final defiant push to the sea.

'Wow,' Leo breathed as they rounded a bend.

The river ran parallel to the sea for a while as it snaked its way to the shore, a long stretch of white-gold sand between it and the ocean. Long rolling waves surged in, wild and beautiful (if you ignored the tourists playing in the surf and lying on towels).

Nina slapped some more sun cream on, revelling in the feel of Leo's hands on her back and shoulders as he rubbed the lotion into the places she couldn't reach, and they dashed off to do their own playing in the sun.

This was indeed a day to remember, and Nina knew, no matter what the future held, she'd never forget it.

Chapter 28

When she thought she'd never forget the day, Nina had specific reasons on her mind, mostly to do with a sexy man who had eyes only for her, and whose mouth tasted sweeter than any baklava, and whose body made her long to be alone with him. They were soon dispelled when the coach stopped at Nina's hotel.

Nina got off the bus, wishing Leo could come with her, but he had his own hotel to go to and she didn't think she'd be able to smuggle him into hers. Instead, they'd arranged to meet at one of the bars on the promenade later. In the meantime, she looked forward to washing the sand, salt, and sun cream off herself, and telling Flossie all about her day. Well, maybe not all of it. She'd not include the details of passionate kisses in the sea.

'Excuse me, lady, are you Nina Clarke?'

'Yes?' Nina looked back at Leo, who had his nose pressed against the glass.

'There is a problem.'

'What?' Nina didn't think she'd heard the man correctly. 'What kind of problem?' She glanced at his nametag, Asdan. It must something official then, and she hoped there was nothing wrong with their visas or passports.

Distracted by Leo's imminent departure, and not wanting him to leave, not even for a second, she turned to look at the coach as it pulled off slowly.

The rest happened in slow motion.

'The old lady, Flossie, she is ill. They have taken her to hospital,' Asdan said.

'What?' she repeated. He wasn't making any sense. He'd just said... oh!

Nina cried out as she realised what he'd said, and she crumpled, falling slowly, her knees giving way. The man caught her and held her up, steadying her.

'I am assigned to accompany you there,' he said. 'We will leave now, yes?'

The squeal of breaks was loud, followed by the noise of the air hissing as a bus door opened. Feet slapped on the road as someone ran towards her, and Nina heard it all from a great distance. Then she was swept up into familiar arms and transported inside the hotel's cool interior.

'What's wrong,' Leo barked, putting her into a squashy armchair and calling for water.

'The old lady, she fell down,' Asdan said.

'Did she have a fall, or did she collapse?' Leo took charge.

Nina was in no fit state to, she knew. She'd be alright in a bit, she just needed a minute to take it in. Flossie in hospital – oh no! Her heart banged out a fluttering, unsteady rhythm, and she felt a little faint.

'Ah, I see, she collapsed.' Asdan stumbled over the unfamiliar word.

A cold glass was placed in Nina's hands. Leo helped guide it to her mouth and she took a long swallow, the water reviving her a little.

'Where is she?' Leo demanded.

'We called an ambulance, they have taken her to hospital in Fethiye.'

'Do they know what it is?' Leo asked, and Nina was grateful for his calm control.

She looked up at Asdan, who shook his head. 'It may be her heart. We do not know.' He crouched down to her level. 'Do you want to go to the hospital now? I will take you.'

'Yes, please,' she said, getting to her feet. She was alright now, it had been the shock. She'd be okay, everyone always said she was good in a crisis.

She reached for Leo's hand. 'I'm sorry, but I have to go.'

'I'm coming with you,' he said.

'There's no need. I'm sure everything will be fine.'

'I'm still coming with you.'

'Asdan,' Nina checked the man's name tag again, 'will come with me. He said so.'

'Okay, I understand.' Leo dropped her hand and took a step back.

She read the concern and dismay in his face, and real-ised he was worried about her, and about Flossie, and she'd just given him the impression she didn't want him there. She did. Very, very much.

'I don't want to spoil what's left of your holiday,' she said in a small voice.

'Silly girl, I want to help.' He put an arm around her waist.

'I will call a taxi, but first does the lady have insurance? The hospital will need to see her passport also,' Asdan said.

'We'll go and fetch what is needed,' Leo said. He glanced at Nina, who nodded. 'How long ago was she taken to hospital?'

223

'Many hours, maybe four or five. We did call the telephone number which was given on the check-in form, but it did not work.'

'It's not your fault,' Leo said to him. 'It's not yours either,' he added quickly, seeing Nina's face.

'It *is* my fault. If I'd made sure to charge my phone,' she wailed.

'Having a charged phone wouldn't have prevented it happening,' Leo pointed out. 'Whatever it is.' He directed his next question to Asdan. 'Could you please ring the hospital to see if there is any news, while we gather anything Flossie might need.'

The manager nodded and dashed off, clearly happier now that he had something constructive to do instead of trying to console distraught young women.

'I knew I shouldn't have left her on her own, I knew it,' Nina kept repeating as she opened the door to her and Flossie's room. 'What if she's... Oh!' She put a hand to her mouth to stop the dreadful word escaping.

Leo held her by the shoulders. 'She's not, the hospital would have rang the hotel and said. Stay positive. It mightn't be anything too serious.'

Yet Nina knew it must be. You don't get carted away in an ambulance for no reason. She just hoped she wasn't too late.

'You find the documents you need and I'll sort some toiletries and night things out,' Leo suggested, as she unlocked the door to her room.

Nina did as she was told, and opened the safe. She had her own travel insurance, and she prayed her grandmother had taken some out for herself when she'd changed the holiday booking to add Nina's name.

Ah, there were the booking details, and the e-tickets. She quickly scanned them, searching for the one she needed. She was about to move to the next piece of paper when something caught her attention – a date. The date Flossie made the booking to be exact, and it appeared to be the date Nina had almost accompanied her grandmother to the travel agent when the old woman went to change the name from Grandad's to hers. Impossible.

She looked at it again, and again, trying to see if maybe the date on the sheet of paper she held in her hands referred to the date Flossie had amended the booking. It didn't. The booking didn't appear to have been amended at all. Grandad's name had never been on it!

Nina sat on the edge of her bed, listening to Leo collecting what was needed from the bathroom, trying to make sense of it all. Why had her grandmother lied? Did her mother know? Surely if Grannie had wanted some company on a holiday, all she had to do was ask, and Nina would willingly have gone with her. Why the charade and had Flossie been aware of the sort of hotel this was, though it was nice enough once Nina learned to ignore the overly sexual overtones and the smell of desperation. She'd been hit on enough times to have become quite adept at letting the opposite sex down gently, and no one seemed to take offence. If they were too persistent, she made her excuses and disappeared off to the loos, knowing her grandmother's forthright and often intrusive questions would put any would-be suitors off.

But that didn't explain why Flossie had booked this kind of hotel in the first place, nor the date on the confirmation letter.

'What is it?' Leo asked, putting Nina's beach bag on the bed next to her. She saw he had filled it with everything he thought Flossie needed for an overnight stay, but Nina had an awful feeling her grandmother was going to be in for far longer than one night.

She showed him the documents.

'I don't understand,' he said.

'The only reason I'm here is because Gran said she and Grandad booked this holiday before he died. When he passed on she wanted to come to Turkey to sort of honour his memory. My mother persuaded me to go with her, but this confirmation says the holiday was booked *after* Grandad died. How do you explain that?'

'Does it matter right now? You can ask the question later.'

Nina sighed. 'You're right.' She stood. 'I think I've got everything.' She double checked. 'Yes, passport and insurance. Thank goodness she took some out.'

Asdan was waiting for them, chatting to a taxi driver. The driver gave Nina a sympathetic smile as he opened the door. Asdan sat in the front but swivelled around to speak to them both as soon as the taxi pulled away from the hotel.

'The hospital would not give me much information,' he began, and Nina held her breath, fearing the worst. 'But they did say she is comfortable.'

Nice to know hospitals all over the world spoke the same language of platitudes and vagueness, she thought, nodding her thanks. As Asdan resumed his conversation with the driver, Nina stared unseeingly out of the window, her hand clutched firmly in Leos as they retraced their steps and returned to Fethiye.

This morning, when their bus had bounced along the same roads, heading for the dual carriageway and Dalyan, Nina had been brimful of supressed happiness and excitement. Now look at her. What a difference ten hours made.

This journey was simultaneously interminable, and over far too soon. The cowardly part of her wanted never to arrive, so she wouldn't be forced to hear the words she didn't want to hear. But another piece of her was desperate to reach her grandmother's side.

Her gran must be so frightened, all alone in a foreign hospital, unable to understand or make herself understood, not knowing what was happening to her.

A sob caught in Nina's throat and she dashed away a tear with an angry hand. Now wasn't the time to fall apart. The episode at the hotel had been nothing more than shock. She was good in a crisis; everyone always said so.

But this was her grandmother. *Hers!* And the old lady was depending on Nina. No one else was here to do it, and for one anger-filled minute Nina wanted to know why her mother wasn't here to deal with it. She felt too young, too unprepared, too scared.

Her mother would know what to do.

Her mother? Oh dear, she hadn't phoned her mother.

Frantic, she squeezed Leo's arm. 'I need your phone.'

'I haven't got it,' he reminded her. 'Who do you want to call?'

'My parents. They should know. They'll tell me what to do and—'

'Wait, my love. Phone them when you know something more concrete. There's no point in worrying them when they're so far away.'

Nina wasn't totally convinced, but she took his advice. Anyway, she wasn't entirely certain whether she wanted to phone home because she wanted to share the burden, or whether she simply wanted to hear her mother's voice.

'We will be arriving soon,' Asdan said. 'The doctors, they will speak to you – though they may have to speak to me first so I can translate.' He sounded a bit put out, and Nina guessed he might have had some difficulty getting information when he phoned the hospital earlier, because he wasn't a relative.

'Thank you,' she said, and a fresh wave of worry swept over her. Did every injured or sick tourist get the same amazing treatment from their hotel, or did Asdan know something Nina didn't, and he wanted the hospital to be the ones to pass on the bad news, so they could deal with her grief?

Chapter 29

Nina stared at Flossie with tears in her eyes. Gone was the sparky, lively old lady Nina had come to know over the course of the last several days. In her place was a tiny, fragile wrinkled bag of bones, who hardly raised a lump under the sheet. Her grannie was wired up to an assortment of machines, bleeping and flashing, keeping the old woman alive.

For now.

'I really do need to call my parents,' she said softly, not taking her eyes from the figure in the bed.

Leo had come in with her, but Asdan waited outside. Leo beckoned him in, and the other man sidled into the room as if they had some contagious disease.

'The doctor, she will be with you soon,' he reassured them, then said something to the nurse, who nodded.

'This is...' Asdan swept a hand around the room, 'I do not know how you say it... special help?'

'Intensive care?'

'Yes. I cannot stay here, I am to wait outside. Only two persons in the room together.'

'You stay,' Leo suggested to him. 'Nina may need someone to translate.' He turned to Nina, holding out his hand. 'Give me your mobile and I'll see if anyone has a charger we can borrow. In the meantime, Asdan, can you find a phone Nina can use?'

'Of course.' Asdan spoke to the nurse again, and she smiled and gestured for Nina to follow.

'Leo? Don't leave her,' Nina pleaded.

'I'll stay with her until you come back. I promise I won't leave her on her own.'

She bit her lip, her chin wobbling, and nodded. She knew he wouldn't stray from her grandmother's side, but Nina so badly wanted to stay.

The nurse had her write her mother's phone number down and dialled it for her, handing her the receiver when it started to ring. Nina clamped it to her ear, desperate to hear her mother's voice.

'Hello? The local madhouse here, chief inmate speaking.'

'Dad?'

'Hello, love,' his voice warmed when he heard hers. 'I thought it was one of those nuisance calls. We're getting them every evening about this time, and they're forever using different numbers so we can never tell if the call is genuine or not, before we answer it.'

'Dad...' Her voice broke and she took a deep breath, fighting back tears.

'Tell them to bugger off,' Nina heard her mother yell in the background, above the noise of dishes clattering. 'Bloody nuisances, there ought to be a law against bothering—'

'Shush a minute, Alice. It's our Nina and I think there's summat wrong. Nina?'

''ere, give the phone to me. Nina? Nina, love? What is it?'

'Gran,' Nina managed to choke out.

Silence. Then, 'What about your gran?'

Nina could see her mother, standing in the kitchen, the phone gripped in her hand, worry on her face and her dad hovering over her shoulder, trying to listen.

'She's in hospital. Oh, Mum, you have to come, I don't know what happened, but it looks serious. She's in intensive care, and is wired up to all these machines, and—' Nina sobbed, 'I think she's going to die.'

'What is it? What's happened? Is Nina alright?' her dad was saying.

'Hang on, Derek, Nina's fine. It's Mum,' her mother said.

'What about your mother? What's she done?'

'Will you shut up and stop blathering in my ear.' There was the sound of a muffled scuffle, then her mother was back on the line. 'Carry on, poppet. Why is she in hospital?'

Her mother's calm, assured voice comforted Nina, and the hysteria threatening to engulf her retreated slightly. 'I don't know,' she admitted. 'I haven't spoken to a doctor yet.'

'Right, listen to me. Call me back when you know something. Derek, get on the internet and find out when the next flight is.' A pause. Nina heard her father speaking but couldn't make out the words. 'No, I don't care which bloody airline or how much it costs. Just book us on the damn thing!' Another pause, then, 'Sorry, love, just trying to get your father organised. Ring me back as soon as you know something more definite, and I might be able to give you an estimated time of arrival. Try *easyJet*,' she called to Derek, and Nina simply knew that once her mother had got off the phone, she'd take over the search for flights, not trusting her father to do a proper job.

That was where Nina got her own practicality and common sense from – her mother – but she didn't have much in the way of common sense right now. Whoever said she was good in a crisis had been blatantly lying.

Nina took a deep breath, held it for a count of ten, then let it out slowly.

'Nina? Nina? You still there, love?'

'I'm still here, Mum. Look, don't book anything yet, let me find out what's going on first and I'll call you back.'

'I'm coming out on the next flight, whether you want me to or not,' her mother retorted. 'I don't like the thought of you all alone in a foreign country.'

'I'm twenty-eight, I can cope.' As soon as she'd said it, Nina realised it was the truth. She *could* cope. Whatever this was, whatever the outcome, Nina would deal with it.

Then her mother's next words brought fresh tears to Nina's eyes, as Alice said in a small voice. 'She's my *mother*, Nina. I have to be there.'

A pat on her arm. Nina looked around. The nurse from earlier beckoned her.

'Doktor,' she said, pointing down the corridor.

'Gotta go, Mum, the doctor is here. I'll ring you in a minute.'

There was no change in Flossie as Nina dashed into the room. She hadn't really expected there to be but…

Asdan was speaking to the doctor, and an elderly man with grey in his hair and a kindly expression. His English, it turned out, was way better than Asdan's.

'Miss…?' He held a hand out and Nina shook it.

'Clarke,' Nina said. 'And this is Leo—' she stopped, mortified. She'd spent the night in his arms and she didn't even know his surname.

'Leo Waters,' Leo said, stepping forward to shake the doctor's hand.

'I am Doctor Macar, and I have been treating the patient. I understand Mrs Gibbins is your grandmother?' He carried on when Nina nodded. 'She has suffered an ischaemia, a stroke caused by a blood clot. We know this because we did a scan,' he added as if he thought he wouldn't be believed. 'The clot was affecting the flow of blood to her brain. Now,' he held up a hand as Nina let out a gasp. 'We have treated her by performing a... how do you say it?' He took out his phone and pressed a few buttons. 'Ah, it is the same!' he said triumphantly. 'We performed a trombektomi this afternoon, which involved inserting a small instrument into Mrs Gibbins groin and up into the brain.'

He traced the path of this instrument with his finger on his own body, stopping and tapping when he came to his head. It must be a really, really small instrument, Nina thought randomly.

'Once in the brain, we sucked the blood clot out, restoring normal blood flow. Mrs Gibbins is lucky – we treated her within two hours of the stroke occurring. The clot was on one of the large arteries,' he pointed to his head again. 'Any more delay and the treatment would not have been as effective.'

'What is the prognosis?' Nina asked, cautious hope rising as she listened to him speak.

Leo slipped a hand in hers and squeezed.

'We cannot tell until your grandmother is conscious and we have run tests. The damage may be minimal or it may be severe. However, we are treating her with medicines to control her pain and to reduce the risk of further clots forming. She may have to take these for some time, but her own doctor will advise her when she returns home.'

Flossie wasn't out of the woods yet, but Nina wanted to believe the doctor was hopeful. Of course, he had to be cautious, she understood that, but he sounded hopeful. Didn't he? She leaned against Leo, drawing strength from him, and he slipped his hand out of hers and encircled her waist.

'When will she regain consciousness?' Nina asked.

'She is not unconscious. She is sleeping. We had to sedate her heavily to perform the trombektomi. She will wake in a while, but may be confused, and may have some degree of paralysis.'

'Will she be able to talk?'

'The stroke was on the right hemisphere of her brain, so her speech will not be affected. She may be paralysed on the left side, she may have memory problems, and her vision may be affected, and there could be some drooping of the mouth. Each stroke is different and no two patients are affected in the same way. At eighty-four, there is the possibility she will take longer than a younger person to recover.'

'*Eighty*-four?' whispered Leo, his lips close to her ear.

'She lied,' Nina said out of the side of her mouth. 'She seems to be doing it a lot, lately.'

The doctor was still talking. 'We have to test for these things when she awakes, though not today. Today I go home to my family and a meal. You should do the same.'

Nina was horrified. 'I'm not going to leave her!' she declared. 'You should go, though,' she said to Leo. 'There's no point in both of us being here.'

'Yes, there is. I'm not going anywhere. I'll stay as long as you need me, or want me to.'

The doctor spoke to Asdan, who nodded. Nina had no idea how much of the previous conversation he'd understood, and she hoped Dr Macar was bringing him up to speed.

'I have authorisation to book you into a hotel nearby,' Asdan said when the doctor had finished speaking. '*Athena Holidays* will cover the cost for tonight, but you must contact your insurance company as soon as possible.'

More Turkish, more nods.

'The doctor says a hotel which is only five minutes from here is good. I will telephone and arrange. I will tell them to expect you.'

'Tell them we might not check in until tomorrow,' Leo said. 'We'll wait here until Mrs Gibbins wakes up and we are sure she is okay.'

Asdan left to make the call, but Nina had one final question before she let the doctor go.

'When can she go home?'

The doctor sucked his teeth and shook his head. 'Not for some days. Ten maybe. I do not like stroke victims flying too soon. Air pressure, you understand.'

Ten days. How was she going to cope for ten days?

Chapter 30

'It's all her fault, I should never have agreed to such a stupid idea.' Nina's mother cried down the phone. 'A stroke. Oh poor Mum.'

'Agreed to what?'

'Your grandmother taking you on holiday. Derek, don't forget your Athlete's Foot cream.' She resumed her conversation with Nina, but Nina noticed it wasn't at the point she'd left it. 'It's the heat, it plays havoc with your dad's feet,' her mother said.

'I thought *I* was taking *her* on holiday, not the other way around.'

'That's what she wanted you to think,' her mother said, darkly. 'Did they say how the operation went?'

'It wasn't an operation, it was a procedure. I think it went well.'

'What's the difference?'

'No idea. Going back to the holiday,' Nina said, more to keep her mind off the tiny figure in the bed in room five-oh-three. 'Why did she want me to think I was taking her? I *was* taking her... well, accompanying her.'

'Do we have to do this now?'

'Do what?'

'Bring up the past.'

'It's hardly the past – it was only three weeks ago!'

'Your dad and I have got a plane to catch.'

'You don't have to leave for a couple of hours. You told me the plane doesn't take off until seven tomorrow. You could have time to have a nap before you leave for the airport, if you wanted.'

'How can I sleep knowing my baby and my mother are on the other side of the world with god knows what's happening to them.'

'I think the happening has already happened. Just tell me, Mum.'

The phone went silent but Nina heard her mother breathing. She heaved in a breath of her own and let it out slowly. She was exhausted and it wasn't even ten o'clock yet. She had the shakes too, though those could be from tiredness, hunger or shock. Leo had gone off to find coffee and food. Not that she wanted food, because her stomach was in knots even though she hadn't eaten anything since lunch. Neither of them had. A coffee would be good though.

'Your grandmother,' Alice began and Nina noticed how Flossie had suddenly become *your* grandmother rather than *my* mother, as if Alice was distancing herself from the events. 'She booked the holiday after we had that little chat about you going away with her.'

'After! Did you know she was lying about it being Grandad's last holiday?'

Her mother sniffed loudly. 'Yes.'

'Why?'

'Because she told me her plan before you arrived.'

'I didn't mean, "why did you know she was telling porkies", I meant why did she tell them in the first place?'

'Because you wouldn't have agreed to go. Not there anyway. You'd have insisted on Bournemouth or Torquay, or somewhere equally boring.'

Oh, Turkey hadn't been boring. Nina certainly couldn't say that about it.

'I wished you had stayed in England. Or Wales even.' The way her mother said Wales, it sounded as if it was out in the wilds where bears and antelopes roamed, not a few miles away on the other side of the Malvern Hills.

'I wish we had, too,' Nina said. 'But you still haven't answered my question. Why?'

'Don't take this the wrong way, or shout at me,' Alice sniffed loudly again, 'but Grannie thought you could do with some livening up. She wanted you to have some fun.'

This time Nina's deep breath was from anger. Here she was, stuck in a foreign hospital, tired, worried out of her mind, still sweaty and salty from the beach, and her grandmother wanted her to have *fun*?

'Fun? Fun! I'm not bloody well having fun now, am I?' Nina shouted, earning a frown from the nurse in charge. 'Sorry,' she said, lowering her voice.

'Apology accepted,' her mother said.

'I wasn't apologising to *you*!'

'Oh.'

'You don't deserve an apology. You're as bad as she is. Are you seriously telling me that Gran concocted some cock-and-bull story about booking a holiday for her and Grandad to get me to go away somewhere *fun* with her?'

'Yes.'

'And when I agreed, she went out and booked a hotel which is supposed to be for people between thirty and forty-five because she thought I needed some *livening up*? Are you aware how ridiculous that sounds?'

'Now you put it like that…'

'Do you know what she's been getting up to on this *fun* holiday?'

'You said you were having a lovely time when you phoned last Saturday,' her mother interrupted.

'That was so you wouldn't worry. On the first day I caught her downing vodka cocktails and playing a game of pin the penis on the man.'

'Was he naked? I bet that hurt.'

'It was a cardboard one.'

'Penis?'

'Man, penis, both, what does it matter?'

'Phew, you had me crossing my legs for a minute, and I don't even have a penis.'

Nina wasn't at all comfortable with her mother saying "penis". It wasn't right. Besides, Alice was trying to turn the conversation.

'She's got me scuba diving, paragliding, going to beach parties.' Nina added.

'It sounds like you had a good time,' Alice said.

Instead of being on Nina's side in all this, Mum was on her grandmother's, seeing nothing wrong with fraudulently getting her daughter to go on holidays with an alcoholic octogenarian who has an adrenalin addiction. God, her mother was so annoying. She got it from Grannie. Thankfully the annoying gene seemed to have skipped a generation. No wonder Nina liked calm and peaceful, orderly and organised. She'd had enough of the opposite while she was growing up. It had been like living in an episode of *Absolutely Fabulous*, with her gran playing the drunken Patsy and her mother playing the other one, what's-her-name, it was on the tip of her tongue.

Which meant Nina must be Saffron. She was, wasn't she? She was the sensible one, the grown-up one, and though Alice was a total adult most of the time, her mother did have a bit of fey about her. Mum hadn't really grown up, despite the sensible, responsible job she had. Take last year, for instance – her mother and father went to Disneyland, two middle-aged people on their own, without kids. Hardly a crime, but most of her friends' parents were going on sedate cruises down the Rhine. Then there was this mad idea they had of selling the family home and going to live in a yurt in Mongolia for a couple of years. Who did something like that at their age? They spoke of retirement as though it was going to be all their Christmases rolled into one and they could act like kids again.

Talking of Christmas, her dad still trod in a tray of flour, donned his work boots, and stamped around the living room, leaving a trail of "Santa's Footprints", and Nina was twenty-eight (though she did spend Christmas with the oldies because her own house was lonely and she didn't fancy cooking Christmas dinner for one), and her brother was eighteen and had stopped believing in Santa Claus when he was ten, and had caught his father in the act of making the man in the red suit's footprints. No wonder Nina's version of fun, and her parents' version, were two distinctly separate animals. And look where their version had got them – Gran in a Turkish hospital, and Nina worrying herself sick. Her family would be the death of her!

Best not think about… you know… *death*…, because it might tempt fate, she thought. 'Just get here, Mum,' Nina sighed.

'Love you,' her mother replied. 'Over and out.'

Dear lord, give me strength, Nina prayed as the returned to her gran's bedside.

'What time will your parents be here?' Leo handed her a cup of steaming coffee and a slice of pizza as she sat down.

'Their flight is at seven, so four hours in the air, an hour to go through passport control and argue with a taxi driver, another hour from the airport, and Turkey is two hours ahead,' she counted on her fingers. 'Three this afternoon?'

She sipped her coffee and studied the greasy mass of bread, tomatoes, and cheese.

'Pide,' Leo said. 'It's like a pizza but not quite. It was all they had unless you wanted a soggy salad.'

Nina grimaced. She didn't particularly want either.

'You have to eat,' he insisted, taking a huge bite out of his pizza.

It's alright for you, she grumbled silently to herself, it wasn't *your* grandmother lying in that bed. An uncharitable thought, Nina knew, considering he was still by her side. He didn't need to be, and she wouldn't have blamed him if he'd gone back to his hotel. After all, they'd only just met, and it wasn't as if they were in a relationship or anything.

She checked the old woman once more (it was weird how quickly she'd fallen in to the habit of watching for the rhythmic rise and fall of her chest), but apart from that small movement, there were no other obvious signs of life. Flossie's skin had lost its tan colour, and verged on grey and sallow, her mouth was open, and her teeth were missing. Come to think of it, where were her dentures?

Nina had to find them – if Flossie woke to discover her teeth missing there'd be the devil to pay. She put her coffee and pizza down, and went to look.

They weren't in the bathroom, nor on the unit next to the bed. They weren't by the sink where visitors and nurses washed their hands. They weren't anywhere. Suddenly her grandmother's teeth were the most important thing in the world. She had to find them.

Hunting with single-minded determination, she searched every inch of the room.

'What are you looking for?' Leo whispered, speaking quietly because of the lateness of the night, or was it the earliness of the morning. She'd lost track of time. All she knew was it was dark and they'd been in the hospital for what seemed like hours.

'Gran's false teeth,' she said.

'They'll turn up, and she probably won't need them for a few days,' he pointed out. 'I'm sure they'll be found before then.'

'I'm glad you're certain, because I'm not,' she snapped, then burst into tears.

'Come here, my love.' He gathered her to him and held her tight, whilst she sobbed as if her heart would break.

'Your parents will be here tomorrow.' He glanced at his watch. 'Today,' he amended. 'But until then you're not on your own. You've got me.'

'How can you be so nice to me, when I'm such a cow?'

His hand combed through her hair, brushing the strands off her face. 'Because this isn't the usual you.'

'How do you know? I might act like this all the time.'

'I may be wrong, but I don't believe you do.'

'I'm boring,' she announced, suddenly.

'Who says?'

'My grandmother, my mother. Probably everyone who knows me, and those who don't.'

'Then they don't know the real you. You're funny, and sweet, and cute,' he kissed the end of her nose, which was brave of him, considering she'd cried so hard. 'And you're not boring, just a little more subdued than Flossie,' he said. 'She takes some keeping up with.'

Nina sniffed and wiped her eyes, though most of her tears had soaked into Leo's sea-stained shirt. 'She should show more decorum, at her age.'

'Which is?' He pulled back to look at her.

'Eighty-four, or three. I'm not really sure.'

'Check her passport.'

Nina checked. 'Eighty-three,' she said. 'I can't believe we threw a party for her to celebrate her eightieth birthday and she was only seventy-nine. She never said a word. I don't care if she's eighty-three or four, Grannie's old enough to know better. Do you know what she did on the first night we got there?' When Leo shook his head, Nina said, 'She waited for me to fall asleep, then she sneaked out and went to a bar with a group of people she'd only just met. I found her dancing on top of the damn bar, lifting her skirt up to her waist, and showing her knickers.' Nina had a feeling she'd be recounting the story for years to come.

Leo sniggered. 'She's cool, your gran.'

'Cool?' Nina spluttered, 'I'd describe her as downright dangerous. She could have fallen.'

'She didn't though, did she, and she could fall anytime, anywhere. At least she's enjoying herself.'

Nina took his comment as a criticism. 'I *enjoy* myself,' she said. 'But I don't have to get drunk to do it, and I don't have to behave like a teenager.'

'Talking of teenagers, why were you booked into *Aphrodite Hotel* anyway?'

'You're not going to believe this, but my mother and grandmother set me up. At first I assumed it was a mistake, but I now know it was deliberate.' She paused for a second. 'The old bat said I needed livening up. Apparently, I'm boring. Ever since we got here she's been telling me to live a little, let my hair down. She's worried I'll get to her age and realise what I've been missing.'

'Is that why you went diving and paragliding, because she thought it would be good for you?'

'Yes, it's why we came on this sodding holiday in the first place.'

'I'm glad you did.' He gazed into Nina's eyes and his expression was unfathomable. 'If it wasn't for her we wouldn't be together now.'

Is that what they were – together? As in, a couple? Or was this merely a holiday fling, and Leo was too nice a guy to abandon her?

Chapter 31

'Wake up, sleepy head, there's someone who wants to see you.' It was Leo's voice, and he sounded far too chirpy.

'Wuh?'

'Your gran's awake.'

Nina sat up suddenly, groaning at the crick in her neck and the stiffness in her back; and her arms, and her legs, and butt, and every other part of her. Even her ear hurt where it had been squashed against Leo's very solid shoulder.

'Gran?' she asked, croakily.

'She's awake,' Leo repeated.

'Thank god.' Nina burst into tears again, and she forced her wooden legs to hold her weight as she got creakily to her feet. She had to see for herself, to believe it. Leo tried to help but she stopped him. She needed to get her body working on its own, no pushing or heaving from anyone else, no matter who it was.

Flossie's eyes were open. She still looked incredibly frail, and old, and ill, but she was alive, which was the only thing which mattered. Nina deliberately tried not to think about how much her grandmother would hate life, if she was trapped in a body and mind she had no control over. She pushed the uncomfortable images to the side; one step at a time.

Nina leaned over the bed, held the other woman's hand, careful not to hurt her, and stroked a finger over the wrinkled skin. 'You gave us quite a scare for a while, but you're okay, you're going to be okay.'

Flossie pinned Nina to the spot with a sharp gaze, but she made no attempt to say anything. Oh dear, oh no, Nina thought, Flossie couldn't speak. Her grandmother was going to absolutely hate that.

'You're in hospital,' Nina said, talking slowly in case Flossie had difficulty understanding her, and as she did so she studied the old woman, looking for a spark, some recognition, anything at all, behind Flossie's steady blank gaze. 'You've had a stroke,' Nina continued. 'Don't worry, they've removed the clot from your brain, and they are going to run some tests to see if it's left any nasty effects.'

No reaction. Nina looked at Leo helplessly. He bit his lip and a crease sat between his brows.

'Mum and Dad are on their way, they'll be here later, and as soon as the doctor says you can travel, we'll take you home,' she said.

Which home she'd be taken to, Nina was reluctant to mention. Probably to Mum's, because there was no way Flossie could manage in her own house, not after this. And that would be another thing her grandmother would hate – she liked her independence too much.

Nina's heart swelled with love. If there was anything she could do to make life easier for her gran, she'd do it.

Flossie's tongue poked out through her lips.

'Are you thirsty? Would you like some water?' Nina frowned. 'Do you think she's allowed any?' she asked Leo.

'I don't see why not.' He poured a drop into a plastic beaker and gave it to Nina. 'Let me see if we can raise the bed a bit.'

He fiddled with a remote control attached to the side of the mattress, and with a whirr the bed slowly moved and Flossie's head and shoulders rose. When she was sufficiently upright to make getting a drink inside her without it dribbling down her front feasible, he stopped.

Nina inched forward with the beaker and slid her hand under the back of the old lady's head, holding her steady whilst her grandmother sipped. Nina examined her closely, searching for any drooping of her mouth or her eyes. To her, Flossie looked fairly normal, if a bit crumpled without her teeth.

With a sigh, Flossie closed her eyes, and Nina carefully lowered her head back onto the pillow. She wiped her grandmother's chin with a tissue, but Flossie lifted a hand off the bed and waved her away. Nina screwed up her face in relief – at least the patient could move one limb. She gave Leo a small hopeful smile, glad he was still there to share that one tiny piece of good news.

'I could murder a cup of tea,' Flossie said quite clearly.

'Gran! You can speak!'

'Of course, I can damn well speak. I can hear, too.'

Her grandmother's voice was gruff but she spoke in complete sentences with no hint of slurring. Nina was elated. Balancing gingerly on the side of the bed, she said, 'What can you hear, Grannie?'

'You two talking last night. You didn't bloody shut up; on and on. And if it wasn't you pair making a racket, it was those sodding nurses, prodding and poking at me every five minutes when I was trying to sleep. I wish you'd all go away and leave me alone.'

Nina let out a huge sigh. Flossie was fine. There was nothing wrong with her at all, thank goodness!

Later, when a different doctor appeared, examined her, and went away again, all without saying a word, Flossie demanded Nina go get cleaned up. 'Have a kip while you're at it — you look like something the cat sicked up. A decent meal wouldn't go amiss either.'

'I'm not hungry,' Nina protested though the thought of a shower made her slightly giddy with anticipation. She could still feel the roughness of the salt on her skin, and if she didn't get this bikini off soon, it would need a crowbar to remove it.

'Not you, me. I could eat a scabby horse, hooves and all.' Flossie's face folded in on itself as she grimaced. 'They'd better give me some breakfast soon. I get constipated if I don't eat regular.'

Leo snorted, and Nina bumped him with her hip. 'Don't encourage her,' she warned.

'Will you be alright on your own for a couple of hours?' Leo asked, and Flossie smiled.

'Go, I'll be fine,' she said, and Leo went off to call for a taxi, fishing the address Asdan had given him out of his shorts pocket.

Nina gave her grandmother a kiss and promised to be back soon. As she made her way to the front of the hospital, she wondered how long it would take to rinse out her only clothes and dry them enough to put back on again. An hour? Two?

'I can't believe she's as well as she is,' Nina said once they'd checked in. 'Bagsy the bathroom first.' She dashed inside and was stripping off even before she'd turned the shower on. Ooh, look, complimentary toiletries, though she would have sold her soul for a toothbrush.

Clean, with a towel wrapped around her boobs and with her clothes dripping in her hand, she scuttled to the balcony and hung them out to dry as best they could. 'Shall I see if they do room service?' she called through the half-open bathroom door.

'Good idea.'

Picking up the menu, she perched on the edge of one of the beds. A movement caught her eye and she noticed his reflection in the mirror, as he pulled his shirt over his head and shucked off his shorts. He wore nothing underneath. Oh my. He was slim, more on the wiry side than burly, his chest defined and his stomach flat; but it wasn't his chest and stomach which had captured her attention – her eyes were drawn south. She already knew he was all in proportion, but she simply enjoyed seeing him in daylight, in all his glory.

A girl can look without having to touch, and anyway Nina's stomach was rumbling now the terrible fear had left her. She reached for the room's phone and chose for both of them.

'How much did you order?' Leo asked, around a mouthful of fries. 'And what is this?' He poked warily at a dish of brown stuff with meat in it.

'Some sort of lamb stew, I think, and there's rice to go with it.'

He dipped a fork in and tasted it. 'Nice.'

She watched as he devoured his share in little more than thirty seconds, hoovering up the rice like a Dyson on a tight schedule. Then he started on the pasta and sauce.

'Will you stay here, at this hotel, when your parents arrive?' he asked.

'Probably. I'll see how it goes. From the way Gran was earlier, I wouldn't be surprised if they let her out sooner rather than later, then we can go home and put all this behind us.'

Leo's fork stilled and she realised how it had sounded.

'I didn't mean…' she paused, not sure how to phrase it. Should she say "us"? Was there an "us"? She'd like to think so, but this was Turkey, they were on holiday, and nothing was real, not like it was back home. What had happened to Flossie was real, and he was still here, keeping her company, but… and that was the problem – she couldn't help thinking "but".

'It's okay, I know what you meant and you're right, it will be good to go home,' Leo agreed after a strained silence.

'I'm sorry you had to… you know.' She shrugged.

'I was glad to help.'

Was, past tense, she noted. He must be eager to return to his hotel and leave the stink of disinfection and illness behind, and resume his holiday. She'd never forget his kindness, but she was selfish keeping him here.

'You should go,' she said. 'Mum and Dad will be here in a couple of hours. I'll be okay.'

'I know you will,' he said softly. 'I'll wait a while if you've no objection, to let my clothes dry, and I'll come back with you to the hospital until they arrive.'

'There's no need,' she protested, seeing how eager he was to be off.

'I want to say goodbye to Flossie,' he said.

'Oh, right.'

The remainder of the food was eaten in silence, except for when Leo switched on the TV, surfed for an English Channel, and the solemn tones of a BBC newscaster filled the room.

'Same old,' Nina said, for something to say. She felt like they were two strangers stuck in a lift, the easiness of earlier having disappeared so quickly she wondered if it had been there at all.

'Yeah, nothing changes.' Leo sounded desultory.

'I'll see if our clothes are dry.' She scooted outside and felt her T-shirt; still quite damp but it would have to do. Not only was she feeling a nagging urge to return to the hospital to check on Flossie, but she suddenly wanted Leo gone. He made her uncomfortable with his calm assurance, his manners, and the way he had of listening to her as if she was the only person in the world. She recalled how her skin tingled when he touched her, and how she felt light and free when she was with him, and safe and excited all at the same time. And how he didn't want to be with her anymore, and how she wished he did.

She really didn't need to feel like this, not now, not ever.

Maybe it was for the best if he did go back to his hotel. They weren't going to see each other again and, in the tradition of holiday romances the world over, it would be a case of nice-while-it-lasted. Home was home, Turkey was Turkey and the two should remain firmly apart and in their rightful places.

Chapter 32

Less than three hours, that was all she'd been away from Gran's bedside. Three short hours. And look at Flossie now.

Swelling of the brain, they said, a cerebral oedema. Quite common after a stroke, they said. But what they didn't say, or couldn't say, was how much of Flossie's brain tissue was being damaged by the pressure inside her skull.

Stupidly, Nina used her newly recharged phone to Google it, and promptly began to cry. The prognosis wasn't good. It was very likely her grandmother might die, and where had Nina been? Ogling a man's naked body and stuffing her face with food, which now sat solidly in her stomach, making her feel queasy. She should never have left her. She wouldn't have if Leo hadn't been with her, but she had wanted to spend a little more alone time with him before they went their separate ways and returned to their separate lives.

Along with the desolation at seeing Flossie so desperately ill, Nina's heart ached at the thought of never seeing this man again. How stupid, she'd done precisely what she vowed not to do – she'd had a holiday fling and had fallen for him, hard. Her world was falling apart, and there was nothing she could do to stop it; she was losing her grandmother and the man she loved, both in a short space of time.

That was the problem, Nina thought – love.

She loved him. She didn't want to, but she did, and it hurt. Cross with herself, she closed her eyes, the tears trickling down her face and plopping onto her chest. Leo's arms came around her, drawing her close to him, but she pulled away and shook him off. He took the hint and retreated to the door, leaning against the frame with his arms folded, leaving her alone with her pain.

A part of her (quite a big part), wished she hadn't done that, but best not to prolong the agony, eh?

Why, oh why, did she sleep with him? She knew the score, she knew one-night stands weren't for her, that she couldn't simply love 'em and leave 'em, as Gran so eloquently described it. She has to take it further, to the extreme. And that meant falling in love with him. Love was never a good idea, despite what her friends claimed. When you're led by your feelings, you're not in control, and Nina hated not being in control. She was so out of control now she could scream.

Look what happens when you let your guard down and let love in – bad things, that's what, like getting your heart broken for instance (one of her smugly married friends was no longer quite so smug, nor quite so married – not so unusual, just look at the divorce rate), but she never expected her nearest and dearest to pay the price of her brief excursion into happy-ville. The simple truth was, if Nina hadn't been so loved up, she would never have gone on that boat trip to Dalyan, and though she wasn't naïve or stupid enough to believe her being with her grandmother would have made any difference to Flossie's health, at least she would have been there for the old lady. Nina would never forgive herself for letting Flossie suffer on her own.

She cast her mind back over the last week. Yes, she had been happy, for a couple of days at least, but even those days weren't consecutive, and the first day, the Elephant day, was mostly one night. The next one had been – yesterday? Was it only twenty-four hours since she and Leo had been playing Katharine Hepburn to his Humphrey Bogart, and life has seemed so simple and carefree?

Well it wasn't either simple or carefree now was it, and Nina suspected life never really had been. Her time with Leo (and what a lovely time it was) had been an illusion, a break from reality, and Nina had been slammed back down to earth with a bloody big jolt.

'Nnuh?'

'Gran?'

'Nunun.'

'What is it? I'm here Grannie, I'm here.' Nina's voice broke as she stroked the delicate skin on the back of her grandmother's hand.

The old lady kept her eyes shut and Nina thought she'd fled back down into unconsciousness, changing her mind when Flossie's fingers curled around her own, in a weak grip. At least the old lady knew Nina was there, and Nina vowed not to move an inch until...

'I wan yuh to geh weh,' Flossie said, her words slurring.

'What do you want, Gran? Water, is it?'

'Nuh, *weh*.' She huffed the last word out.

Nina glanced at Leo, who remained by the door. He shook his head. He didn't understand Flossie either, but he stepped forward, a speculative look on his face.

'Does it begin with "W"?' he asked.

'Yeh.'

'Wuh-ah?'

'Nuh.'

'Wuh-eh?'

'Yeh.'

'Wuh-eh-ah? Just say "yes" when I get to the letter you want,' he told Flossie.

Nina raised her eyebrows and puffed out a breath. She would never have thought of doing that, and once more, almost against her will, Nina was grateful for his presence.

'Yeh, tha.'

Leo had been working his way slowly through the alphabet, giving Flossie time to speak after each letter and he hadn't got very far. 'Wuh-eh-duh? Is that it?'

What was Flossie trying to say? Nina mouthed the letters, and as Leo spelled them out, she realised what her grandmother was trying to tell her.

'Wed? I don't understand,' Nina said.

Flossie huffed, her cheeks expanding, the sunken cave of her face filling out. 'Muh,' she started again.

'Married,' Leo said. 'You want someone to get married, or they are already married?'

'Geh.'

'Get married?' Leo asked.

'Yeh. Nuhnuh.'

'You want Nina to get married?'

'Yeh. La wshh.'

'La? La-buh? La-cuh? La-duh?'

'Last wish,' Nina interjected. 'She's saying "last wish". Isn't that right, Grannie?'

'Yeh.' The old lady sighed and seemed to sink back into her herself. No, please, no. Nina watched, waiting desperately for the next breath, holding her own. The seconds grew longer.

Flossie sucked in another lungful of air, and Nina let hers out in a rush. She studied the old woman's chest for a few minutes more, making sure there was a rhythm, then leaned back in the chair.

'I can't believe she said that,' Nina stated quietly. 'What a thing to say. She'll have many more wishes; she's not going anywhere, except home. Why is she so intent on finding me a husband?'

'Perhaps she wants to see you happy and settled?' Leo suggested.

'I'm happy now. It's not like it was when she was young and women had to have a husband to validate themselves.'

'I don't think it's got anything to do with validating yourself as a woman. Flossie strikes me as the kind of lady who doesn't need anything or anyone to validate her. Did your grandparents have a happy marriage?'

Nina shrugged. 'I think so. Gran was certainly devastated when he died.'

'Maybe she wants you to have what she had?'

'Marriage isn't always a bed of roses, you know.'

'I expect she's aware of that, but I think she's trying to tell you that nothing is as important as family, and maybe she wants you to start one of your own, and experience all the joys it will bring.'

'I don't want to get married,' Nina protested, trying to make Leo feel less uncomfortable. She hoped he didn't think she felt the same way as her grandmother; talk about putting the poor bloke on the spot. They'd only known each other five minutes and she hadn't known his surname until yesterday, and she still didn't know much about his life back home, and here was Flossie talking of marriage. Nina also hoped he didn't think he was the designated groom.

'Nuhnuh?'

'I'm still here.'

This time Flossie opened one eye and regarded Nina balefully.

'We–d. You 'n' hi.' Flossie's single eye sought Leo out.

'Me and Leo?' Nina's voice was flatter than a wet Monday morning. Don't do this to me, Gran, she begged wordlessly. She was acutely conscious of Leo standing by the door where he'd retreated to, once his odd conversation with Flossie ended. It looked like he couldn't wait to escape, and Nina wondered why he persisted in staying, especially with her parents about to arrive at any moment.

She half-turned to him. His expression was impassive. He just wanted to get out of there, she could tell, and she wished she had the freedom to walk away like him, to return to normality, to let life trundle on as it had before, forgetting about love, and death, and heartache, but it was love which made her stay, and duty which kept her anchored and held her firm.

She would see this out to the end.

Flossie sighed, stirring restlessly, and once more Nina resumed her vigil, and once more Leo remained a solid rock in the river of her fear, giving silent support from his chosen place by the door. She didn't know how she would have coped had he not been there.

A commotion, a disturbance in the force, and Nina knew without looking, that her parents had arrived.

She stood, her eyes blurring with tears, and stepped into her mother's embrace as they entered the room in a flurry of bags and discarded sweaters. The two women hugged fiercely. When Nina found the courage to loosen her hold, she noticed her mother's gaze was fixed on the tiny woman in the bed.

'When did she get to be so old?' Alice whispered. 'She doesn't look like your grannie.' Sudden hope flared in her eyes, to be extinguished as quickly. 'For a second, I thought there'd been some kind of mistake and it wasn't her. Oh Derek, I can't bear it.'

Nina took her bottom lip between her teeth to stop it from wobbling. Flossie might be her gran, but she mustn't lose sight of the fact that this was her mother's *mother*. Nina could only appreciate a fraction of what Alice was going through. Lord protect her from the day Alice died, she thought.

'Right love, what has the doctor said, assuming you was able to understand him.' Her father took charge and Nina was grateful – she was heartily fed up of being an adult.

'It was a her,' Nina said, 'and her English was very good.'

'Yes, but are you sure you know what's going on? Did they explain it to you?' her dad persisted.

'I'm sure. Gran had a stroke, as I told you on the phone. They did this procedure where they go in through an artery in the groin and up the body to the brain. Once there, they sucked the clot out.'

'What went wrong?' This was from her mother, always ready to do battle, and if anything *had* gone wrong, Nina definitely didn't want to be in the shoes of the person responsible.

'Nothing,' she said. 'It went perfectly well. Grannie was even sitting up and having a conversation with us this morning. She seemed fine, considering.'

'So what happened?' her dad persisted.

'We went to the hotel for a couple of hours to shower and have something to eat, and when we came back, she was like this.' Nina's voice broke, and she sagged against her mother. 'She's got an oedema, a swelling in the brain. It's quite common after a stroke, apparently.'

'I'm sorry you had to go through this on your own, poppet. We're here now.'

Her mother patted her back, though Nina sensed Alice's own tears were very close to the surface, and she wondered who was comforting who.

'What now?' her father asked.

'We wait. Apparently, the oedema gets worse before it gets better, and only time will tell the extent of it, and to top it all off, there's the very real risk of pneumonia in these cases.'

'Oh.' Alice's voice was small and her eyes once again filled with tears. She busied herself with wheeling their case around the other side of the bed where it wouldn't be in the way, and taking out an assortment of objects.

'She likes lemon barley water,' Alice said, placing a half-used bottle on the over-the-bed table. 'I wanted to bring grapes, but your father refused to stop off at the supermarket on the way.'

'You wanted to get to the airport in time, didn't you?' He turned to Nina. 'We wouldn't have got here at all if your mother had her way and we'd "popped" into Tesco' (he used his fingers to make quotation marks). 'There's no such thing as "pop" where your mother's concerned. She'd have done a weekly shop once she got in through those doors.'

'You're exaggerating, as usual. I only wanted a few bits and bobs, nothing much.'

'Go on, show our Nina the list you wrote. It's two sides of A4. We'd have needed to buy another case.'

Nina tuned out the bickering; she was used to it and her parents actually seemed to enjoy it.

'Who is "we"?'

'Eh?' Nina had been studying her gran's chest again, when her mother tapped her on the arm.

'I said,' Alice repeated, 'who is "we"?'

'I've got no idea what you're talking about, Mum.'

'You said, and I quote, *we went to the hotel*. Who did you go with?'

Shit, she'd forgotten to introduce them to Leo in all the flurry surrounding their whirlwind arrival.

But when she looked towards the door where he'd been leaning a few minutes ago, he'd gone.

Chapter 33

One or the other of them always stayed with Flossie; usually her or her mother, and her dad was used as a gofer ('go fetch some fresh water, Derek'; 'go and find the nurse, Derek, the smiley one' and so on). By that evening, Alice had sent Derek to book into the same hotel as Nina, had argued with the insurance company, and had persuaded Nina to return to her original hotel back at the resort.

'Get a taxi and stay there tonight. I'll ring you if...' Alice trailed off. 'You look shattered. Try to get some sleep. Your dad and I will take it in shifts to watch your gran.'

'I'd have to collect our stuff anyway soon — we're due to fly home tomorrow, so I'll have to fetch our things and check out.' Nina's lip wobbled again. She didn't want to go, but it had to be done.

'I know, and your dad and I have been talking about that. We think you should fly back as planned.'

'You what?'

'You can't do anything here. You've done enough already, and those damn people,' (Alice had been refer-ring to *Holi-Days Insurance* employees as "those damned people" ever since she'd made her first phone call to them, and by now she'd made several) 'will only cover the costs of one of us. Your dad will have to pay for himself. Damn cheek! They'd be singing a different tune if it was one of their mothers in a hospital bed, let me tell you.'

Before Nina had chance to fight her corner and insist on staying at the hospital, her mother had bundled her out of the door.

'Wait.' Nina walked back into the room. 'I must say goodbye to Gran.'

Her parents knew what she meant. With a significant look at her father, her mother pushed Derek into the corridor. 'Let's stretch our legs for a minute, shall we?' Nina heard Alice say. She also heard the grief in her voice.

Nina waited until they'd gone a safe distance and approached the bed.

'I'm sorry, Gran. I should have been a better grand-daughter. I could have visited you more, spent more time with you.' Tears streamed down Nina's face and she could barely get the words out for sobbing. This might be the last time she saw her grandmother, the last time she had a chance to tell her she loved her. Even now it might be too late, as it was unclear whether or not the old lady was aware of the world around her. Nina convinced herself Flossie could hear her, and did understand; it was the only way she could say goodbye without totally breaking down.

'I want to thank you,' she said. 'For your love, for your support, and for your faith in me, but most of all I want to thank you for forcing me to come on holiday with you. I've loved spending time with you and I'll always treasure our time together.' Nina smiled, her face wet with tears. 'I love you, Grannie.'

'I love you, too.' Flossie's voice was as clear as an anchor-man on TV.

'Gran?'

'I'm here.' The old woman hardly spoke above a whisper, but there was no slurring, no having to force the words out. Nina understood her perfectly.

'Go after him,' Flossie breathed. 'You love him.'

'I do not!'

'You do, I can tell, and he loves you. Don't waste it.'

Nina stared at her grandmother in wide-eyed astonishment. 'He loves me? How do you know?'

'I've not lived this long without learning a thing or two.' She paused and Nina wondered if she was still conscious. 'He told me,' Flossie said, finally.

'He did? Oh.' A kaleidoscope of emotions surged through Nina's mind: Leo loved her; Gran was dying; Gran might live; she loved Leo; her gran was right; her gran had no idea what she was talking about…

Too much all at once, and Nina resorted to the one thing which usually worked for her – she crept back into her sensible shell and dealt with one thing at a time. She needed to say goodbye to Grannie, and if the goodbye happened to be a permanent one, then so be it. Flossie might be awake and lucid but, as Nina had discovered once before, it didn't mean the old lady was out of the woods.

'I love you, Gran,' she said, pouring her heart into the words, this time with the knowledge that her grandmother understood her, and if those were the last words Grannie heard coming out of Nina's mouth, then Nina would have to accept it. At least she had a chance to say goodbye.

A noise at the door made her glance up from the figure on the bed.

'Mum, Dad, look, she's awake and talking!' Nina leapt to her feet, grabbed Alice's hand, drawing her closer to her grandmother. 'She – Oh!'

Flossie lay motionless and silent, her eyes and mouth half open.

Nina's voice broke as she said, 'I think she's gone.'

Chapter 34

Nina remembered nothing of the taxi-ride to her resort. She remembered very little of the rest of the day at all; it had been awash with red-tape and paperwork. When Nina felt she could be of no more use, she got in a taxi and went off to pack up the detritus of her holiday.

'Miss Clarke, welcome.' Asdan greeted her at the desk, coming out from behind it to pull her to him and kiss her on both cheeks. 'If the hotel can do anything?'

'I fly home tomorrow,' she let out a big sigh. 'I just need to pack our things and check out in the morning.'

'No need to check out. It will be done for you, and I personally will arrange private transport to the airport for you.'

'Thank you. Will you pass on my thanks to all the staff, you have been wonderful.'

'You and Mrs Gibbins have been in our thoughts. *Allah rahmet eylesin* – may God's mercy be with her.'

Nina nodded her thanks and left him staring after her with his liquid brown eyes. The hotel management had been brilliant, considering they weren't used to dealing with elderly people. They were probably more familiar with cases of alcohol poisoning and broken limbs from guests falling over whilst drunk. She must remember to send them an email thanking them when she got home.

The room was as she left it. It even smelled of Flossie – an aroma of Chanel No. 5 and mothballs. Only the best for you, eh, Gran?

Nina scanned the inside of the wardrobe. Was it necessary to pack all her grandmother's things, the swimwear, for instance? It would just be more for Alice to deal with when she got home, and Flossie certainly wouldn't be wearing those darned bikinis again.

Decision made, Nina called reception and arranged for someone to bring a cardboard box or a bag to her room. They knew of someone who would benefit, rather than throwing them out. Though Nina imagined the look on the recipient's face when she opened the bag, expecting to see old lady clothes inside, and instead coming face to face with a lurid pink scrap of cloth.

The memory of Flossie wearing it made Nina smile sadly. She had the feeling her grandmother had worn it to highlight Nina's staid middle-aged choice of swimwear. She had a feeling her grandmother had worn, said, and done a great many things she might not have if Nina had been less set in her ways and more youthful in her outlook.

Flossie had been holding a mirror up to Nina's face, but Nina had steadfastly refused to look in it.

She was looking now alright, and what she saw dismayed her. As a child, she'd never been one to take risks, or to throw herself wholeheartedly into something. She'd always hung back, letting others test the water for her, and even then, she didn't always dip more than a toe in. She'd been a spectator, watching life from the sidelines, never really taking part. She was the same now that she was an adult she realised, too cautious to take chances.

Not anymore. Flossie might be in her eighties, but her grandmother's life was fuller and more exciting than

Nina's had ever been. Flossie might have done most of the things she'd done lately to prove a point but, dammit, the woman had had fun whilst she was doing them. Nina recalled the look of sheer happiness on her grandmother's face when Nina enthused excitedly over the octopus. Flossie hadn't dived herself, but she'd seen her granddaughter's joy and it had made her happy.

Apart from this holiday, Nina couldn't remember the last time she'd felt so light, so unburdened as she had since they'd arrived in Turkey (she deliberately didn't include the last couple of days), and it was all thanks to her grandmother for showing her how precious and wonderful life could be, and the potentials it held.

She didn't have any intention of fulfilling Flossie's wish for her to marry; not Leo nor anyone else. Not any time soon anyway, unless a suitable man could be magicked out of thin air, but she did intend to take life by the tail and hitch a ride. She intended to start by seeing if she could retrain. For her, teaching had run its course. She'd only fallen into the profession because she had lacked the balls to make a less safe choice and follow her heart. Nina didn't have a firm idea of what she wanted to do, but archaeology definitely held an appeal. Maybe she could do some volunteer work on the weekends and in the school holidays, just to make sure she liked it. There was no point in jacking in a well-paid, secure job for a new career just yet – better to give it a trial run first, and if she found she didn't like it, she could always give something else a go. Besides, teachers had to give at least a half term notice, which meant she wouldn't be able to start a course until a year September – plenty of time to plan and prepare.

Plan and prepare – it looked like some things would be more difficult to change than she anticipated. Leopards, and spots, and all that.

Her busy hands found the bottle of duty free vodka, and she remembered Grannie buying it at the airport.

'To have a little tipple in the room,' Flossie had said, returning from a visit to the loo with the vodka and two hundred cigarettes, having made a detour on the way back, the sneaky madam.

'We're going all inclusive,' Nina remembered pointing out to her, and her gran's reply was 'you can never have too much booze.'

Nina unscrewed the top and tipped the neck of the bottle to the heavens. Cheers, Gran, she said and took a hefty swig, spluttering as the liquid burned the back of her throat, and her eyes watered. That stuff had bite.

Nina stopped at one drink; she wasn't about to abandon all her caution in one fell swoop. She'd done enough things which were out of character already in the past week or so. She'd take it slowly and become more used to the new improved Nina. Plus, she'd tried the off-her-face thing and she didn't particularly like it. It wasn't simply the loss of control, it was the ill feeling afterwards. Why would anyone deliberately want to give themselves a pounding headache and make themselves feel nauseous?

A knock at the door. When she opened it a man in a polo shirt with "Maintenance" on his chest, held out a large plastic bag. She tipped him and resumed sorting through Flossie's clothes.

There wasn't much to sort – everything went in the case, except for the stupidly high sandals, the ridiculously small bikinis, and other hot-weather holiday stuff which Nina intended to give away, along with some toiletries which went in the bin. Nina nearly came undone when she picked up Flossie's denture tablets. They still hadn't found her grandmother's false teeth.

The hardest part done, Nina sorted herself out. She stripped off the over-large top she'd borrowed from her mother (she couldn't have kept on wearing the T-shirt she wore to Dalyan, though she put her foot down at borrowing a pair of her mother's knickers, so she'd swilled out her bikini yet again, using it instead of underwear), and the trousers which hung off her despite the elasticated waist, and stepped into the shower.

Water cascading down her face, she tipped her head back and let the memories flow over her, her tears mingling with the spray from the shower. She cried until nothing remained except hiccupping sobs, and slid down to sit in the bottom of the shower, her arms wrapped around her knees, letting the water wash away her tears.

Her own suitcase finally packed, Nina sat on the edge of the bed wrapped in a towel, and wondered what to do now. She couldn't face going to the dining room for dinner in case anyone tried to chat her up, but she needed to eat. She hadn't had a proper meal in days. She'd go out, and have something to eat in one of the restaurants on the front. She wished her despair was as easy to wash away as her tears, remembering strong arms and a loving smile.

Enough moping, she told herself sternly. Crying over spilled milk wouldn't make it any less spilled. Besides, Leo had made his position very clear.

She slipped a dress over her head, walked out of the hotel, and into the bustle of the evening. Picking a place at random, she ordered a Caesar salad, and sat back to people-watch. Flossie loved doing that, commenting on anyone and everyone: what they wore, how they walked, what nationality they could be, what jobs they held, were they drug-dealers (the man on that particular occasion had looked a bit like a gangster, or what Flossie thought a gangster should look like), were they straight or gay, lonely or in love...

Talking of love... maybe it was right and proper that she sought Leo out. Purely to thank him for his support and kindness, of course. She felt bad at allowing him to slip away, though she understood his reasons.

They had unfinished business, and though she had no intention of doing what her nutty grandmother wanted, Nina felt she had to see Leo again to put this thing to bed, whatever this thing was.

Closure, that's what she needed, a proper goodbye, a wish you well for the future, whenever I think of Elephant I'll think of you, sort of goodbye. Hope you have a good flight and the weather back home isn't too much of a shock to the system, sort of goodbye. But her main reason for seeing him again, she convinced herself, was to tell him about Flossie. He'd want to know how she was. He'd taken a shine to the old woman, and after spending all that time in the hospital, it was only right he was kept updated. And maybe he'd want to say his goodbyes to her too, because there had definitely been something between Nina and him, a definite connection, and it wasn't just all lust and holiday antics.

Salad finished and paid for, Nina grabbed her bag, checking her phone yet again (no missed call from him, no text) and wondered where she should start. There were many, many hotels in the resort, and she couldn't possibly check them all, but she knew the coaches tended to pick up from the far end of the town, and work their way towards the main road (the only road) leading up the side of the mountain and out of the valley. Leo had already been on the bus when it had collected her and Flossie for the Elephant and Pinky Moon trip, so by deduction Leo's hotel must be to the left of the resort.

Retracing her steps to *Hotel Aphrodite*, Nina started with those hotels on the road nearest the sea, figuring she'd work her way inland in a grid pattern, making sure she didn't miss any.

Fingers crossed, she entered the lobby of hotel number one.

'Sorry, no. We do not have any guest by that name,' the woman behind the desk said.

The man on reception in the next hotel said more or less the same thing, as did the one after that. By hotel number nine, Nina was hot, tired, and her feet hurt. Not expecting good news, and beginning to wonder if the staff manning the front desks were really checking, or they were just saying "no" because they weren't allowed to give out any information about their guests, Nina had to hold on to the wooden counter in shock when the elderly gentleman behind it checked his computer. She'd almost passed the place by because it looked more like a bar from the outside, and it was only when she'd glanced inside the practically empty restaurant area, she noticed a sign saying "rooms free". With scant hope, but in the interests of being thorough, she popped inside and asked the question.

'No, sorry, no Mr Waters here,' the gentleman had said in stilted English.

Nina expected nothing less, and smiled her thanks, turning wearily on her heel. This was quickly becoming a thankless task. Leo had her number and hadn't called, so what was she doing chasing after a man who obviously didn't want anything to do with her, when the man said, 'He left yesterday. Sorry.'

She stopped. 'Yesterday? Are you sure?'

He nodded enthusiastically. 'Yes. Yesterday. They go to England.' He made a taking-off motion.

'Thank you.'

Yesterday. He'd gone. He was home now, wherever home was, practically on a different continent. Back to normality, back to his everyday life. No wonder he hadn't contacted her. For him, the holiday was clearly over. Maybe he'd tell his friends how he was a knight in shining armour to Nina's damsel in distress, and maybe he'd remember the night they spent together, but she wasn't counting on it.

Their brief fling was exactly that – a fling, a holiday romance, a fleeting connection between two people who could pretend to be someone else for a short while, before they were catapulted back into their everyday lives.

To Leo, Nina realised, she was now nothing but a holiday memory.

Time for her to go home herself, and forget all about her holiday romance.

Chapter 35

Funerals were supposed to be sombre, no matter how much the deceased insisted on it being a celebration of their life. You might wear red and dye your hair purple, but there was always going to be a darkness inside, no matter how colourful the outside. After all, it was death's party and death was the belle of the ball.

'It's your party and I'll cry if I want to…' Nina crooned under her breath, as the mourners made their way out of the chapel and into their cars. The day was overcast, just like her mood and the black dress she wore suited her state of mind.

She glanced at her phone again, hoping for the unlikely.

Still no call, no message.

Though she knew it was fruitless, Nina kept hoping Leo would get in contact. Ever since her return, she'd been checking her phone to make sure it hadn't abruptly lost all its charge since the last time she'd looked, ten seconds ago. She'd gone from a woman who wasn't too bothered about her phone and often forgot it, or couldn't be bothered to charge it, to having to have the damned thing surgically removed from her hand if she wasn't careful.

'Hurry up Nina, and put that thing away – it's disrespectful.'

Her mother was right. Nina took a final glance at the screen, slipped the phone in her pocket, and climbed into the funeral car, to be sandwiched in the back seat between her father and her mother, who clutched a hankie in her hand. Nina had yet to see her mother use it – none of the family had been close to Aunt Mabel, not even Gran, who'd predicted her sister's demise with a certain detachment, even before they'd gone on holiday. Flossie had been dry-eyed throughout the entire service, and the rest of them had headed back to the car, leaving Flossie basking in the mourners' attentions. Her brother Ben, awkward in his newish suit (he'd gotten to wear it for their grandfather's funeral and now he got to wear it again – he'd taken to calling it his death suit) sat on a backward-facing seat. Nina hoped he wouldn't throw up on the way home.

The turn-out had been impressive, even if half of Aunt Mabel's friends had already passed-on ahead of her. Nina wondered if she could command the same volume of mourners if she died tomorrow, and came to the sober conclusion she couldn't. It was disconcerting to think she'd be missed less than a little old woman, who had outlived most of her family and nearly all her friends.

'Who are all these people?' Nina asked, not recognising most of them and wondering if there could be a lost relative or two in the throng.

'It's the Farewell Committee,' her mother said, fussing as her father got out of the car for a second time. 'He's got ants in his pants today,' she added, frowning sternly at him.

'The Farewell Committee?' Nina asked.

'The Reverend calls them that because they often turn up at funerals. There's a whole gaggle of them. This is only about half, so we're lucky.'

'Lucky so many turned up?'

'Lucky there aren't any more of 'em,' Nina's mother stated. 'We haven't got enough sandwiches to feed the full quota.'

'They're not all coming back to our house, are they?' Nina still called the family home "ours", though she moved out four years ago.

'If they can wheedle the address out of someone, and if it's not too far away. Some of them still drive, god help us!'

'It's not that bad—' Nina began.

'You haven't seen them behind the wheel, they're a menace, the lot of them. Someone should revoke their licences. And they're like gannets once they scent food. They can strip a table bare, faster than a shoal of piranhas on a corpse.'

'I meant, we can pick up some more bread and ham, and I'll make more sandwiches.'

Alice gave Nina an incredulous look. 'Are you suggesting we ask the funeral car to pull over at the corner shop?'

Ah, now it was put like that, maybe not.

'What can she possibly be doing?' Alice grumbled, craning her neck.

'Stop fretting, Mum, she's alright. Gran's indestructible,' Ben piped up whilst frantically thumbing his phone with both digits.

'Why is it okay for Ben to play with his phone, but I can't check mine?' Nina whined.

'He's younger than you.'

275

'He's old enough to know better,' Nina retorted.

'What was your excuse then?' Ben chortled. 'You're, like, ancient.'

'Twenty-eight is hardly ancient!' Why, oh why, did her family make her act like a twelve-year-old, her brother especially. It was a wonder she hadn't cried, 'Tell him, Mum', though if she had to endure her annoying brother's company much longer, she just might.

'There you are!' Alice cried, pushing her way out of the car, and relieving the Reverend of his talkative burden. Nina's dad hovered uncertainly, wondering whether to take over the reins – Flossie had screeched at him before for taking charge of her wheelchair when she wanted someone else to be the favoured person to push her. The Reverend didn't give her father much choice, handing Flossie over eagerly, and Nina saw the relief on his face.

She might be wheelchair-bound, but Flossie's mouth worked just fine, and since she'd had a new set of dentures fitted, she didn't stop using it.

'If I lift her out of the chair, will you help me swing her round and get her in the car?' Alice asked Derek. 'Ben, sort out your Gran's chair.'

'What do you want me to do with it?' Ben asked, sitting in it once Flossie had been hoisted out, and moving the contraption backwards and forwards like a kid in a go-cart. 'Does it do wheelies, Gran?'

'Stop it, Ben, don't encourage her. She's bad enough as it is, without you making it worse.' Alice shooed him out of the wheelchair, making "wind-it-up" signals at him.

'When can I go home?' Flossie asked in a whiny voice, as Derek bundled her into the front seat and fought with the seatbelt.

Nina's heart went out to her. Her gran hated the nursing home, even though she understood it was a temporary situation. She'd been lucky, the damage was minimal and could be rectified (more or less) with intensive physiotherapy.

Alice said, 'Not for a while yet, Mum. You've only just started treatment. Try not to run before you can walk, eh?'

'Don't talk to me about walking, that's cruel, that is.' Flossie shuffled around to give her granddaughter a cheeky wink.

'Oi, stop wriggling. I can't do up the seat belt with you squirming like a cat in a sack,' Derek protested.

Nina winked back. There was nothing her grand-mother enjoyed more than winding Alice up. 'Bites every time, she does,' Flossie was fond of saying, and Nina guessed Gran had to have some fun in her life, because the nursing home was a bit of a joyless place.

Nina had taken to smuggling miniature bottles of brandy and whisky in (vodka was a summer drink, appar-ently), and was in the middle of trying to show the old lady how to use a laptop. It was hard going and Nina had been forced to hide Flossie's bank card, but at least it gave the pensioner a line to the outside world. Though her gran trying to use Skype was proving to be more interesting than Nina anticipated, having had Flossie Skype her whilst the old lady was in the bath.

It would take a long time before those particular images were erased from Nina's mind, and Flossie had got into a shedload of trouble for "a) taking a bath on her own, when she could barely manage one with an auxiliary helping her, b) taking an electrical item into the bathroom and balancing it on the toilet lid, and c) sending indecent images over the internet, even if it wasn't for pornographic purposes".

'That nursing home manager has no sense of humour,' her gran had declared. 'She could probably do with a good seeing to.'

The telling off only served to give Flossie ideas – the old woman hadn't realised the internet could be used for that, and had spent the whole of Nina's visit one afternoon wondering whether there was a market for Flossie flashing her knickers ('It went down well in Turkey. They loved it!' Flossie kept saying). Looked like a bar full of tourists hadn't been enough of an audience for her!

'It'll be my turn to die next,' Flossie announced, sucking on a sticky sweet she'd wrestled out of her coat pocket. 'I said Mabel wouldn't last the month, didn't I?' The old woman sounded positively delighted she'd outlived her sister. 'I'm the last of the Varsey girls. There were three of us sisters, you know.'

'We know, Gran,' Ben sighed. 'You keep telling us.'

'Don't be so cheeky, young man, and if I keep telling you it's because I'm never sure whether you're listening to me or you're concentrating on Grindr, or summat.'

'Grindr?' Ben spluttered and turned an odd shade of puce.

It was left to Nina to explain to the wrinklies what the site was for.

'Why didn't Aunt Mabel ever get married?' Nina asked, as the driver finally pulled away from the church grounds. She hadn't known her aunt all that well, but she felt a little mean leaving the coffin in the chapel all on its own ('no graveside service for my sister,' Flossie had insisted. 'It's ghoulish to gather round the hole she'll be planted in').

Flossie clacked her dentures as she thought about the answer, and Nina imagined stories of unrequited love, or a man who was unobtainable because he was married to another woman, one he didn't love but who he was tied to until death did them part…

'She was a lesbian, that's why,' Flossie said.

Ben choked on his astonishment.

'The younger generation didn't invent woman on woman action,' the old lady said, seeing his incredulity. 'You didn't invent sex either. We old folks did it too – where do you think your mother came from?'

'Oh, gross, Gran.' Ben grabbed at the headphones hanging around his neck and plugged them into his ears, but not before Gran said, 'I miss sex.'

Nina seriously wondered if her brother would ever recover from hearing that. His eyes bugged, and he kept opening and closing his mouth. She was relieved when his phone beeped, snapping him out of his shock and disgust.

'I thought I'd go before her,' Gran said, 'after that episode in Turkey.'

"That episode" was how Flossie referred to her stroke, and the rest of the family had thought the same thing. For a while there, it had been touch and go, but as soon as the swelling had diminished, Flossie rallied within the week and had been allowed to fly home. Though to her intense annoyance, she'd been sent to a nursing home to convalesce, rather than her own home, which was what she'd demanded.

When the car drew up at the kerb, Ben was the first out, shooting out of the vehicle like a man being chased by a hive of angry bees, followed closely by Nina. 'I'll check on the sandwiches,' she called, leaving her parents to deal with Flossie.

With no children of her own, Flossie was Mabel's closest relative. It was only right that Alice hosted Mabel's wake. She'd opted to hold it at their house, rather than a sterile church hall, or the upstairs room in a random pub, and Nina had spent all the previous evening buttering bread for sandwiches and slicing lemon drizzle cake. She'd been up so late preparing for Great-Aunt Mabel's send-off that she stayed over, sleeping in her old room, and wondering where all the years had gone.

It was also a good excuse not to go back to her own house.

She had no such excuse once the wake ended.

Nina volunteered to take Flossie back to the nursing home first, assuring her for the thousandth time that the old lady wasn't going to be left there to rot. It was a perfectly nice nursing home, as nursing homes go, Nina thought. And yes, Flossie would return to her own home, and no, they hadn't sold her house from underneath her nose and were planning on running away to Australia on the proceeds. Nina said for the thousandth time, that first Flossie would need to relearn how to walk again, which was why she was having physio on her weakened leg and arm.

Once she returned her gran to the expert care of the nursing home, Nina ran out of places to go, and things to do.

Home it is then, she thought, pulling out of *Happy Hills* carpark, though she'd promised to check on her gran's house on the way, and as it delayed doing lesson preparation for the start of term, Nina was more than happy to oblige.

Post littered the mat behind the front door. One letter carried an imprint of Ben's size ten footprint; the lazy sod hadn't bothered to pick any of it up the last time he'd been here. They were supposed to take it in turns to make sure no one had broken in, that the roof hadn't blown off, and the plants were watered. Nina poked a finger into the nearest pot. Dust dry.

Post sorted (Nina put anything she thought might be important in her bag – she'd give it to Mum to take to the nursing home), plants watered, and windows opened to let some fresh air blow through the stale house, Nina wandered from room to room.

She hoped Gran would eventually return home. The old lady was fiercely independent and hated that damn nursing home. Mind you, she'd hate living with Mum even more, Nina thought. Two alpha women in one house – it would drive them both batty.

She trailed a hand across the worktops in the kitchen, thinking that the next time Gran came home it would probably be to supervise the packing up of her possessions. None of the family had mentioned it to the old lady (they were too scared) but they were all thinking the same thing – assisted living. Bagsy Nina wasn't the one to have that difficult conversation with her!

Duty done, and if the said duty left her slightly tearful there was no one around to witness it, Nina drove to her own little house.

Home; where she felt safe, contented, cocooned. Home, where she enjoyed her own company and binge-watched box sets.

So why did the place feel so empty and bleak now?

Chapter 36

The first day back was often a shock to many teachers, but never to Nina. Oh no, not her, because, ever since she graduated and secured her first teaching post, she'd always popped into the school at least a couple of times a week during the long summer holidays (usually more), so for her the start of term was an anti-climax, merely a continuation of the end of the last academic year.

It said an awful lot about the state of her personal life.

She didn't have one, not unless going to the gym, having the occasional drink with friends, lunch at Mum's every Sunday, and most nights spent curled up in her favourite chair reading a dry tome on ancient history, passed as a personal life.

Since she'd returned from Turkey, Nina had been forced to admit she'd been living life one step removed from it. Yes, she loved reading about the Greeks and the Romans, and it wasn't as if you could go back in time and immerse yourself in their cultures, was it, but she could be on a dig, or working in a museum where she might actually be able to hold one of those fabulous artefacts in her hand, and feel something touched by a person who lived two thousand or more years ago.

To carry out proper research, to make her own deductions and discoveries was as far removed from reading about it, as hanging thousands of feet in the air and experiencing the thrill of gliding back down to earth was, compared to watching a paraglider on TV.

And if nothing else, Nina had Leo to thank for opening her eyes. She'd never met anyone with such passion and dedication to what they did to pay the bills, and she wanted a piece of it for herself. She wanted to wake up in the morning thrilled to be going to a job she loved, and not to a job she did because it occupied the time between waking and sleeping, using up the long hours in between. She wanted to feel alive.

It was with mixed feelings (and heavy eyelids, because she'd spent all of the evening and much of the night trawling through course after course on the internet) Nina unlocked her classroom and stepped inside. Breathing in the familiar smell and staring at the carefully decorated and copiously adorned walls, she wished she was anywhere but here.

Of course, her house would have to go, maybe her car, definitely the expensive gym membership, the Marks and Spencer ready meals for one (Tesco value for her from now on), and she'd have to resign herself to no more expensive haircuts or nice clothes. She'd be living in a hall of residence with teenagers only a year older than those she taught, eating little more than toast and drinking cheap beer, and wearing whatever happened to still be clean. Welcome to student-land.

Nina shuddered. It would be as if the last ten years hadn't happened. Except she didn't fancy having a skin-full of booze every night, staying up 'til dawn and not washing for days on end, again. Oh wait, she hadn't done that the first time around either, had she?

Conscious she was getting ahead of herself, she went through the rest of the day on autopilot, trying to imagine how it would be to have no money, except for the statutory student loan. She'd hardly started paying off the loans for her first degree yet! The way she was going, she'd be in debt until she was as old as her gran.

At lunch, instead of joining the others in the staffroom as she would have done in the past, she hid in the faculty office, Googling local dig sites, trying to find out if anyone needed volunteers. So far, no luck, but Nina understood that with autumn fast approaching, the dig season was more or less over. Maybe she could put her name forward for a dig in the spring and spend the winter months volunteering at a museum, or offering to do free research. She knew she was being rather vague, but this was all new to her. Excitement fizzed in her veins – she didn't care what she did, as long as she did something.

Day two of the pair of training days before the hordes of pupils returned was a repeat of day one, except for the additional excitement of visiting the reprographics room and placing an order for photocopying. Oh, and a phone call from a company who organised school trips.

'Message for you.' Sue, one of the receptionists, handed her a pink slip of paper. 'Your email doesn't work, everything I send you keeps bouncing back,' she told Nina. 'I've written it down instead.'

Nina glanced at the paper.

Man called from a company organising school trips.

Asked for Nina Clarke.

Didn't leave his number.

'Did he say which company?' Nina asked, not really caring. The last thing she wanted to do was take a load of hormonal teenagers on a school trip.

'No, I didn't get much out of him at all,' Sue said, and Nina wondered why the other woman bothered to give her the message in the first place.

Scrunching it up, and hurling the crumpled paper at the bin, Nina checked her pigeon hole, to find she didn't even have any post – nothing, nada, zilch. Maybe the god of education was trying to tell her something; email not working, no post, and useless messages. Perhaps the universe was trying to give her a great big hint.

Sitting at her desk with the intention of familiarising herself with this year's pupils, Nina wondered if maybe a change of exam board with a different syllabus would inject some life back into her work. It was too late for this academic year though, she'd have to go with what she had. Damn it, but she was bored!

She found herself clicking on images of Ephesus on her phone. She hadn't taken many photos, and to her continuing dismay she didn't have any of Leo. Smiling, she recalled how he'd tapped his head and said all his memories were in his mind and that he didn't need a photo to "see" them.

Funnily enough, neither did she. Every second in Turkey was as clear as if she was still there, especially the days (and night, don't forget the night) she'd spent with Leo. When she closed her eyes, every inch of him was seared on her mind: the way he scratched his head when he was thinking, making his hair stand on end; the gentle way he had with Flossie; his laugh and how his eyes creased when the smile reached them; the desire on his face when…

She blinked and sat up straighter. There was a time and a place for those kinds of thoughts and it wasn't now, so she steered her wayward thoughts into a safer direction.

He'd had nice hands, she remembered, strong, with a tiny smattering of hair at each wrist. Hands that—

This time she cleared her throat and got up to make a cup of coffee.

The strong liquid did nothing to warm her or fill her up. Her insides were hollow, except for an ache where her heart used to be. The dull pain in her chest was almost physical, and until she realised what it was, she'd considered taking an aspirin.

So this was what it felt like to have a broken heart?

Goddammit Flossie! Couldn't you have decided to liven me up in Brighton, or Scarborough, or St Ives – anywhere but Turkey? Anywhere so she wouldn't have met Leo and fallen in love with a dream. She knew she should have refused to go.

She Skyped her grandmother, needing to hear her voice. Flossie was her only connection to Turkey. To Leo.

'It's all your fault,' she said as soon as Flossie answered the call.

'It always is, you'll find that out for yourself when you're a wife and a mother. You'll never be able to do anything right.'

'Don't you want to know what I'm blaming you for?'

'I already know.'

'Go on then, what is it?'

'That nice young man of yours.'

'He's not mine.'

'He is.'

'Why hasn't he called then, or sent me a text?'

'He'll have his reasons. Did you call me just to have a go at me?'

'Yes,' Nina said sulkily.

'Haven't you got some kids to bully?'

'It's a teacher training day.'

'Another one? I wish I had as many training days as you do.'

'Ha, bloody ha.'

'Why don't you stop arsing about and phone him?'

'I haven't got his number.'

'Oh.'

'See?'

'I see.' Flossie's tone became less belligerent. Nina wished it hadn't when she heard the pity in her grandmother's voice. 'We all get our hearts broken, dear, sooner or later. The first cut is the deepest.'

Nina swallowed hard. 'That's such a lovely thing to say.'

'Rod Stewart said it first.'

'Who?'

'A singer from the seventies. He's right though, the first time you get your heart broken you think you'll never get over it. At least you're mature enough to deal with it, and not a drama queen of a teenager.'

'Thanks for the words of wisdom, but they don't help.'

'Nothing will,' Flossie declared, cheerfully. 'You have to suck it up and get on with it. Now, have you finished?'

'I still want to shout at you.'

'No, you don't, you want to shout at Leo. Anyway, you can't shout at me, I've got witnesses.' Flossie turned her phone around. She was in the nursing home's day room, which was chockfull of elderly people all staring at her.

'Better than Jeremy Kyle, that was,' a whiskered old gent in a bobble hat yelled.

'Thanks, Gran, glad I amused somebody today.' It was only when the call ended, that Nina wished she'd thought to ask why the old bloke was wearing a bobble hat indoors at the beginning of September.

Bugger, the phone in the office she shared with five other staff was ringing. For a minute, she considered not answering (the way the day was going it wouldn't be anyone for her, anyway), but a remnant of the old, conscientious Nina raised its head, and she shot out of her chair to pick up the call.

The receptionist said, 'There you are. I'd almost given up. I wish people would tell me when they're expecting visitors, or at least have the courtesy to come to reception so I don't have to phone all over the school looking for them.'

Sue was a bad-tempered Rottweiler disguised as a human. No one wanted to get on the bad side of her, least of all the head teacher. Nina, a lowly teacher with no power, had no chance, so she grovelled.

'Sorry Sue, I'm honestly not expecting anyone.'

'How do you explain your visitor then?'

'I don't?' Nina grimaced at the phone, not sure why she phrased the statement as a question. Fear, probably.

'Hang on.' Sue must have put her hand over the receiver, because all Nina heard was muffled mumbling. 'He says it's about a school trip.'

Nina took a deep breath, blew out her cheeks, and took the proverbial bull by its sharp and dangerous horns.

'Sorry, he's not got an appointment. Can you please tell him I'm about to go into a meeting? With Mr Blake,' she added for good measure. Maybe mentioning the head teacher's name would make her lie sound more plausible. 'Could you also tell him I'm not interested in organising any trips at the moment, but if he wants to leave a phone number I'll call him if the situation changes.'

Nina waited for the fall-out, an expression of abject terror on her face.

'Hang on, he says, not even a visit to Ephesus?' Sue sighed dramatically down the phone.

Nina heart skipped a beat making her cough. 'A visit to where?'

'Ephesus,' Sue shouted down the phone. Her voice became marginally quieter as she asked the visitor to spell it. 'E-P-H—'

Nina interrupted her. 'What did you say his name was?'

'I didn't. It's Mr Waters.'

'First name?' she squeaked.

'Leo. Now do you want to see him or not, because I can't spend all day on this blasted phone, I've got work to do.'

'I'll be there in a sec, just give me a minute.' Nina darted out of the office before being yanked back by the telephone cord. 'Don't let him leave, whatever you do!'

She hung up and pelted into her classroom. Should she brush her hair first, or put some lipstick on? Oh no, she hadn't worn any make-up this morning, she thought, frantically rifling through her bag. He's going to think she's a right gargoyle.

When the office phone rang again, Nina stared at it as if it was going slither across the floor and bite her. Sue was getting impatient.

Taking a deep breath, and with her head held high Nina marched off down the corridor to meet her future.

Chapter 37

It was him, really him, as large as life and twice as gorgeous. He had his back to her as she strode into the school's lobby, but she knew that backside anywhere, and what a lovely backside it was too. Firm, and muscular and just the right shape for a bloke's butt.

He turned and caught her ogling his arse. Nina blushed.

His expression was guarded.

'You could have warned me, I'd have...,' (worn a dress, washed her hair, put mascara on at least, made sure she didn't have her scratty old bra on – not that Nina intended for him to see her underwear right this minute...) '...informed reception you were expected.'

'You didn't answer your phone,' he said.

'That's because you didn't call,' she countered.

Sue pretended to do some filing, but Nina could tell the woman was listening intently.

'Let's go into the meeting room,' she suggested, giving the receptionist a pointed glare. 'It's more private.'

Closing the door behind them, she repeated, 'You didn't call.' She didn't offer him a seat and he didn't take one.

'Yes, I did.' He sounded weary. He looked it too, through what was left of his summer tan. 'I called and I texted. Look.' He showed her his phone.

Ninety-four calls.

'That's not my phone number,' Nina said.

Leo looked at the screen in confusion. 'Whose is it?'

'I have no idea.'

'Are you sure it's not yours?'

'Quite sure.'

'Oh great. That explains why the last time I dialled it I got a Scottish bloke on the other end, accusing me of stalking him and threatening to call the police. I thought you might have put a friend up to it, to get me to back off.' He stared at the little black box as if it might burst into flames in his hand.

Bursting into flames was remarkably what Nina felt like doing. Her heart hammered and her mouth was dry. There was a tremble in her left leg, and something was doing cartwheels in her stomach. She hoped she wasn't going to throw up.

The pair of them stood in silence for a couple of seconds. Nina examined the floor; the carpet needed a good clean, she noticed for no apparent reason. She couldn't believe he was really here. Why? What did he want? Hope and fear took turns to bounce up and down in her chest.

She shot him a swift glance. He looked good, if she ignored the weariness. Much more than nice (how had she ever thought him just nice?). He'd lost a bit of weight too, like she had. She'd tried her favourite jeans on this morning, to discover she had room in them to grow. She wasn't complaining though – she might be wearing the most disgusting bra in the world, but her bum was a size smaller.

The silence grew until both of them spoke at once.

'I didn't think you wanted to see me again,' Nina said, at the same time Leo stated, 'I thought you were giving me the cold-shoulder.'

Both of them ground to a halt.

'Go ahead,' Leo offered.

'No, you.' Nina didn't want to be the first to speak, in case she made a total arse of herself.

'Okay.' Leo took a deep breath. 'I wasn't ready for you, I'm probably still not ready for someone like you. You scare me. No, listen,' he said, as she opened her mouth.

Scare him? A big bloke like him, scared of her? He was almost twice her size, for goodness sake!

'I mean, I'm not ready for the way you make me feel,' he continued. 'I'm frightened by it, but from the moment I saw you on that coach, I simply knew I had to get to know you better, though it went against every bone in my body.'

Nina opened her mouth again.

'Let me say what I've come here to say, and if you want to say anything when I've finished...' he trailed off.

Nina shut her mouth with a snap. She really, really wanted to hear this. Or did she?

'That night, I knew it was wrong, but I couldn't help myself.' He cleared his throat and paused.

Nina thought, he's come to apologise...

'I wanted you so badly, and not just for the sex, though that was pretty wonderful, but for *you*. You're cute and beautiful, and funny and...' He heaved a sigh. 'Anyway, I didn't think you felt the same way, and in the hotel near the hospital I was sure you didn't. It almost killed me to leave you there with your parents. Walking away from you was the hardest thing I've ever done, but I did it because I love you. There, I've said it.' He sounded defensive, defiant almost.

Nina's throat closed up. She couldn't speak now even if she wanted to. The backs of her eyes pricked with tears, and the trembling in her left leg moved to her right, until both were shaking as hard as a couple of saplings in a hurricane.

He loved her.

He *loved* her!

That *was* what he said, wasn't it? She heard him right, didn't she?

'Is that what you came all this way to tell me?' she asked.

He lifted his head so he was staring down his nose at her. 'Yes.'

'If you thought I was avoiding you, why did you come? How did you find me anyway? And where did you get that number from?'

They paused and stared at each other. 'Flossie,' they chorused.

'She must have read it out wrong, or I mis-typed it when I put it in my phone,' Leo said. He was still tenser than a frog about to be prodded (not that she tended to prod many frogs nowadays, but she had done so when she was younger because they spawned in her dad's garden pond, so she knew a tense frog when she saw one), but his face had lost a bit of the wariness it held earlier.

He said, 'To answer your other questions, I came because I wanted to hear you tell me you weren't interested from your own lips. I couldn't believe that after that night and those days we spent together, it all meant nothing to you. I had to hear you say it. I found you because I called every high school within a ten-mile radius of Worcester.'

'You did?' she choked out.

'I did, and after the first couple, I became a bit cannier, otherwise I got nothing out of those creatures manning the phones. They're bulldogs, the lot of them.' He shuddered. 'I hit on the idea of telling them I was from an educational visits company – it was the only way I could get any of them to confirm whether you worked at their school or not.'

He stopped. Nina worried at her bottom lip with her teeth. Should she say it? *Could* she say it?

Damn and blast, just say it Nina, she told herself.

'I love you too.'

Chapter 38

The volcano hung in the air, shimmering purple-grey in the distance, looming over the landscape, brooding and deadly, but only when its potential was understood did you realise how great was its silent threat, Nina realised. It was magnificent now; how much more majestic would it have appeared in 79 AD before it blasted its top to smithereens.

Nina put her hands to the small of her aching back and stretched. This history business was proving to be hard work, and here she was thinking she'd be having fun.

There was still so much more to see.

'Can we come back tomorrow?' she pleaded, all big eyes and pouty lips. She knew he'd be unable to resist.

'We're supposed to be going to Capri,' Leo reminded her.

'Meh.' Nina shrugged. 'If you've seen one island, you've seen them all.'

'You could say that about Roman ruins,' Leo countered, dryly.

'Noooo,' she wailed, twining her arms around his neck, trying to pull his face down to her level. If she could get her lips on his, she knew he'd admit defeat. 'Pompeii is totally different to Elephant. It's got enormous penises for a start.'

'Yeah, that's really gonna do it for me. I need an attack of penis envy like I need a hole in the head.'

'You do know they're paintings, don't you, and they're not taken from real life models either.'

'How do you know? They might have been. Anyway, it's still demoralising. A man can't help but compare.'

'You've got absolutely nothing to worry about in the trouser department, Mr Waters.'

'No?'

'No.'

'Fancy testing it out later, just to make sure?'

'It'll be my pleasure.'

'I'll do my absolute best to make sure it is, *Mrs* Waters.'

'Say it again.'

'Which bit?'

'The missus bit.'

'*Mrs Waters.*' Leo dragged the words out while he nibbled at the side of her neck just to the south of her earlobe.

Nina wriggled in delight.

'Oi! I thought you was supposed to be showing me round Pompeii, not showing me how babies are made. I know how that's done already, and in case I've forgotten, Mr Sneldon has been reminding me.'

'You what?' Nina held the tablet at arm's length in case Mr Sneldon decided to remind her too. 'Which one is Mr Sneldon?'

Gran might have moved back into her own house, but she spent more time visiting the nursing home inmates than she did seeing her own family.

'Him what wears the bobble hat,' Flossie said.

'Oh, gross.'

'He's not gross, he's lovely. He keeps his hat on for a reason though.'

'No need to share the details with me, Gran.'

'Why not? You shared everything with us last night.'

'*Us?*'

'Everyone at *Happy Hills*. We all watch you on the telly.'

'We're not on telly, Gran, we're on your computer.' Bless her, Flossie tried so hard to get to grips with technology and she was doing her best, but some things seemed a bit out of her grandmother's reach.

'Yes, you were. I used an HDMI cable and plugged you in. Had both of you on wide screen and in HD. In all your glory.'

Hang on, 'What do you mean, *all our glory*?'

'Put it this way – we could all tell you are newly-weds. You forgot to turn Skype off.'

O.M.G. *She didn't!* Nina's face flamed as she recalled what she and Leo had gotten up to after they'd finished Skyping Flossie, and she nearly dropped the tablet as a series of cackles and suggestive comments came out of it.

'Nina? Nina? Are you still there?' Flossie called.

'I'm still here,' she said, gritting her teeth. At this moment, she was extremely glad her grandmother wasn't, for fear of what she might do to the old bat.

'Ha Ha! Gotcha! I turned it off,' Flossie squawked, 'when I saw what you pair were up to.'

'Thank goodness for that! I thought for a minute—'

'I know what you thought, young lady, and I'm not that daft. Besides, I don't want Mr Sneldon ogling you when he should be ogling me! Right, where are we off to tomorrow then?'

'We'll still be in Pompeii, Gran.' Nina glanced at Leo, who nodded and smiled. She knew she'd be able to talk him round. Pity she couldn't say the same for her grand-mother.

'I wanted to go to Capri.'

'We'll go soon, Grannie, we will, but first I want to see a bit more of this place, it'll help me when I start my course on The Roman Empire in September.' Excitement swirled through her tummy when she thought of it, not to mention all the lovely field trips it promised, Rome being one of them.

'Get a move on, then, I'm not getting any younger,' Flossie cackled. 'Today could be my last day on earth, and I wanna make the most of it.'

'Told you we should have brought her with us,' Leo whispered, his breath tickling her ear.

'On our honeymoon?' Nina gasped. 'No bloody way!'

And as for it being Flossie's last day, Nina suspected the old lady had a lot more days left in her yet. Fingers crossed!